Flotilla

by

Daniel R. Haight

TELEMACHUS PRESS

Flotilla

Cover Designed by: DM Illustrations – DMIllustrations@gmail.com

Cover Image:
Copyright © Jeff Dickerson-Dickerson Photography, Auburn, CA

Published by Telemachus Press, LLC
http://www.telemachuspress.com

Visit the author website:
http://www.flotillaonline.com

ISBN: 978-0-615-56254-4 (eBook)
ISBN: 978-1-938701-84-9 (Paperback)

Version 2014.08.31

Printed in the United States of America

10 9 8 7 6 5 4 3 2 1

Dedications

To N.L and T.T.L.—*This is for you.*

To LYNN + LANE —

Awesome TIME. w/ YOU @

Wizard World!

Best Wishes,

[signature]

Acknowledgements

I also want to take a moment to thank some people who were influential to taking Flotilla from project to product:

Joe Quirk—*From our first conversation two years ago until now, you've always been an unflagging supporter to a first-time novelist. Thank you for your kindness and your help.*

Allen Steele—*I picked up <u>Orbital Decay</u> over twenty years ago when I was in junior high school. I never imagined that I would be approaching you for help in getting published or that you would be so helpful. Thank you, from the bottom of my heart and a little to the left ... this is truly humbling and awesome.*

Amity Westcott—*my un-official editor who did more than any official editor ever could.*

The Creative Convention forum at Somethingawful.com—*Their advice and feedback were vital at different stages of this novel and always managed to tell me what I needed to hear—even if it wasn't what I wanted to hear. Thanks, guys.*

Cpl Mike Marshall—*2nd LAR Delta Company USMC—Your time at the Castle did not go to waste.*

TABLE OF CONTENTS

Flotilla

Prologue—Is This Thing On?

I DON'T KNOW how much longer I have to live.

This speech-to-text thing gives me something to talk to and I don't feel like dictating a will. Can you do me a favor? If you happen to find this, will you please contact Rick Westfield or Theresa Bowman and tell them what's happened to us? I have no idea where they are. Theresa is my mom and she lives in West Covina so I'm hoping that if there's any central evacuation place for Los Angeles that you can find her there. Rick Westfield is my Dad, he was taken ashore and we're trying to find him now.

Me and my sister Madison are on board this old yacht. It's called the Horner C. It's my Dad's boat and it's a beast. I spent a lot of time swabbing decks but I've never driven (sailed?) it before. I've been at sea for over six months but I have almost zero experience at how things work when the boat is under power.

My name is Jim, by the way.

It's about 2230 right now, 10:30 to everyone besides us. The weather is pretty bad, but I'm not complaining—if it wasn't for this storm Madison and I would have been grease spots on a deck somewhere. I'm hoping that the boat can handle it, but we're getting water under the door to the bridge and the wind is blowing us around on the water like a cheap kite. I can't hold my course to more than 20 or 30 degrees ... that might be the wind or the fact that this old tub hasn't moved in the last 10 years.

I'm trying to watch our GPS, the black night outside our windshield and Madison all at once. She's asleep at the chart table next to me ... I'm afraid she'll slide off the chair and crack her forehead on something.

I don't know how else to say it so I'll say it: the world has come to an end.

At first we heard the news that it was a virus of some kind. That was bad enough. Then more news started rolling in. There were coordinated attacks in several major cities. It just kept getting worse and worse.

We watched it all happen: riots in the Bay Area, Phoenix and St. Louis. There was a bug that was killing people in Baltimore and here in LA. Dirty bombs were set off in Reno, Plano and Vicksburg.

Everyone on the Colony had family in one of those places and we were all riveted to the feed hoping to hear something, hoping they were okay. Hope started to dwindle when we caught the reports of the shootings. People outside the infected zones were killing people because they might have been sick. Nobody bothered to check first, though ... they just started shooting.

We personally were out of danger, as in 'not about to die of the plague or nuclear contamination', but we had other problems. The place where we lived until very recently, Pacific Fisheries Colony D, is, well ... strange. Because it's strange, the problems you experienced there were strange. It's a long story, but the only thing you need to know right now is that it is my home and it's the most dangerous place on earth.

Sorry, not 'is,' 'was.' I have to get used to talking about Colony in the past tense now. Half an hour ago, the Navy came along and sunk it to the bottom of the ocean.

Anyway, my dad got himself in the middle of something that I still don't know the half of. They took him away. He went ashore with everyone else looking for 'survivors', but that's a load of crap. It was pure suicide but they didn't give him a choice.

Dad gave us a hug and said: "If you don't hear from me in a day, send a message to your mom. If you don't hear from me in four, take the boat, the docks and anyone else you can and go north. Find a place called Puget Sound and look for a small island to hang out. You can stay for a while. I'll find you there and we will be together again."

That was four days ago. Now he's gone and some drug pirates tried to kill us. Like I said, it's a long story.

Two days later after Dad left, we were leaving messages for Mom that we never got a response to. We dodged the pirates and some really scummy people Dad screwed over. Two days after that, I cut the boat loose and we were headed out to sea—just ahead of the Navy. We got out of there just by the skin of our teeth and that's no lie.

I'm not saying things were great out on the Colony but at least nobody was trying to kill me. Not until four days ago. This app posts all my speech-to-text stuff to a blog page. Hopefully, someone will find it. I'll post our coordinates as we go and if you haven't seen a post from us in more than 24 hours, will you call the Coast Guard, assuming we still have one?

*Our coordinates on the Colony were **33°24'9.37"N 120°13'2.10"W**—if you are sending a rescue party, start looking for us here.*

Chapter One—Shipping Out

"YOU'RE REALLY NEVER going to give me an answer, are you?" she said. We were eating breakfast at a Denny's off the 110 in Rancho Palos Verdes. The boat would meet us in the Port of Long Beach on some dock that Pacific Fisheries used as a point of embarkation for Colony visits.

So let's talk about how we get from there to here. When I first came to the Colony, it wasn't under happy circumstances. Sure, I wanted to visit my Dad out on the Colony and see its weirdness for myself but not like this. I was forcibly admitted to a 21-day session at a drug and alcohol treatment center. I got there because it was the third time I had been arrested for underage drinking and the first time that I was violating the terms of my probation by getting drunk. I wasn't even supposed to be out of the house—I was still grounded from getting probation two months ago.

They had to admit me for borderline alcohol poisoning. I passed out at a party and woke up handcuffed to a gurney while some RN the size of a fullback rammed an IV into my veins. Not my proudest moment.

Now she wants to shoehorn some therapy in as a going-away present.

"You didn't tell me that you were going to send me to Dad's," I replied.

"If you want people to be honest with you," she said, "you have to start with yourself. Why, Jim? Just tell me that much ... why?"

I was officially under arrest at the treatment center and about to do 6 months in YA, but Mom managed to convince the PO that she had an alternative option. She convinced my probation officer—this ugly white lady with dead eyes—to let me come out to be with Dad on the Colony. The PO said that coming to the Colony would be "part" of my community service and they'd discuss the remaining details when I returned. Dad was to give weekly reports on my "progress."

I'm reviewing all of this history because there's no way I could tell her what I really thought. She'd blow up, I'd blow up ... I don't want to walk to the pier. I was still trying to consider all my options when she pulled out of her parking slot at the rehab center and started heading toward the Denny's. The Lexapro made it hard to think.

I was feeling gross and I had a headache—this was definitely not the time to be doing an all-day boat trip. Mom had my stuff in the car and she gave me some clothes to wear for the ride. After two weeks of wearing sweat pants that kept falling off of my butt and hospital slides, it was weird to be dressed in jeans and sneakers.

My doctor put me on Lexapro to 'try it.' If that didn't work, he said, they'd give me Cymbalta. So many different medications for depression to choose from that it's almost like going to the salad bar. Just find the right mix to balance out the bad stuff in your head, kid. "Teach you to live life without chemical dependency," he said, without a hint of irony.

I'm such a mess right now that all I can do is sit there in the passenger seat like a sack of Jell-O. Please don't ask me to do anything, please just put me in my bed and let me sleep. Please ... please don't ask me to go for a car ride and please, whatever you do, don't ask me to get on a boat and go 120 miles out into the ocean. I am so not up for this today.

But you aren't really listening, are you, Mom?

"It didn't have to be this way," she said.

"Not that again," I said, trying to sound like I wasn't terrified. My mom was sending me away—is there anything that makes your 'nads shrink up more than that?

"I hope you find the answer, Jim. You almost killed yourself. You're becoming an alcoholic."

"Mom, I'm not an alcoholic ..." I started, but she cut me right off.

"You're binge drinking and you're 14, Jim. Let's not kid ourselves." She looked away and I could see that she was about to cry. "I'm such an idiot. I can't believe I didn't see it. I … I just feel like I've failed you, Jim and I need to know where I went wrong."

Nice one, Mom. I know you want me to break down and beg your forgiveness and admit that I'm the one who's stupid. But you're sending me away to live out on the ocean with my Dad and right now I'm not feeling that charitable.

So I didn't cry in front of Mom. I felt like it, but we're past the point where tears would have made a difference. After a few minutes, I noticed that Mom was crying quietly but it didn't really affect me. It should have made me feel something. I know people were watching and the waitress was giving me the stink eye. I felt some buzzing in my head, that's all. I blame the meds … it's as good an excuse as any. She got it together eventually and we finished breakfast in silence.

It took a few minutes to find the dock in the Port of Long Beach once we got there. I don't know if you've ever seen it but Pier F Avenue is really hard to find in that zoo. Close to half an hour tracking among the docks, Navy boats and container ships to find the squat building and docks that owned by the Pacific Fisheries' business office.

Mom pulled the car into the lot, popped the trunk and sat there. Maybe we were both waiting for the other person to say something. She silently handed me an envelope with some 'walking-around money' in it and I got out. I pulled my duffel bags that she had packed and closed the trunk. I walked around again to her side of the car, looking for a 'good-bye' or a kiss or both. She looked at me through the glass and took her foot off of the brake. She left me standing there in that parking lot without a word.

I had that buzzy feeling again—like I wanted to cry—but then she was gone and that was that. Here I was about to leave to go to sea and do the first 'adult' thing I'd ever done in my life. You don't cry at a moment like this. Even if you want to … you just don't.

"Help you?" a woman called from the door of the office. Maybe I'm not the first transportee that she's seen. I was processed through the office in about five minutes and then pushed out to the dock to wait for the ferry ride.

I paced up and down the planks smelling salt, tar and diesel fumes. Something hot to drink would have been nice, but I didn't know where to get it and I wasn't going to go back inside. The Pac Fish rep paid as little attention to me as possible when I was inside and hinted that she might drop-kick me into the water if I kept her from the mystery novel she was working on. I sat there, cold and numb, for half an hour waiting for that boat to arrive.

When it did arrive, it was not impressive. The ferry boat itself was a small pilothouse that had a cabin for up to 10 people to sit in and it wasn't here to take on passengers. Two silent Mexicans pulled stevedore duty and stuffed packages into the cabin until almost every cubic inch of space was filled. It took me a minute to realize that they were hauling groceries. Somehow I was supposed to find a place to sit in there.

"All set?" a gravelly voice asked. The old Filipino pilot waved me onboard, helping me step onto the boat without dropping my duffel in the water. My first taste of colony hospitality was of him jerking his thumb to the top of the bundles that filled the cabin and saying "You can sit *there*."

He immediately cast off by waving to the guys on the dock and hitting the starter switch on the motor. It grumbled to life and in a couple of seconds we were on our way. I was suddenly reminded of a memory: waiting in line at Magic Mountain to board a rollercoaster I wasn't thrilled about. There's a small pit in your stomach where all of your fear and doubt lives and it steadily grows as you wait for the ride to start. You want to get off, maybe talk your way off of the ride without looking like a wuss, but you know in your heart that there's simply no escape. You stew in your own fear and doubt until it's your turn to go.

The cargo was mostly food and the air filled with the smell of coffee and oranges. It hit me that I was really doing this. If I weren't feeling so crummy, I would actually be excited.

I tried to shift my weight during the loading only to hear corn chips or something crunch under my butt. The pilot yelped and made me get up while he checked the load. "I said *don't move!*" He snarled while repositioning something under the bags. He stabbed the air with a crooked old finger. "Okay. now sit there and don't move!" Meekly, I sat as ordered—the old fisherman spat some bitter words in Tagalog and refused to look at me for the rest of the trip. It was foggy and misty, with water streaming from the windows and a view that was only slightly less gray than the ocean. It was impossible to see where I was going to spend the next three months.

The Pacific Fisheries terminal is pretty close to open water at the harbor. After a few minutes of threading between a sailing yacht and a container ship, we were pointing toward the horizon. It would still be 10 or 12 hours before we reached the Colony itself. Most of the day with no one to talk to and express orders not to move—was I allowed to pee? I tried to make small talk with my host, but apparently he was deaf. Between radio checks with the Colony because he would never acknowledge that he heard anything I said.

The pilot was dressed in a green rain slicker and khaki trousers. He made adjustments to the console with hands that were like dark polished wood. The lack of any visual references outside the boat was disorienting to me, but it didn't seem to bother him. He kept his eyes fixed to a large flat compass and a GPS at the helm to keep us on course throughout our trip. We were on a course south from the LA harbor and would turn west after skirting Santa Catalina Island. I toyed with the idea of being washed overboard near Avalon. They let you stow away home on the ferry, right?

I knew roughly from Dad's emails that the Colony was out in the open ocean south of the Channel Islands, but this boat trip gave his description a much larger sense of scale. The ocean was rougher and the crack of waves against the hull started to sound like gunshots. We were going out there, way out there, and if I wasn't convinced that I would be on my own before, I was now. The sinking feeling in my stomach, the rollercoaster feeling, was growing into a full-on panic attack. I was definitely off of the reservation this time and nobody was going to fix that.

Motoring for ten or twelve hours on the ocean can be a rude awakening when all of your previous water experience comes from wakeboarding on the lake. I mean, I didn't get seasick but there was nothing to recommend the journey. Halfway into the trip, the old guy let me get off the groceries and take a piss off of the rear of the boat when I thought I was going to explode. There I was hanging onto the railing on a pitching deck and trying not to fall overboard with my schlong out. If they ever make pissing an Olympic sport, this would be one of the events. He talked me through working the little galley stove and I heated up some ramen in cheap foam cups for the both of us. He threw in a Coke from stock he was hauling. The day felt two weeks long but finally the colony appeared before us, pitching in and out of the rain.

At first glance, the Colony looked less like a business than it did floating wreckage. This is where my Dad lived? It looked like a naval disaster. I could see the lights of the different ships, but it was clear they were there to provide the minimum amount of illumination and only if one stood directly below or around them. The wind started to moan and whip the ocean into whitecaps. The old fisherman wildly spun the wheel and nosed the boat away from something. I craned my neck to see what had happened and saw a set of nets he'd nearly run into. Where were we supposed to dock?

The network of docks in the colony had been designed to allow the ferry boat to nose in and tie up directly at the colony. I knew this from Dad's emailed descriptions, but I couldn't see where that point was. As we neared a single boat, the pilot spun the wheel and goosed the engines slightly. I was certain we were about to crash but soon saw what the old fisherman had seen. The small opening presented itself and allowed the ship to come inside to dock in the center.

Riding up to the main dock let me get a closer look at my new home. The picture coalesced and I could see the boats and the people on them preparing their evening meals. The rain caused individual scenes to fade in and out of view. Open cook fires and people huddled around them. Men, women and children moved in and out of the shadows wearing cheap plastic rain gear if they wore any at all. Orange plastic work lights twisted in the wind over decks made out of cheap plywood covered with cheaper non-skid yellow plastic. Was it like this on purpose? An old Asian woman sat on a milk crate peeling potatoes. With her hair soaked and plastered to her head, she let the peels fall right into the water. She disappeared in the rain and then I was watching a group of Mexican men standing around a gas grill. Their cooking location was the back deck of a barge-like ship and they paused to look at me watching them. Then they were gone again as the boat motored through another turn.

I was either an alien visitor to a new world or the world's most pathetic tourist. The Colony being the jumbled mess that it was, you felt disoriented just looking at it. Brand new yachts rubbed fenders with broken-down houseboats. Trim plastic-and-metal docks touched puke-colored sheets of splintered pressboard sitting on top of sawed-off telephone poles. Cheery groups of Mexican or Asian families went about their business next to each other, ignoring the sullen-looking white guy across the water with the thousand-yard stare.

It took a while but finally the boat pulled up to dock next to the *Phoenix*, the ship at the center of this disaster zone. Dad had told me that he would meet me there. In our conversations, he had told me a few things about the ship. It was strange to see it finally in person. It was like seeing the Golden Gate Bridge in San Francisco for the first time after looking at it for years in pictures, movies and television. I was here ... after two years, I had finally arrived. I stepped outside to look at the grey cliff of steel, getting my face immediately soaked by the rain.

"Hey, j'wanna gimme a hand?" the old Filipino said. "Your Da' said you would help—that's why I didn't charge him." I turned around to see my two duffel bags airborne and flying at my face. I managed to catch them but staggered under the impact. I recovered before I could go flying off of the dock and into the water. Looking down, I saw that but there was no dry place to drop them. I could only set my bag onto the deck which was already puddled with rainwater.

"That's good," the pilot remarked, watching me vainly try to find a way to keep my stuff dry. I gave up and set it in the smallest puddle on the dock, hoping Dad had a dryer or something. "I always send out the laundry first—if you can't handle that, no way am I letting you touch the food." He began tossing other bags to me in the same way. Some of them were easy, like the pillows in sealed plastic bags and others were not. I struggled to find a place for a forty-pound bag of dry dog food that he suddenly tossed in my direction. My first ten minutes onboard the Colony and I am supposed to move cargo for this quietly violent old man? Hardly the welcome that I was hoping for.

I worked in silence and considered my situation. The sinking feeling in my stomach was getting worse. During the treatment center period, I developed this gut feeling that I had crossed the line from a comfortable level of trouble into something much deeper. It never got any better even though I was waiting for that time when things would be on their way back to normal. I wasn't there yet. That gut feeling got worse when mom told me I was leaving to go see Dad during the breakfast and riding out here had not improved things. Now, standing on the teetering dock, soaked to the bone, this bad feeling was larger than my whole stomach. I don't think I've ever felt so lost or so alone. I didn't want this … I wanted to go home. I wanted my *Mom*.

Whoa. Did I just say that? This wasn't the time or the place to go to pieces. Stop it, I yelled to myself. I looked around quickly and saw the dock and the gangplank leading up to the destroyer. The pilot was busy doing something on the boat. Either he was ignoring me or maybe he forgot I was there. I toyed with the idea of pulling a runner while he had his back to me. I was carefully picking up my duffel and preparing to sneak away … find a boat or a phone and beg Mom to arrange transport. My feet were shifting into *out of here* mode when I heard a voice over my shoulder.

"How was the trip?" I turned around suddenly hoping to see Dad. A kid was talking me from the gangplank of the *Phoenix*. He stepped carefully off of the aluminum gangplank and started toward me. The boy was younger and smaller than I was but wore a leather jacket I could have camped out under. He sauntered up to the cargo stacked on the dock and started rummaging through a double-bagged sack of oranges like he owned them. Maybe he did, how was I supposed to know? The pilot caught him after he placed the second one in his pocket and reacted swiftly.

"Hey, gimme 'dat!" the old man screamed and made a show of waving a large rusty boat hook at us. Faster than I would have thought possible, the kid pirouetted on his toes and darted off down the docks without another word. In a second or two he was gone in the silvery sheets of rain.

The fisherman was cursing in Tagalog, searching for the equivalent in English and too angry to find it. I heard the word "Craphead!" in among another long string of angry foreign cursing while he looked at the damage. Gesturing at me, he continued his tirade while slapping the wet sides of his boat and stabbing his finger in the direction of the departed thief. Bystanders looked at me like I was to blame. I kept my mouth shut and stood there; too tired and too scared to care. I was wet, tired and hungry— now maybe my free trip was gone because of this shoplifting kid.

"Problems?" Dad had appeared at my elbow and I had been too distracted and frightened to notice. He didn't seem surprised by the screaming or how I looked, dripping wet and ready to start swimming for home. He didn't seem to notice the weather or the heaving deck. In fact, Dad looked comfortable wearing a ratty pair of thongs and a bright Traffic Yellow slicker. It had been a year since we had seen each other. He had a goatee now and his traditional high-and-tight was starting to include some streaks of gray.

The pilot was still steamed, but he finally calmed down enough to communicate in English. "Your kid's a thief!" the pilot yelled. I jumped at the accusation, but Dad put a restraining arm on my elbow. "You can pay me off later, Rick but the kid owes me a new bag of oranges. I want my boat fee for hauling him out here, too!"

"That's crap, Ignacio," Dad said shortly. He was a short guy, but he had the shoulders of a linebacker. I don't know why but his balanced stance on the dock felt somewhat predatory to me. "Jim didn't steal your oranges and that kid sure didn't make off with a whole bag. Jim didn't know he was boosting until he was gone."

The boat pilot wasn't about to back down and I suddenly noticed his hunched and leathery neck … kind of like a turtle. "In the old days," he commented darkly. "We'd just take his hand."

"And you're welcome to," Dad replied wearily. "As soon as you find the hand." He picked up the duffel in a single hand and began to move away. "Thanks for the lift, boss," he called back over his shoulder. "Com'on, Jim." Dad moved off almost as quickly as the shoplifter.

I had to run on wet and treacherous docks to catch up. The Colony was laid out in concentric circles of docks—A through E—We walked on our way to the E-ring where the *Horner* was and it took 20 minutes to make our way out there. Dad took a dizzying set of rights and lefts I knew I wouldn't be able to remember.

As we walked along, I tried to take everything in. The place had a vibe to it like this flea market we used to go to every Saturday over at the Rose Bowl. People were moving all over the place and you had to squeak through them balanced against the motion of the sea. People were busy eating dinner—the cuisine looked like it had come from every corner of the world. The smell of curry mixed with smoky barbeque and hot cornmeal. Onions, garlic and hot soup—my stomach started to growl. Kids were all around us chattering in different languages. At first I couldn't understand why these people would be out in the rain like this but then I realized that some of the places we passed on the docks were actually restaurants. Lots of little counters and stalls with two or three stools but then we passed one with tables and a waiter. *Stranger by the minute*, I thought.

The docks were wide and inviting in some places and other places they crowded you almost to the water's edge. Dad seemed to be an expert, he moved through the crowds without breaking stride while I bounced around like a drunken acrobat. My initial fears of dying before I could find Dad were replaced by my fear that Dad would somehow get me killed before we could get to the boat. I was certain I would never be found again if he wandered off and stared so hard at his back that my eyes began to hurt.

It was dark and wet in some spots but in others, they had rigged lights and rain cover. The clear plastic sheets were stretched across the open space, sagging dangerously with water. *They won't last long as as rain shelters*, I thought. The weight would eventually cause them to burst. With my luck, it would happen while I was standing right below them. Then I saw that I wasn't the only person who saw it … but where I saw a problem, he had seen an opportunity. A squirrelly-looking white guy came along with a huge equipment dolly that held a compressor hooked to a large plastic tank. He reached up with a J-shaped rubber hose and started to suck the water out each rain shelter.

I watched him move from shelter to shelter and I had to be impressed by the simple genius of a shelter/water trap. It was an 'oh, wow' moment for me, cut short when I realized suddenly that fresh water was probably something we didn't get a lot of out here.

I felt an elbow in my ribs and turned: Dad had realized I was not behind him and came back to get me. We weren't going directly to the boat. He took me to dinner at one of the full sit-down floating restaurants. Pho and egg rolls—simple stuff but it was hot and tasted great. Dad kept introducing me to everyone in his line of sight. We couldn't go more than a bite or two before Dad was waving someone over and going "This is Jim, my son … the one I told you about!" Then an ancient Chinese woman would be patting my cheek or I would be shaking some old white guy's callused, weathered hand.

Dad's introductions continued through the dinner and the rest of the walk to the boat. Some people were all smiles and handshakes, others were a little distant and still others were glazed over, like Dad was introducing them to a hamster. It wouldn't have mattered if they gave me wads of cash or beat on me—I was so overloaded with names and faces that I wouldn't be able to recall any of them a day later. I was more tired than I'd ever felt in my life. I was ready to collapse on the soaking deck when Dad announced: "Here we are!"

Based on Dad's pictures, I was expecting to find it easier. The *Horner C* was moored with the aft swim platform up against the E Ring dock and looked almost invisible against the dozens of boats I'd already passed. I could barely make out the upper deck in the dripping gloom. Somewhere inside, a light burned making it look friendly and welcoming. Dad led me up a small set of stairs where he then unlocked the rear salon door and waved me inside.

"Drop your stuff here for a moment," Dad said, and disappeared downstairs somewhere. I stood there, dripping wet and exhausted, looking at the boat Dad had been describing to me for the last two years. We were in the salon, a large rear lounge area that was as wide as the ship. Cheap furniture faced a small flat panel screen that hung over a fake fireplace that didn't look like it burned anything in decades.

I moved forward up some stairs into the galley area. You could see the boat had been expensive at one point, but it had suffered years of abuse. The scratched and scarred faux granite countertops told me that evidently, nobody had ever heard of a cutting board on this ship. Most of the LED lights overhead needed replacing but the ones that worked showed wooden cabinets that were splintered and warped from decades of contact with the sea air. Forward of the galley was the bridge. A single faded and torn leather chair sat in front of the large chrome ship's wheel. The console was filled with different buttons and readouts, but I had no idea what any of them did. They looked broken anyway. Two chairs had sat there at some point in the past, but only one remained, leaving a chair mount I would constantly have to avoid tripping over.

Stairs disappeared below somewhere and I saw another set of stairs heading to the upper deck back in the salon. Boats are really three-dimensional and even though it was half the size of my mom's house back in West Covina, I felt lost and enormously out of place. Finally, Dad reappeared in the galley and beckoned me downstairs. Out of all the cabins on the boat, the only semi-available space was the crew quarters. Dad had the Master Stateroom at the head of the passage and the other stateroom was completely full of junk.

"Guess things happened too quickly," Dad said, sweeping stacks of old newspapers and books roughly to the floor with one arm. With the other, he dumped a bundle of old, nasty blankets onto the bare mattress. It was cold and cold and wet in this cabin … I could almost see my breath. Someone had left a porthole open and so that any heat in the room had disappeared hours before. "You'll be staying here," he continued. "One of your first jobs will be to get this cabin in shape." He turned and disappeared back up the passageway.

I sat down on the bunk and took in my new room. It was large by boat standards but since it was crowded with junk I had only enough room to stand up and turn around in. When they ship a dog on a plane, the dog crate has more space than what I had to work with. *What am I doing here?* I kept asking myself that question over and over again while I tried to shift the junk enough so I could put my bags down.

The buzzing in my head had gotten worse and on top of that, the rolling below decks was making me nauseous. I was supposed to take some meds that were back in my bags somewhere—Dad may not have been told about my prescription. Hungry, tired, had to pee and miserable … that was me at that moment. The rain was actually the opening act on a full-blown storm and this was how I was introduced to life on the sea.

I'm going to pause this thing for a second and drive or pilot or sail— whatever you want to call it. I'll pick it up again in a few.

Our current position is: 33°50'21.60"N 120°16'17.53"W

Chapter Two—Gardens and Guns

I PLANNED ON going straight to bed, but Dad had other plans. We were up until midnight catching up. He drank beer and smoked half a pack of cigarettes while I told him all about the trouble I had been into.

"Your mother hasn't been keeping me in the loop," he said, his hands working to repair a green nylon net.

"She told you about the rehab, right?" I asked hopefully.

"Sort of. Why don't you tell me?" I had a lot of details to fill in. I tried to be as up-front as I could but the whole story made me want to die of embarrassment. I'm a real doofus when you stop and think about it. I could tell that some parts of the story were upsetting, especially when I got to how I almost died.

"You had alcohol poisoning?" he asked. "How much did you drink?"

I had to admit the truth. "A lot."

"What does that mean?"

I didn't know how to answer that and shrugged helplessly. He gave me an ugly look but didn't comment. In my embarrassment, I kept peppering my conversations with a bunch of 'you knows' and 'uhs'. Dad said absolutely nothing throughout my story until I finally ran out of things to say. He stared at the ceiling for a while.

Finally, he brought his eyes back to me. "Pen patrol starts at dawn," he said while crushing out his cigarette. "Get some sleep." He slapped some light switches and the upper deck of the boat plunged into darkness. I had to find my way to the stairs by touch and the dim light from other boats. Dad's voice followed me down the hole: "Tomorrow you are going to work harder than you've ever worked in your life."

I stumbled below to my stateroom. Dad disappeared into his cabin and shut the door. I wasn't sure where the bathroom was. Dad would start with the nautical terms in the morning and I was expected to call it a 'head' like everyone else. I would learn its dirty little secret soon enough. Ever been desperate to piss and too tired to make it to the john or is that just me? Just before falling asleep I discovered that with a little ingenuity you could actually crack the porthole open and take a leak by bracing yourself against the bulkhead. Thankfully, nobody saw me bent against the window trying to take a piss … I'm sure I looked like an idiot. By the time I was done I was panting from the effort of holding myself up like a drunken gymnast.

My duffel was on the bed and I pushed it to the floor. As it landed, a plastic bag full of meds fell out and I picked them up. Mom had packed all of the stuff the doctor gave me into a freezer bag, along with typed dosage instructions. I couldn't handle thinking about that right now. I sank back onto the bed, wrapped myself in blankets and fell asleep almost instantly.

It felt like I had barely shut my eyes when Dad was shaking me awake again. It was still dark outside, what were we doing up? "Wakey-wakey … Eggs and bakey." Didn't I hear that line in a movie? I groaned and rolled over.

Dad poked me hard in the ribs. "Get 'em up. On your feet."

I groaned again, from the fatigue as well as the poke in my ribs. "Is it morning already?" I asked groggily to his departing profile.

"Yes." He was gone before I could say anything else.

When I stumbled upstairs to the galley, Dad was leaning against the fridge while drinking coffee from an old enamel mug. Smoke from his cigarette curled upward and clung to the ceiling. Dad had changed into a wetsuit that stank of fish and cigarettes.

As for me, I was shivering, half-asleep and barely aware of anything. When you're fourteen, days don't start this early. The boat was dark, cold and about as welcome as a pitcher of ice water dumped on your junk. I had finally changed out of my rehab clothes, but I couldn't find my jacket. Dad's only nod to the cold weather was a cheap fleece jacket and an ancient Yankees cap so I thought (incorrectly) that it would be warm outside.

"Are we going to have breakfast?" I asked.

Dad shrugged and pointed toward a blue windbreaker hanging on a peg next to the bathroom door. "Food second, chores first. Put that on."

No breakfast? This was ridiculous! After that, Dad communicated in hand gestures and grunts. I took the cup of coffee he offered, but it was too hot for me to drink. I blew for several minutes on the hot coffee to cool it but I still singed my tongue when I tried my first sip. He finished his butt and dropped it in an overflowing tin bucket on the counter next to the sink.

Over another cup of coffee, Dad started to explain the rules of Pen Patrol, one of the principal duties of mariculture. Mariculture, Dad explained, was about raising fish for sale while living on the ocean. They raised the fish by maintaining them in pens and his personal catch of fish lived in the nets he had connected to the *Horner C.* He had explained most of this in his emails over the last two years but somehow I couldn't make the connection until I was standing here in the galley. Raising fish for sale. *Raising them while living on the ocean. Living on the ocean to take care of the fish.* I had to say it a few times in my head until it started to make sense.

"It's like this," Dad said arranging his gear. "Mariculture is what they call raising fish on the open ocean, instead of raising them on a fish farm. Commercial fishing's been in a nosedive over the past 50 years. Overfishing, pollution … catches get smaller and smaller. People can't agree on solutions and meanwhile the problem just keeps getting worse. No end in sight.

"Then different companies like our company, Pacific Fisheries, start to experiment with mariculture and sea-ranching. They've been doing it in Japan and Canada for decades, but nobody really gave it a shot over here until now. The fish grow in their natural habitat free from predators. They get big enough, they get transported back to shore for processing. Simple, right?"

Dad continued with the brief history of "Pac Fish", the different colonies on the California coastline and then he moved onto some Pen Patrol rules while he finished suiting up. Finally, we stepped out onto the deck. The *Horner* is connected with the rest of the Colony at the E-Ring docks. Like every other boat on the E-Ring, it's moored so that the stern of the boat faces the dock and the bow faces outward. We have to exit to the rear and then walk between the *Horner* and the neighboring ship, the *Key*

West Forever, to the 'fishing porch.' This would be our work area. The fishing porch was a leftover piece of vinyl deck was clumsily strapped to the cleats of the *Horner* and our pen system was strapped to that with zip-ties and heavy wire. *A real piece of White Trash art*, I thought. Since we were out on the ocean, the deck was never stable and I had to constantly balance myself to avoid going off into the water. The deck creaked quietly under our feet and Dad motioned at me to keep the noise down as some people were still asleep.

Or maybe not … I could look across the docks and see the lights on in the galleys of many other boats. "I guess you aren't the only early bird here," I said.

"Hmm?" Dad was fooling with some of his air hoses.

"Nothing."

"Right." He knelt to strap on his fins. He started to explain other aspects of Pen Patrol—watching the regulator for alarms and holding the signal cord. "One tug means are you okay?" Dad grunted while tugging on a fin. "One tug back means 'everything's cool' or 'okay.' Two tugs going down means 'come up' or 'help me' and three tugs means 'emergency'." He paused and poked a hole in my shoulder. "If you feel three tugs, that means drop everything, got it?"

I nodded since my teeth were chattering. I was wearing the windbreaker but no shoes. The dank morning air had started in on me when I came out and now Dad saw me shivering. "Try some shoes, if you want," he suggested. I looked out at everyone else out there working and shook my head. They didn't seem affected and I didn't want to look like a wimp. Dad shrugged and got his stuff together ready while I slowly froze. He finished his prep, handed me his signal cord and took a giant step off of the dock and into the water.

He hadn't warned me. I was standing too close and his landing soaked my pants. Thanks, Dad.

The fishing porch had an old potter's bench that Dad had bolted to the deck as a work table. I leaned against it while holding his signal cord and watching it lazily pay out into the water. As the minutes passed Dad's diver light grew dim and as he moved deeper into the pens. The breeze was blowing in from the water and my goose bumps were starting to develop goose bumps. I wished for a refill of that coffee, but Dad said not to leave the line. Could I leave him for a minute? I felt a sharp tug on the signal line—just one. It made me smile … Dad was making sure that I was there and hadn't gone to sleep. I gave a good yank back on the line. Yeah, I'm still here.

The sky grew grey, then red—I found a plastic lawn chair to sit in and moved next to each of the pens he was working on. I kept nodding off— his sharp tugs would wake me long enough to pull back and then I'd nod off again. I started to get a headache and there were those meds I needed to take. Dad would occasionally surface and I'd hand a tool or a roll of nylon line that he pointed to. He took no breaks and so neither did I. Tending the signal line was so boring that you couldn't help getting drowsy and yet you couldn't leave. The second I even thought of leaving I'd get a sharp little tug or Dad would pop up. It felt like a torture designed by Buddhist monks: sit here, be uncomfortable and hold this piece of string. Under no circumstances are you allowed to move.

It felt like Dad was deliberately trying to drive me crazy. Maybe he wanted to start things off by getting back at me for being in rehab. The thought made me mad and that knot of anger helped me to stay awake.

Two geological ages later Dad climbed out of the water, stiff and cold from his morning workout. He spat spitting his regulator into his hand. "Thanks for doing that," he said, his sinuses were clogged with salt water. "Lemme dry off and we'll get some breakfast." He led me inside and stripped off his gear right there in the salon without a word of warning. I was a few seconds behind him closing the door and was shocked to see him suddenly buck naked and using a wet towel to quickly rinse all of the salt water off.

He saw me standing there. "You mind?" he growled. I quickly moved past him and into the galley. He finished with the wet towel and then dried off with some dry old rag that looked like it belonged in a dumpster. Then he put on some dry clothes and started putting together something to eat. My first meal aboard the *Horner* was a breakfast of frozen waffles and reconstituted eggs. I sat with him, drinking a cup of coffee that tasted much better to me than I thought it would. Coffee, if you're having it for the first time, is disgusting. However, I was at a point of fatigue and cold where I wasn't focused on the taste, just the heat. I never understood before why people were such freaks for it.

"Dad, I have some pills I have to take," I finally said as he was putting the finishing touches on our meal. I neglected to mention it last night or this morning, but Mom said part of my responsibility was to take them every single day. Dad barely looked up from the frying pan he was stirring.

"So take 'em," he said. "Want me to count them out for you?"

"No."

"Where are they?"

I pulled my luggage up from the stateroom and together, we went through the bag Mom had packed for me—it was really the first time I'd looked inside. My heart sank as I realized my laptop and my music were not in there. Just some clothes, a toothbrush, underwear and socks. This wasn't like her at all, I thought. A clue about how mad she was, perhaps? I tossed the freezer bag full of pill containers to Dad. Inside was a hand-written note from Mom and he scanned it briefly.

"You were supposed to take some last night," he commented. "No biggie. We'll start you off now and it'll be your job to take them after this." He showed me how to read the prescription and count out the pills. It was something of a learning experience to me; I just assumed after the stay in the treatment facility that all meds were dosed in those stupid paper cups.

Dad returned to his cooking and we ate shortly afterward. I realized while eating that it was a frozen-dinner version of the one Mom had sent me off with. Weird. I wanted to go back to sleep after breakfast … I needed to sleep worse than I ever had before in my life. I told Dad that but he shook his head.

"This is a working ship, son," he said. "We sleep after the job is done." I must have looked awful, but he couldn't let me sleep. On top of that, he was working me like a day laborer out of the Home Depot parking lot. What was this all about?

After we had cleared the dishes, we started cleaning the lower-half of the *Horner*. Dad gave me a lecture on the proper maintenance of a boat's interior and how to clean it 'stem to stern.' It was obvious that the place hadn't seen the wet side of a dishrag before I showed up but I wasn't in a position to argue. "I'll do the galley," Dad said, "if you'll take the head." I agreed, appreciating Dad's generosity - he knew how much I hated doing dishes. I went to get started on the bathroom. This would also be my first chance to use it.

When I opened the door, the stink just about blew me away. I sagged back against the door. Imagine your old uncle just *unloading* on the toilet and then leaving it unflushed for several days in the middle of summer. Fetid, stinking—it smelled like … like *death*. I felt my breakfast come up and thought I was going to puke right there.

"Get that door shut!" Dad hollered from the galley distracting me from my nausea. "That thing will stink up the whole ship!" I slammed the door shut and leaned against it like I was afraid the stench might try to break through and kill us.

"What happened in there?" I whined. "Did someone die?"

"Shaddup," Dad replied, moving quickly to open the salon door and let some fresh air in. "You said you'd clean the head, now get going." He set the salon door it on some kind of built-in latch so it would neither slam open or closed in the constant breeze. Meanwhile, I was slow to move … I'm serious: this stink was *bad*. Dad turned around and saw that I was reluctant to carry out my orders. I had been aboard less than 24 hours and already we were doing the Battle of the Wills. Dad knew how to win, though.

He took a single step toward me what appeared to be violence in his eyes. Choosing death by stink over death by Dad, I flung the door to the head open and locked myself in—I didn't even get to take a deep breath. I was locked in with the worst smell I had ever smelled in my entire life. I started gagging immediately. Inside the head, the smell wasn't any worse but now there was no fresh air to find. A small window had been opened and I put my nose up to it, breathing big lung-filling gasps of fresh air. I spent about five minutes at that window like a dog trying to sniff under a door. Then I hiked the neck of my t-shirt up over my nose … it was better than nothing.

I heard a fist thump against the door. "I don't hear movement!" he called. "You won't die. Get moving!" He punctuated this with another fist thump and I heard him move outside.

Realizing that there was no way I'd get out of this without cleaning this horrible room, I looked around to see if I could locate the source of the stink. Maybe someone had taken a dump but missed? I gingerly checked the small space to see if I was right. The thought alone was nauseating, but the head was so small that it took me no more than two seconds to dismiss the possibility. No major evidence of a poop crime scene ... what had happened? I gave up and moved on to the rest of my chore.

While taking time-outs to breathe in the fresh air and cleaning the bathroom down, I was able to at least make use of an important lesson Mom had taught me: the proper way to clean the bathroom. I didn't want to have to do any of this over again if Dad didn't like the first pass.

Dad knocked on the door about fifteen minutes after I had closed it, I was nearly done. "You still alive in there?" he asked.

"Yeah," I replied. I finished wiping down the shower and mirrors with ammonia (which helped cut the smell) and then stepped outside. Dad was quick to shut the door behind me. "Phew!" I exclaimed melodramatically like I a coal miner suffocating from dangerous gases. "Is this what I get for drinking at parties?" I was trying to be funny, but it was the wrong thing to say.

It turned out to be poor timing on my part. Dad had turned from the door he was about to open and gave me a smart crack on the crown of my head with his knuckles before I was even aware it was happening.

"No," he said. "*That* is what you get when you drink at parties." He pinned me to the wall with his stare. My stomach clenched involuntarily ... I've never seen this side of Dad before. The tension in the room went from a 3 to a 10 in the space of a second. "Don't ever joke about that to me. Not even a little bit."

I didn't know what to say. My brain just disengaged and hung there in Neutral while my face got hot and itchy. No ... it definitely was not going to be fun and games out here. Dad didn't wait for me to respond. He pulled open the door to the head, gave a cursory glance and slammed the door shut. "Very good," he pronounced. "Now do that to the rest of this boat. I'm going to give you"—he glanced at his watch—"four hours. This boat had *better* be clean by then." He disappeared through the salon door without another word.

I was still in shock from the smack he gave me. After a few moments, I sat down on the couch to consider my situation. It's like I was suddenly put into boot camp or prison. Just arrived, no sleep, bad food and I'm getting worked me like a slave. Was this guy *really* my Dad? Where was the guy who chatted with me over email and helped me with my homework?

After about twenty minutes, I looked up at the clock and realized that I was losing time. I got up and started cleaning. It felt good to be focused on something besides my own fear and uncertainty. I spent a lot of time thinking about everything I knew about him. For those ten seconds it was like he was going to kill me. Was I really in trouble or was he just trying to fake me out? Reconnecting with him had given me an impression of him that he was going out of his way to destroy. Why would he do that? The email conversations we had left no indication that things would be like this when I visited.

I felt like I had gone crazy or that my Dad had been replaced by aliens. Was this some kind of a prank? Everything I knew about him, every conversation we had over the past two years and everything he told me about living out here. Nothing ... *nothing* was like what I expected.

Mom had built up a picture in my mind about him: smart, funny and a screw-up. "Like you, kiddo," she'd laugh. She showed me the pictures she had of him—the one where he was smiling through a scuba mask on a beach somewhere in Mexico was my favorite.

She'd talk about his jail time, the failed businesses and the times she'd caught him cheating more often than anything else about him. He disappeared from our lives three months before Madison was born. For ten years, it was just the three of us and my grandparents and then Marty came along. During that time, Mom didn't find anyone permanent in her life and the thought of Dad just made her angry more than anything else. She barely said anything about him but if she did, it wasn't nice. It usually something like, "I'm not saying I don't love him. I'm saying he's a hard man to love." I think she thought I was supposed to be satisfied with that. It still doesn't make sense to me.

Dad's personality came up a lot after I got into trouble. Mom, Marty, my probation officer and my counselor ... everyone was very certain that I was 'acting out' because he left. My whole point was 'why did I wait twelve years to act out?' but nobody was really listening.

During one of the family sessions, Mom and I had a really bad argument. She came very close to saying that she was sorry she met my Dad. It was one of those moments where you're yelling at each other and then other person is about to say something. They almost say it and you know it's going to be really mean, but then they just clam up. They stop short and at the moment they're staring into your eyes, you know exactly what they're about to say. Not saying it doesn't change anything. Something about wishing she'd never met Dad and never met me - I think that's where she was going to go.

Mom and I stood there, eyeball to eyeball, knowing that she was about to say something really ugly. The counselor ended that session early, but a cloud of funk hung over every other time he and I talked. Mom and I didn't talk again until she handed me that email printout telling me that I was coming here.

So ... now we're here. Between the fact that he's been gone and then he suddenly showed up when I was 12 and now this, I guess I really didn't know how I was supposed to feel about him. Maybe that's why I wanted to come out here ... I thought it was supposed to be a chance to get to know him. Does that make sense? It's like begging your parents for a new bike or something and then getting it and realizing you don't really want it. You aren't supposed to feel that way about your Dad.

I was putting the finishing touches on mopping the deck when he returned. "Nice work," he said. He was carrying a shopping bag, folded shut, under his arm. Silently, he set it on the counter out of the way and started to inspect my cleaning job. I think he wanted to make sure I wasn't hiding piles of laundry in closets somewhere. His inspection was a little more detailed than the one he did for the head. I guess he was pleased because all he said was: "Come with me." He picked up that folded shopping bag again and headed outside.

Out of the *Horner* for the first time today, I started to relax and take in the scenery. The entire colony was up and hard at work at whatever it was they were up to. We walked along the dock with Dad introducing more people to me and giving mini-lectures about 'how things worked.' "Each boat has its own network of nets, grows its own fish and essentially is responsible for everything in between."

We stopped and he introduced me to the two old gay guys who lived next door to us. Their boat was named the *Key West Forever*—they grew calamari and tuna. The younger one was over 50 and built like a small grizzly bear. He reminded me of that old guy in Pete's Dragon some reason. What was his name? Mickey, Mickey something. Anyway, the other guy was tall and thin and I would later find out, did a lot of naked yoga positions on their back deck. Completely gross. It earned him his nickname: Naked Yoga Guy. NYG was into the whole neo-hippy thing … tan as an Indian with a salt-and-pepper mullet and never without the silver and turquoise pendant around his neck even if he was wearing nothing else.

Dad continued the tour around the E-Ring. It took us a half-hour to get to the other side because of the introductions and Dad pointing little things out to me.

"We're going to raise tuna on the next catch cycle," Dad said.

"What's a catch cycle?" I asked.

"Catch cycles are the amount of time you spend raising fish that will be sold off and sent to the mainland," he replied. "Getting the fish that you can raise isn't that simple, though. You can't just pour a bunch of fish eggs in the water; you actually have to get juveniles from somewhere. Some of the other boats raise fish from eggs to larvae to juvenile fish just so that other boats like the Horner can raise them in the larger, ocean-facing pens. It's a complex little economy we have going on out here. There are a lot of ways to make and lose money."

Dad introduced me to some fat Hawaiian guy who turned out to be a connection on juvenile tunas. For the next half hour, they went back and forth on prices and details that made no sense to me. Gradually, it became clear that they were negotiating prices for the fish. "I want 500 against 5 percent of the take," the Hawaiian guy kept saying.

"You've never wanted 5 percent—last time you were at 3 percent," Dad argued.

"What can I say, Rick? The prices have gone up."

They went back and forth for an hour, finally agreeing on six hundred dollars or 7 percent of the take, whichever was more. By that time, I was stumbling with fatigue but Dad didn't seem to be affected. He jabbed me in the ribs repeatedly to keep me awake. Then we continued the tour where Dad had left off. At one point, he nodded toward the *Phoenix*. "The company provides pretty much everything you need ... at a price," he said. "Other people have a side business, along with growing fish. Like the restaurant we ate at last night."

"What's your side business?" I asked.

"I don't have one yet," he grinned. "That's the problem." Dad had only been here for a couple of years and had yet to settle into one scam or another. He dabbled here or there but couldn't make anything successful. "Straight fishing is difficult. You can eat, but you don't eat well. I'm trying to build some contacts here and get something going."

He turned suddenly down a very precarious-looking section of docks that separated the E and D rings. I moved to follow him but stopped when I saw what he was up to. A home-built pontoon bridge had been installed as a shortcut between the rings using only the most 'scrap' of scrap wood available. Sawed-off pieces of telephone pole and large logs had been randomly chained together. On top of them, sheets of plywood and particle board had been nailed or attached to give footing. No handrails, not even a rope to hold onto. It looked like the work of a drunken teenager and yet it was a major thoroughfare? The sheets of wood were splintered from months or years of foot traffic. Dad waved impatiently from the other side. "Come on!"

I knew I was going to regret this. Gingerly, I started to make my way across and almost immediately found myself stumbling. Just before I plunged in, I managed a shaky dismount back onto the deck. I don't know how Dad managed to walk across as easily as he did, I could barely hold on.

Looking across, I could see Dad and he was laughing at me. "First time's the worst," he called. "Com'on over!" Gingerly, I half-crawled across the pontoons and moved from one platform to the next making about a foot every minute or so. I'm sure I looked like an idiot, inching my way across this monkey fence on my hands and knees, but it was either that or swim across. I was half-way there when I heard some laughs and looked up. A crowd of people was waving and snapping pictures with their phones on a completely functional bridge that wasn't more than 20 feet away. You couldn't see it until you were where I was and by that time, it would take longer to go back than suck it up and finish your journey. They clapped and cheered for me when I reached the other side.

"Congratulations, you made it," Dad said. "Doing the pontoons is part of the initiation around here. Fun, huh?"

"Cute," I replied, trying not to snap. "Was that really necessary?"

Dad simply shrugged and continued on as if it never happened. We continued to pass boats of different sizes, shapes and conditions … Dad had a story for each of them. As we passed a rusting converted car ferry, Dad told me about the vats of fish larvae it sold and the guy who lived in the tiny wheelhouse. In the next berth was probably the nicest looking boat in the place, a fishing trawler that looked like it belonged on the cover of a fishing magazine. I paused to admire it, but Dad quickly waved me along.

"You don't wanna hang around with those guys," he said.

"Why not?"

Dad shook his head. "Weirdos, kid."

The cleanest boat was the weirdest? I didn't question him. A few minutes later, Dad stopped at one particular berth and said, "Here we go. Right here." He stepped onto the deck of an ancient-looking houseboat and led me inside.

The smell of chlorophyll and fertilizer hit me like a wall as we stepped through the door. From the outside, the boat itself looked normal but inside was a wall-to-wall hydroponic garden. Vats were stacked on top of each other to the ceiling and the floor was littered with leaves and junk. Purple lights were casting weird shadows and buzzing gently.

My vision adjusted to the dark and I could start to make out what was growing here. Vegetables … lots of them. I could pick out the carrots and radishes easily enough. Then here were potatoes, lettuce and a variety of other stuff I wouldn't be able to identify until it was full-grown and in the Produce aisle. It smelled great in an earthy kind of way.

"Marie?" Dad called. Whomever he was calling, she was in the boat somewhere.

"Maybe she's buried under all of this," I offered.

"Quiet," he ordered, shooting me a look. He tried again: "Marie!"

I was wrong, as it turned out. A female voice responded "Coming!" and presently an old woman shuffled in from the back. "Richard!" she said brightly. "Is this the boy?" She was an older white lady, in her 60s or so. Graying hair had been twisted into dreads under a wine-colored hat. She wore old granny glasses complete with a chain around her neck. Her smock was stained with dirt and other stuff—I guess she was the primary person behind this operation.

"That's him," Dad said proudly.

"Hello," the woman said. "I'm Marie. You must be James."

"Jim," I said.

"Of course," she said. "Your dad is helping me with my operation here—it's so gratifying to have someone else on the colony with a green thumb."

I smiled politely but was thinking: *Dad? Green thumb? What did he tell her?*

"I brought that pH balancer I promised you," Dad said. "Jim here is pretty handy with plants. In fact, I've taught him everything I know."

Oh God—what was he doing? Dad was getting me into something and I didn't even know what I was supposed to do. I started to say "Are you high?" when he shot me a look. I guess whatever I wanted to say was going to have to wait.

"Oh, well that's wonderful," she said. "How much experience do you have with hydroponic systems, Jim?"

"Umm … well …" I floundered. I'd heard of hydroponics at some point—all my friends' research into pot had led to intense discussions about grow houses and using hydroponics to farm the green, but that didn't mean I knew how it all worked. Growing plants in vats of water with chemicals dumped in, right? Sounded easy but I couldn't put it together. Thinking on my feet would have been simple if I weren't exhausted and feeling those pills kick in. I was dying here.

"He's more experienced with conventional gardening," Dad explained smoothly, putting his hands on my shoulders. "Jim here can weed a garden like nobody's business." Marie led the way giving us a tour of the plants she was growing here: fruits, herbs and vegetables. The top level of the boat was a hothouse where she kept her prize-winning roses and orchids.

"I hope that I can count on you from time to time," Marie said as we were leaving. I turned to see her looking at me expectantly and again, I was puzzled. There was obviously more to this story than I was being told but again I had Dad there talking before any awkward questions could be asked.

"He'll be glad to, Marie," Dad said. With one hand firmly on my shoulder, he guided me outside and shut the door.

"What was that all about?" I asked as we left.

"What, that? That was nothing." The conversation and the fact that I was just volunteered to help in a hippy-dippy farmers market seemed forgotten to him. Dad was purposefully walking on to another appointment. He continued to point out other neighbors and boats but made no mention of whatever it was he had going on back there. Did that just happen? Maybe I was hallucinating from exhaustion.

A jet ski blasted past us suddenly, moving recklessly fast. I realized that we were standing next to the same waterway I had traveled the day before. I caught a flash of tan or Asian legs straddling that old Sea-doo and I zeroed in on the fact that there were girls here on the Colony.

Hot girls.

My teenage male eyes locked onto that pink bikini bottom just barely visible under her ski vest. "Niicce!" I heard a voice suddenly say and then I realized in horror that it was coming from me. That's never happened before. She obviously heard me ... she was moving crazy fast, but she managed to glance at me while not wiping out into someone's boat. Compared to the dead-slow way Ignacio piloted the boat yesterday, screaming through here seemed like someone's idea of a death wish. Still ... beautiful women on jet skis. What was all this about? I looked at Dad and he shrugged.

"She's practicing," Dad said by way of explanation, which didn't explain anything at all. "Life on the colony is just like life on land but with the safety tags ripped off, Jimbo." Up ahead, I heard the sharp sounds of pistols and the *boom!* of a shotgun. Now what?

We drew closer to the source of the gunshots, a very dirty and rundown houseboat. Dad stepped confidently onto the forward deck that was touching the dock. While he knocked at the sliding glass door, the wood of the deck sagged under our feet. I could see water and daylight through some of the holes.

The door slid open and a short, squat Mexican peered out at us. "'Sup?" he inquired.

Dad pointed at me. "*El burro*," he said. The Mexican grinned.

"The mule?" I asked.

"Yeah," the Mexican replied. "I just rented you." He grabbed me by the shirt front and pulled me inside before I could say another word.

Dad left me there and disappeared. I was ushered into the salon area of the houseboat where ranchero music and three separate soccer matches were punctuated almost constantly by gunshots. It was like being inside a bowl of Rice Krispies. I was disoriented and more than a little afraid. Dad had obviously negotiated with some friends to use me as free help. He just neglected to tell me.

This was to be my introduction to Miguel—the guy Dad would be doing a lot of business with. Miguel ran the *Barco de Arma*—otherwise known as The *Gun Range*—one of the biggest non-official recreation facilities on the Colony.

The *Gun Range* was Miguel's second boat. I never saw the inside of his normal living quarters and he was usually here anyway. This was the boat that housed his family when they came in for seasonal work around harvest-time. When they weren't there, he ran markers out 50, 100, 200, 300 and 500 feet and people went at it firing with their own hardware or with guns that he rented at a shameless markup. Tethered orange buoys ran out to a thousand feet, rusted and scarred by stray bullets. Miguel had rigged them to stay more or less in place as the colony rotated around the axis of the *Phoenix*. They marked out the large, pie-shaped wedge that designated where shot and bullets would be landing in—with a reasonable degree of accuracy. Nobody was dumb enough to come anywhere near that side of the Colony ... they referred to it as "The Danger Zone."

Other than the Danger Zone, Miguel had a clay pigeon launcher that sent biodegradable orange disks out to be pulverized by eco-friendly buckshot. He set up the trap range on the upper deck and the rear deck was used as a 4-station pistol and rifle range. Of course, it was still incredibly dangerous but Miguel said, "So far, no major disasters."

I feel so much better now.

He left the outside of the *Gun Range* looking sad and rundown, but inside Miguel installed a comfortable lounge area with flat-panels and sound for the customers who wanted to hang around before, after or in-between a shooting session. He played music constantly, even if it only played Tejano or Ranchero. I would be working the snack bar and gun desk, Miguel explained. My job would be to check guns in and out of the rental case, sell sodas and candy bars but otherwise stay out of everyone's way.

The job training was extensive and he rattled off all kinds of information about guns, bullets and fire safety. I don't think I understood half of what he was talking about. The lack of sleep was getting to me. *Great, another crap job from Dad*, I thought. The second in 20 minutes. Having been up since 4:30 in the morning after maybe four hours of sleep, I wasn't in the mood to get sucked into working in a place I had never seen doing a job I didn't know how to do. "I don't suppose my Dad told you that I've never done something like this," I said, hoping that it would stop his lecture about ballistic properties in its tracks.

"Oh?" he said, sounding surprised. "You've never done this before?" I nodded hopefully—maybe I could go back to the ship and head straight to bed. My heart sank when he shrugged and said "You'll learn."

"But—" I started, thinking he misunderstood.

"But nothing," he said. "Talk to your Dad. You're on my time." He continued the discussion, pointing out how the cooler was stocked, as if I never said anything. Miguel explained that he could always use the help and other kids drank more sodas than they sold. Somehow, I could be counted upon to keep my skim to the bare minimum. As Miguel was talking, a loud gunshot exploded from overhead and we both jumped.

"Julian!" he yelled. He took up a broom and used it to poke the ceiling. "Quit playing army sniper and *tell me* before you shoot that thing!" Miguel swore something in Spanish and grumbled, "I need a new pair of *chones* every time he pulls that trigger!"

He shook off the interruption and continued the orientation, showing me the launchers, the extra beer fridge that you had to buy beer and ice for in advance. We talked about safety, not allowing loaded weapons inside. I still wanted to get out of this somehow and the fact that I was around all this dangerous equipment seemed unreal. Did they really expect me to handle all of this on my first day? "I dunno ..." I began. "I think my Dad-"

He gave me an irritated look and shut me down. "He says you clean the head pretty good. Would you like to do mine before we move on?" Translation: *shut up or it's about to get worse.* I didn't need a mind-reader to see where this was going. I shook my head after a moment and he continued on, rattling off about the *Gun Range*, my job and anything else he cared to throw in. Please, God, let there not be a pop quiz on any of this.

He beckoned me outside and we climbed the almost-vertical ladder on the rear deck to the second level. "We don't sell guns but we can rent them. Or people can shoot what they bring and that's about it. Or they have a gun, but no ammo—then I can sell it to them at a 400% markup of what it costs on land. People are so bored out here that they need something to do. Free enterprise is what it's all about." A tall, slim black guy was lying prone on the deck aiming a rifle at a floating target in the distance. Beside him, lying in an open gun carrier, was another rifle—largest one I'd ever seen. He didn't seem to notice us; his concentration was total as he stared through the scope. Finally, the rifle popped—not the same sound we had just heard. He peered through a small scope on a tripod next to him.

"Hit," he said simply.

"Yeah, hit is right," Miguel said. "You let that thing off and I hit the roof."

"That's a lot of work, considering how short you are," the black guy replied. He returned to his place, studying the target through his scope and before long the rifle popped again.

"He's hopeless," Miguel said. "Guy was a sniper for the Marines and he brought that gun in from somewhere—it's completely illegal back on shore. Now he spends too much time lying on my roof and not enough pulling fish out of the water."

"Not what you said the last time they swung by through here," Julian responded obscurely. He got up from his prone position and stood. He ignored both of us and set to work packing up his weapons.

After a quick demo on how to work the clay launcher and where the pigeons were stored, Miguel put me back on the counter and I stayed there for another three hours. "Sit here," he instructed, pointing to a worn red

Naugahyde bar stool. The top had been cracked and replaced with many layers of ancient duct tape. He didn't speak to me again for that entire period. He changed the channel to a Spanish news station and we watched the President's speech, dubbed in *Espanol*, before moving onto whatever else he cared to punch up.

The sky was darkening when Miguel released me. Sitting on a bar stool gave me a stiff back and a numb butt. He fished out a twenty and handed to me. "Go," he said.

"Twenty bucks?" I was shocked. Did he really think I was going to go for this?

He looked confused. "You still here?" he asked. "Get going—tell your Dad I want to talk to him about that thing tomorrow." I was pissed and about fifty things ran through my mind that I wanted to say, including what he could do with that bill. It was probably poor manners on my part to cuss out a business associate of my Dad. After all, how much can you argue with a guy who owns his own gun range?

His instructions didn't make any sense to me. "What 'thing'?"

"He'll know. Good work. Catch you around sometime." It took me half an hour and asking for directions three times before I made it back to the *Horner*.

Dad was eating a microwave ramen bowl, smoking and reading a copy of *The Art of War* when I came inside. "The working man returns," he commented. "How'd it go?"

"Okay," I said, barely able to contain myself. "Why didn't you tell me you 'rented' me out?"

He looked at me over the cigarette. "Does it bother you when I do things like that without telling you?"

"Yeah."

"Karma," he said.

"Huh?"

He sighed and looked back down at his book. "Look it up, Jim."

Our current position is: 33°57'59.26"N 120°16'50.08"

Chapter Three—Career Opportunities

WE'RE PASSING BETWEEN the Santa Rosa and San Miguel Islands right now. Maybe this is a bad idea but I know nothing about sailing and something inside me wants very, very badly to be near land. It's stupid to get hung up on being near shore. After I pass these islands, we're right back out in the water again and heading north toward the coast beyond. I don't have much of a strategy. I want to stay away from Los Angeles and anywhere else that sounded like trouble. I'm watching our depth gauge to make sure I don't bottom out or something so … wish me luck. Where was I … ?

Anyway, things started to settle into a routine after that first week. I went through the SCUBA safety course they put on at the *Phoenix* and Dad let me start practicing with the hookah rig. I got my feet wet, literally, with the underwater part of Pen Patrol and we quickly got to the point where he became my line tender and I did all of the swimming.

About three weeks after I arrived, so did the sun. We had a weeklong heat wave out here. Out on the ocean, the sun is merciless. The colony was almost silent for the three hours after lunch except for the grinding of air conditioners. The *Horner* did have an air conditioner but, unfortunately, it had seen better days. The compressor motor had seized up and, according to Dad, a replacement was out of our price range.

We tried to make things livable. We rescheduled pen patrol on the hottest parts of the day. Dad had to sit under this huge golf umbrella the entire time and he felt like it made him look stupid. The hookah line was a problem, too. It had never worked really well—Dad bought it second hand and never had it checked for maintenance. I was getting light-headed from all the time, but he kept insisting that the line was perfectly fine. Then one day I almost fainted.

"Such a pansy," Dad grumbled. I was taking two or three times as long to finish my chores and we were losing daylight that Dad wanted to use to get to the other errands. When I didn't stop 'farting around' he got so mad that he ordered me out, right then and there. He took the hookah line and mask from me and dove into Pen 2 to catch up on what I was falling behind on. I sat there next to his signal line watching the bubbles come to the surface. It had taken a few minutes before I noticed something was wrong. I felt the first tug and tugged back, to let dad know I was there. Then, I felt a second tug … and then a third that was much weaker.

I knew what three tugs meant: Dad was in trouble. I started hauling in on the signal line, but weight was too much—it was cheap nylon cord and not there for hauling in almost two hundred pounds of weight. It sank right into the meat of my hands and left purple streaks across my palms. Seconds ticked by and still no sign of Dad. I finally saw Naked Yoga Guy in the boat across the way and screamed for his help. He came running up to where I was a few seconds later.

"Okay, slow and easy," he commanded. "Here, I got it." He took the rope from me and started hauling in. He was able to hold the cord without hurting himself—I thought that was a pretty neat trick—and for an old guy he had a surprising amount of strength. Dad's face was gray when he broke the surface a few moments later.

Dad was too weak to swim to the ladder. I was shocked at how bad he looked. NYG and I had to dive in to pull him out. There was a certain surreal quality to the rescue. It was scary, but nobody was panicking. Yoga Guy tucked his arm under Dad's armpits like a pro and pulled him along while all I could do was paddle along behind them.

Once on deck, I was going to run for the infirmary but NYG stopped me. There was no sense calling for a medic, he explained. Hookah mishaps were a fact of life and a medic was only useful if the victim wasn't breathing. The medic could revive them if he got there in time, or provide a body bag if he didn't. Naked Yoga Guy stayed with us until Dad was able to sit up on his own and then returned to his interrupted day on the *Key West Forever.* Dad complained about having a blinding headache and that was the end of pen patrol for the day.

Dad didn't say anything until almost bedtime. I wasn't sure if he was angry at being saved by Naked Yoga Guy or if he felt guilty because he didn't believe me. For me, I was upset because Dad had come so close to dying and everyone was just kind of 'meh.' My Dad almost died—didn't anyone care? In any case, Dad finally broke down and bought a new hookah rig. Pen patrol was down to what we could accomplish by free-diving while we waited a week for a new rig to show up.

But back to this heat wave—it was miserable. The sun was beating on us like never ending heavy-metal drum solo. We slathered sunscreen and continually soaked our clothing, but it only helped so much. The *Horner*'s insulation was old and collected heat like an oven. It seeped out so slowly that we continued to bake indoors long after the sun had set.

I tried to make a swamp cooler. I found some plans online and we built a cooler made out of several box fans, an old ice chest and several dozen meters of clear plastic tubing. An old aquarium pump sat in the ice chest amid several bags of ice and water. The cooled water was pumped out of the chest and through a series of pipes that were zip-tied in tight circles around the intake the fan. After it had finished with one fan, it moved onto the next. By the time the water had reached the far end (and therefore was at its warmest) it was at the front of the fan stack. It worked. Sort of.

I barely wore clothes during the day. After chores, I took to stripping down to my underwear and a t-shirt for a nap under the sunshade on the flying bridge. Dad always knew where the air conditioners were working and I wouldn't see him until things had cooled off. Sometimes I went with him but you had to balance being cool versus being under Dad's constant attention. Even when he wasn't cracking the whip over chores or pen patrol, it just seemed like he kept you busier. He'd remember every chore I forgot and rarely missed a chance to find 'new and novel ways for me to demonstrate my value to society.'

"What does that even mean?" I argued, the second time I heard him say it.

"You're here to prove that you're worth something," he said in a fatherly tone of voice. "Don't forget, I have to provide updates to your probation officer. I'd like to be able to say that you're well on your way to being a productive member of society." What*ever*, Dad. Call it what you want, but all it meant to me is work, work and more work.

After the third or fourth day like this, he was gone and I had declared it to be a day for enjoying some peace and quiet. Dad would be gone for hours. I caught a shower and decided to give sleeping naked outside a try. I was about to drift off to sleep when I was suddenly interrupted.

"Excuse me," a voice called from somewhere below. I quickly wrapped a towel around myself and moved to the railing. Down below, an older woman in a wetsuit and snorkel had surfaced and was treading water between the *Horner* and the *Key West*.

"Yeah?" I asked. Whether she could see me or not, I couldn't tell, but it was awkward to be talking to people when you were almost naked and I wanted her to go away. She was cheerfully oblivious and the questions continued.

"Which boat is this?"

"The *Horner C*," I answered.

"Oh," she said. "I was doing my afternoon swim and got lost—is this on C or D ring?"

"E Ring," I said. Man, was she lost. Even I knew which ring I was on.

"I swam right underneath a whole dock," she exclaimed. She waved cheerfully and splashed away. Just as she dipped under the water she goes, "Nice butt, by the way."

Oh God …

I decided to get dressed and go for a walk, maybe somewhere far away from the boat so I could pretend I was never there and the lady was making it all up. The heat was still miserable so I decided to find Dad and started with the *Gun Range*. I never had trouble finding my way there—I just had to listen for the shots.

It was cool when I walked in. The lounge had this old blue AstroTurf left over from a mini-golf course in Mexico. A soccer game was going and Ranchero music was playing from somewhere outside. I saw some faded words still visible in the carpeting I didn't notice the last time, but I couldn't translate them.

"It says, 'Please stay off the statues and windmills.'" I turned to see Miguel finishing the longneck he had brought in from outside. He fished another out of an ice-water-filled washtub and wiped the rim of the bottle with his Senor Frog's tank top. "Greetings, Jamie Santiago. Que paso?"

"Have you seen my Dad?"

"I may have observed him from time to time," he replied with some weird, elaborate courtesy. He was already buzzed and it was ten in the morning. "You wanna know where he is? It'll cost you."

"Aw, come on, man. It's hot outside."

He grinned and jerked his head toward the rear. "He's out back—grab yourself a Coke."

Dad was firing at the armored target boat Miguel would rent out from time to time with a .22 rifle. It towed a complex floating target around the Danger Zone and was fun to watch if you were out of ammo or bored. "There he is," he said to me when I saw him. "Done for the day?"

"Yeah," I said. I didn't know who the swimming lady was and I was hoping Dad didn't, either. I didn't want to tell him that I was done for the day, but I couldn't go back home. Not yet, at least. I didn't want to say that I was bored. I learned quickly: telling him that would get me something like "Fine, you're working over on the Herman's Hermit" and then I would be on some old sloop scrubbing decks all day. Sometimes money was involved but other times he would just go "Ya gotta let me get you back on that one." He never told me ahead of time whether I was getting paid or not.

"If you're free, how about a paid gig this time?"

"Really?" I was shocked. Dad was actually talking money this time.

"Sure, I got you a gig on the Phoenix Grill with a friend—you'll be working for him starting tomorrow."

I brightened a bit—the grill was a popular spot and I had stopped by for a burger once. I didn't know that Dad was friends with the people who ran it or that he was working on getting me a job there, but it didn't matter. I mean, obviously, it had something do with Dad and his scams. That was the only reason I was working at the Gun Range. Dad was trying to get something going with Miguel, but he refused to say what it was. Dad told me one time that his scams were based on the 'pickle test' method of business development.

"It's like this, Jim," he said, picking up a couple of pickle chips from the counter where we were making burgers one night. He flipped both pickles straight out where they smacked against the window. Slowly, they began to slide downward.

"You take an idea and throw it against the wall," Dad continued. "If it sticks or it slides down, that tells you how good it is. If it's a good idea—you go with it. If it isn't, you let it go and pick something else." Grabbing the pickles before they hit the sill, he popped them into his mouth and then cleaned the window with the front of his t-shirt.

"That's disgusting," I said.

"That's economics." He went on to describe some of the schemes he had been involved in. Dad and Miguel would occasionally run supplies in from the mainland. Other times people would abandon their stuff sometimes and head for shore—he would go through it, sell off the interesting items and dump the rest.

"Remember that guy who collects the rainwater? You saw him your first day." I nodded. "He has to get that water before anyone else does and make sure that it's drinkable. Not a big profit margin."

"There are easier dollars to be made," Dad explained. "But they're usually illegal. I try to avoid that. It's never worth the hassle. It's a lot easier to make money if you already have it. You can do stuff like investing in other boats and buy stock in the Pacific Fisheries company." Dad grinned weakly. "I don't have that kind of capital to throw around."

Dad's plans seemed to be centered on his friends: Miguel, Marie the Plant Lady and his fat Hawaiian friend. It didn't make a lot of sense to me but then, not much about this place did. His little lecture was probably designed to make everything clear to me, but everything actually made less sense after that. Did everything have to be so dramatic, Dad? Skip the prop-comic act and just tell me what we're doing out here, please.

I admit: I wanted to come out here. But from the second I hit the deck here until now, I've been rolling from one zany misadventure to the next. Not exactly what I would call a stable atmosphere. I was out here because I didn't have any choice—what was Dad's excuse?

Dad, being the joker he is, told me that you started at the Grill as 'cabin slave' and slowly worked your way up. The next morning I walked into the Grill, ready for some hard work to find a fat Mexican kid smoking and reading a girlie mag at the cash register.

He was nonchalantly leafing through a truly hideous photo spread—trashy blondes with bad skin—while looking out at the roiling mass of the colony going through another day. I could smell a dozen cook fires and grills going—mixed with the salt air, barbeque smells wonderful. "Um, hi," I said uncertainly. He looked up, bewildered. "I'm Jim. I guess I work here." The kid's response was to fart. Loud.

"I'm Riley," he said. "First off … oh, geeze!" He ran toward me as if pursued by monsters. I was a little slow to respond until it hit me. The worst fart I had ever smelled. Gagging, I ran for the fresh air.

"It wasn't me!" Riley said indignantly. "The sewer main is backed up again!"

"I've heard that before," a voice behind me said, making me jump. A small white guy was standing there with a cigarette butt dangling perilously from his lower lip. I hadn't heard anyone come from behind me—usually the iron deck vibrates with footfalls and noise all day long. He was skinny and looked like someone who belonged on the Megan's Law database. He stepped inside the grill and immediately opened the refrigerator. He studied the cans of beer inside and then checked a tally chart next to the cash register. Satisfied that any missing cans were paid for by customers, he popped one open.

"Ever worked a grill before?" he punctuated his question with a burp.

"We grill all the time on the boat," I replied.

"Fine. You're the grill man, then," he said. To the Mexican kid, Riley, he said, "I guess you're free, then." The kid smiled happily and busied himself with prepping the front. What made him so happy?

"You're Jim, right?" he asked. I nodded. He took a sweat-stained painter's cap off of his head and ran a cheap black comb through what was left of his gray hair. "Jeb Francis," he introduced himself. "The walking stink over there is Riley."

Riley bristled. "Mom said you weren't supposed to call me that!"

"She says a lot of things," Jeb replied. He opened the door and stood well clear, allowing the air to circulate. His not-so-friendly eyes gave the horizon another sweep. "Your dad said you know how to work. Hope he's right." Having decided that it was safe enough, or maybe that time was wasting, Jeb began the job training.

The orientation lasted five whole minutes. "Clean this. Stock that. Register works like this. Don't give me any crap—I can get five kids to replace you. Any questions?" He hadn't looked at me once since he arrived and even then, I wish he didn't. Like I said, he didn't look friendly. I shook my head. Jeb nodded and disappeared through the flip-up section of the counter. He sauntered off in search of another pack of cigarettes.

"What's up with him?" I asked.

"He's a jerk," Riley said. "Only reason I work here is 'cause he's my step-dad. I can't quit and he can't fire me." He brightened. "I keep waiting for him to fall overboard 'cause then I'd own the place." He started slicing onions while I looked around a bit.

Riley talked about how many girls he'd met working here and hinted that they didn't just invite him out to their boats for fishing. It was a small place, but set up like a ship's galley—not a spare square inch. The cooking area was the size of a truck bed and most of that space was for the grill. Up front was the cashier/dining area.

The Grill was small, but it still had a bar counter with five stools, a front area where we made sandwiches and refreshed a box of cold drinks that lived on a bed of shaved ice. The painted stools were of the home-brew variety; the paint job looked like someone filled their nostrils with different shades and then sneezed on it. From the cashier to the railing was about ten feet of deck and that gave the location plenty of foot traffic. Beyond that, I could see the colony spread out almost like a map.

As the day wore on I got started making burgers on the grill and serving them. If you've handled the gas grill at home, there's really not much else to it. Riley had to show me how to work the deep fryer for fries and corn dogs but after that he kept his distance. The heat was murderous in that little shack.

The sun knifed off the water and cooked the corrugated steel roof of the Grill, turning it into an oven. I realized what Riley was so thrilled about when he heard I was going to be the grill man. By two o'clock, it was over 115 degrees in that shack and would peg the little lawn thermometer next to the grill out at 120.

Riley gave me a battered Camelbak that he had filled with ice water. After I had sucked down the first one, he added some Gatorade powder—it kept me from passing out. At the end of the day, my clothes were soaked and caked with salt. This was a hot, miserable job.

I was so worn out at the end of the day that I collapsed in a sweaty, smelly heap on the couch in the salon. I was supposed to help Dad with Pen Patrol when I got done, but I was in no shape to suit up and go swimming. Dad said nothing and did it all by himself. I guess it wasn't that big a deal—he's been caring for these fish long before I got here. I was back at the Grill again the following day.

After about a week, I had the process down. It was still hot and miserable, but even rotten jobs can be fun. Good jobs have you focused on what you're doing. A bad job makes you focus on what you can get away with. If there was a 'Good Job' out here, you better believe they weren't wasting it on me. We would take turns hosing off the deck with a saltwater hose but Jeb stopped this after our fifth hose fight. We started had impromptu snowball wars with the leftovers from the shaved ice bin. When girls would cruise by, we'd try and talk with them—we kept score on numbers, email addresses and anything that suggested we might get past first base.

The girl operation was pretty simple—between the two of us we had a sex appeal factor of zero and thus, it was more of an obnoxious extreme sport. We thought up the weirdest pickup lines and then dared each other to use them. Some girls laughed, some tried to slap us. I tried one on this hot white chick who was a few years older than us and here visiting with her boyfriend. He got mad and then tried to pick a fight with me after the grill shut. Jeb saw what was going on but refused to give me up.

"If you catch him, he's yours," he said and it was all I needed to hear. The guy had just arrived and it was nothing to lose him in the colony—after you leave the gangplank there's about eighteen directions to run in and it just goes from there. I guess you could say that I was learning the lay of the land out here. The guy was a retard, though. He showed up the next day to start some trouble but Jeb told him that the offer expired at midnight.

We ran out of propane for the grills one Tuesday, but Jeb refused to let us leave early. Riley had screwed up the cash register and he was pissed off about it. Neither one of us was allowed to go. I was bored out of my mind and re-reading a 20-year-old hunting magazine when I heard something scuffle behind me.

"Heads up!"

I looked up just in time to get a raw squid slapped across my face. The gooey, briny mass slithered off my face and landed on the deck. I immediately stuck my face out of a nearby window and started dry-heaving. Sometimes I kid like that but not this time—I really lost my lunch.

Pranks grew crazier and weirder over time. The only rule we had was: don't get caught. If you get caught, you're on your own—we both agreed to not narc on each other. Riley built a launcher out of some surgical tubing and we'd find leftover fish or other disgusting junk to send out over the water. This led to a formal complaint from the *Phoenix* after two boats reported being pelted with rotting fish.

The more stuff we screwed up on, the angrier Jeb got and the angrier he got, the harder we laughed. Behind his back, that is. Jeb would yell at me, yell at Riley and then yell to my Dad who either ignored Jeb or made me sleep in the cold on the top deck, whichever one he felt like. He yelled at me, but he refused to fire me. I didn't understand why until later.

I was finishing up with scraping the grill one afternoon when Riley appeared. All that crap that builds up on the flat cooking surface of our grill filled a 5-gallon bucket by the end of the day. It was every bit as disgusting as you can imagine.

"I have an idea," he announced. Reaching into the bucket of greasy, sooty junk that I just scraped, he grabbed a handful and started painting his face with it. I stared at him—had he finally snapped?

"Now, you," he said. I thought to myself: Why not? I took some and started gingerly dabbing it onto my face, but Riley shook his head. "No, you gotta get serious." He took a handful of sooty grease and smeared it across my forehead.

I gagged on the smell. It was completely nauseating. "That's disgusting!"

"I know, keep going!" He finished his paint job (if you could call it that) and reached for a stack of cheese slices that I used to top the cheeseburgers. He put one or two on top of his head and then put a burger bun that he'd added mayo and mustard to on top of that. "Now you," he said. The race was on to make myself into the grossest food nightmare ever seen on the Colony.

I tried to outdo him but once he saw what I was up to, Riley went back and started adding to his own hamburger. I ended up dabbing long streaks of mayonnaise and mustard to my face, Indian-warpaint-style, topping my 'burger' with tomatoes and lettuce and using the ketchup bottle to paint a nice big smiley-face on my shirt. Soon we were ready for display.

I let Riley do the talking when we went back out to the front where a couple of customers were waiting. An older white lady was waiting to buy a cold drink and started laughing as soon as she saw us. "What on earth is going on?" she asked.

"It's a new promotion from Jeb," he said. "He wants us to dress like our food."

"Exactly," I added. "He thinks it'll bring us more business." She laughed, bought her drink and left. Before long, a crowd started to gather to see what she was laughing about. We did end up getting a lot of business and not a few pictures taken by the Pacific Fisheries Admin Office for the next company newsletter. *'The Phoenix Burger Boys Really Get Into Their Work.'* I still have a copy of it somewhere.

The attention eventually attracted Jeb, who was so used to having little or no business that a crowd in front of the grill could only mean that we were up to something. He stormed up to the front of the grill and started to shout when Riley stopped him cold. He punched a button and the cash drawer flew open, giving Jeb a good view of the take we were bringing in.

"That was a good idea, Jeb," he said softly. Jeb stared at the money for a long minute and then back up at Riley. He turned around and walked away through the crowd without another word. For Riley, any attention was good attention and any time he could make Jeb look stupid, well, that was just the cherry on top.

I finally got fired after the streaking incident. I still don't know why I fell for this—Riley dared me to streak, run naked, on the *Phoenix*. We needed a tie breaker after running neck and neck for the most girls talked to and pranks pulled in a week. "I don't know anyone who has the guts," he declared after he suggested streaking to me. "But if anyone did, it'd be you, bro."

It was almost seven in the evening. The walking traffic was dying down and we'd be closed in 15 minutes. It was getting almost dark enough to turn the lights on. I had to run around the entire afterdeck and back again—maybe 20 yards total—to win. He'd already spent a couple hours trying to convince me but when he said he'd proclaim me winner and throw in fifty bucks, well, what can I say? I did make him show me the money, though. I wasn't that stupid. I started getting ready.

"Go!" he shouted and I was off.

To keep me from getting caught, I found an old paper bag in the back and poked some eye holes in it. I must have broken the record for the 20-yard dash as I tore off. I was moving too quickly to hear any screams; I don't think anyone really noticed. I was coming around the other side and within 5 feet of the grill when I saw that the joke was on me. Riley had rolled down the steel doors we used to close the grill up tight at the end of the day.

I could only yell 'Oh—' before I slammed full speed into the metal roll-up doors. They crashed like cymbals and I fell to the deck. Riley was inside, laughing his head off. My paper bag came flying off and now it was obvious who it was, if it wasn't before. I jumped up like a shot and started slapping the metal doors for Riley to let me inside.

Riley responded by flipping on the music we played to attract people. I was doing the Full Monty to some Tejano music. I heard a woman scream and start laughing—I pounded on that door like I was on the inside of a burning house. "Com'on, man!" Riley's response was to turn up the music louder.

This naturally attracted everyone on board and I'm sure a few out on the Colony, too. I've never been more humiliated in my life. Finally, after a minute he opened the door and I could go inside. I screamed and swore at him while I dressed, but he was laughing too hard to really notice. Riley was decent enough to pay me the fifty bucks which I had more than earned. The crowd outside was laughing, too; it was the best joke they'd had all month.

When Riley rolled up the doors again—a great cheer rose up in the crowd. At that moment, there was nothing else for me to do but raise my arms up like a champion boxer and take a bow. They cheered some more. My butt was certainly getting a lot of attention out here.

Jeb, on the other hand, wasn't amused. He fired me for 'gross insubordination' or something. Dad was kind of mad at Jeb but more so at me. "When we've got a thing going, I don't need you to draw attention to us," he said.

"Thing?" I asked. "What 'thing'?"

"Never mind," he grumbled and that was the last I heard of it. Later, Riley told me that Jeb's friend, Virgil, had heard about the incident and was threatening to pull his money out. Dad had to go over there and calm him down. It sounded like a big problem, but I still didn't know what it was all about. Business deal? Scam?

At first I felt guilty, but then I decided not to worry about it. Dad's scams were his business—when he wanted to cut me in on the action and tell me what was going on, I'd be more careful. I told him as much and his response was to make me sleep on the upper deck out in the cold air.

The next day Riley came by and told me how the girls were asking about me. When I told him about being fired, he waved it off. "You don't need Jeb," he said. "I'll get you some more hours at the Range." Miguel was a second-second cousin to Riley. His farts were horrific but he was turning out to be a gold mine.

With my increased notoriety, the day jobs started rolling in. I started doing some gardening work for Gramma Alice. Like Marie, grew hydroponic vegetables on board the *Green Thumb* but she also grew fish on the E-Ring like we did. Some people said she had something to do with the old Hippy days, but I never knew what. She was always out there working her rows of veggies and fruit and wearing a big, floppy sun hat. Our deal was for whatever she was growing—I never saw a dime. Out here, vegetables are almost worth their weight in gold.

Gramma Alice always had an air of mystery around her. The rumor was that she maintained a pot grow house. She would get visited all the time by Pac Fisheries, the Coast Guard and the DEA whenever they had an excuse. She always came back clean as a whistle … she was always polite and never had a problem.

They pulled a surprise inspection on her one morning when I was due to go over there. I spent an hour cooling my heels on the dock outside until the Security guys in their yellow windbreakers finished looking for whatever they thought she had. She was always sunny and cordial. To their faces, anyway.

As far as the Pac Fish employees—it was very much an 'Us vs. Them' kind of thing. The official employees of Pac Fisheries lived on the *Phoenix* and certain designated craft nearby. Some of them were pretty cool and others acted like the cranky managers of an RV campground. Part of that came from the memos out of corporate and it was up to them to decide how broadly they were to be interpreted. Some of the Pac Fish people were willing to put the hammer down rather than lose their job. It would have been the height of embarrassment to lose your job and then contract to come back out and work as one of the people you were in charge of only a few months before. So there was a sense of following the letter of the law and that made the relationship between the colony bums and the Pac Fish people a little tense.

I approached her tentatively thinking that maybe, she wasn't up for company. The search was immediately forgotten and she was as nice as she could be. "Hi, Jim," she said. "How's your Dad?" She had a soft spot for Dad, I realized.

"He's good. What am I doing today?"

"I got some new bags of fertilizer," she said, "and some chum work." 'Chumming' was a miserable job and didn't hunting sharks. She would take dead fish from other boats, put them through a wood chipper and use what came out to feed her fish. It might sound interesting, but she never cleaned the chipper out and, as a result, it smelled like the world's worst outhouse.

I groaned about the chipper—it was my least favorite job. I was pleasantly surprised not to get a lecture, though. "I got a cure for that," she said. She went to the sink and pulled out a small jar. Opening it, she held it out to me and said: "Take a dab and smear it on your upper lip."

"What is it?" I asked. It smelled strong, like eucalyptus or something.

"Vicks Vap-o-Rub," she announced. I'd seen it before in the store. I took a smear of it on my lip and the overpowering scent made my eyes water. I couldn't smell anything else, though. "Get to it," she said—waving me toward the back porch and the waiting fish.

I left the boat and started navigating the docks toward her pens. Some places were more intricate than others—we were satisfied with large, football-field-sized pens, but others thought smaller. Gramma Alice had dozens of smaller pens that she used to grow different varieties of fish. Her dock system was huge—maybe fifty yards from the boat and the rest of the colony. It had taken her years to get things where they were and it wasn't likely she would ever leave. The pens were organized by the size of the fish that lived in them. The larger, carnivorous fish were in pens farther from the boat and it took a few minutes to reach them.

It was far away from any boat and for good reason: The stink from the chipper would have caused complaints if it were any closer. It ran on biodiesel and always took a minute or so to start up. I used that time to slice open the shrink-wrapped bales of fish and get them ready to go in. She had whole bales of rotted fish that were shrink-wrapped for transport and came apart in your hands when opened. As absolutely disgusting as it was, it wasn't much of a surprise that she didn't want anything to do with it. My feet were sliding on rotted fish guts and bird poop—the seagulls always visited on days we were chumming. I was feeding her stock of tuna with this junk and they boiled to the surface as the food splashed in. In seconds, seagulls were landing on the surface of the water and squabbling for anything that floated to the surface.

I finished the chumming in time to see that girl on the Jet Ski scream by on her way to another 'practice run.' She was close enough to smell the chipper and made a face as she went past, but she still waved to me. I still didn't understand what the practice runs were all about, but she was seriously hot. She wore an aqua blue bikini under her life jacket that showed off sun-kissed legs and a booty toned by hours of swimming.

Jessica had all the right junk in all the right places. Anytime she wanted to show that off was fine with me.

After the chumming, I had to haul those bags of fertilizer in from the dock. The 50-lb bags of fertilizer were really bags of coir—peat made from coconuts. It was still miserable lugging them up her tiny ladder-like stairs. She was filling over a hundred identical terra cotta pots with the fertilizer and then hanging them from some cool little wooden holders. She was using the side of the *Green Thumb* to make more room to grow. Between trips, I remembered a question I wanted to ask.

"HMS *Green Thumb*," I read aloud so she would overhear me. "What's 'HMS' mean?"

"Normally, His Majesty's Ship," she replied, "in the Royal Navy. But I'm the duchess of this yacht—so it stands for Her Majesty's Ship. Me." She tossed me a cold bottle of water that she had brought out and disappeared again. I took the opportunity to sit down with my feet hanging over the side of the top deck. I hadn't realized how tired I was. The green smell of the gardens wafted over to me through the salt air—it was really chill to just relax here and enjoy the day.

Dad wandered by as I was finishing the Gramma Alice job. They talked for a bit while she filled two grocery bags with fresh veggies. Dinner that night was a couple of freshly-caught tilapia from the pens and some of the carrots, done up tempura style. We had a quiet evening at home, which probably sounds boring but after the last few weeks it was a welcome change.

Our current position is: 34° 6'54.35"N 120°17'31.99"W

Chapter Four—Main Street and The Big Fourth

BECAUSE DAD WAS a long-timer, 'a lifer' he would say, I got a lot of latitude in people treated me. I found out just how far I could push it during the Big Fourth when Miguel found me passed out on the dock and hung me up by my ankles.

The Big Fourth was the weekend where 4th of July, the Pacific Fisheries Founders' Day and several large fish harvests fall on the same weekend. A three-day weekend was declared by silent majority and the party lasted all 72 hours of it. Everyone went crazy and I could only remember what happened up to a point. The next week, productivity was down to almost nothing as people recovered from whatever their substance of choice was. We were lucky that nobody died.

The Big Fourth hit about a month after I arrived—I had gotten used to the place and my time at the Grill had ended. I was starting to come out from under the hoodoo that mom put on me at the Denny's way back when. The pills weren't making me as sleepy and things were generally getting dialed in. I wasn't supposed to be drinking: sobriety was a condition of my probation. Then I had a slip-up.

The Colony is a weird place. While you are here, you're constantly involved in this bizarre human experiment. Dad says that you can't read too much into it. We were hauling supplies back from the dock—enough food for an army. Dad was busy organizing a barbeque of meat that included a special shipment of mesquite charcoal in from the mainland. He wanted to celebrate in style.

Once inside, we were chopping vegetables for salsa and measuring out ingredients for the three different kinds of marinade he wanted to use. "The collision of bohemian and blue collar in a space smaller than the footprint of your average shopping mall," he said over a sizzling pan of roasting garlic. We were having eggs and hot dogs for dinner. "This is a melting pot full of people who refuse to melt."

"What does 'bohemian' mean?" I wondered out loud. Dad grumbled something about my 'lack of vocabulary.' I'm not an English major so it's like, get off my back already.

I gradually understood that he was talking about the different cultures we had out here. The fishermen who had left the East Coast were from Gloucester were these throwback square-jawed types and they were constantly at odds with the 'Children of Black Rock City' who used their catch money to finance art projects and annual trips to Burning Man.

Dad and I were out in the Colony yesterday, looking for a few items he forgot to order. He located the kosher salt we needed at one of the floating restaurants. The owner was an old Asian guy who told us over a lunchtime plate of egg rolls about sailing junks on Victoria Harbor while growing up in Hong Kong. Now he is here, experiencing the *mañana* culture of the Baja fishers who lived on the boat next door.

"Everything is a bit new," he said in a British accent, which was a surprise to me.

"Are you from England?" I asked.

"No, Hong Kong."

"Why do you sound like you're from Eng—" I began, but Dad hissed and gave me the cut-throat sign.

"Eat your lunch," he broke in before I could embarrass myself further. The old guy was laughing and I think Dad was amused too. It would be easy to say that a constant state of conflict existed on the colony, and some conflict did occur. For the most part, everyone just wanted to make it through another day and live to see their catch get hauled in. Getting used to everything, figuring out how to grow the fish and sell them at a profit didn't leave you with the time or energy to be angry at that guy next door with the weird accent.

I got upset one night when we found a logo tagged on our porch with yellow mustard. It was from the 'Children of Black Rock City' over on B-Ring. I was upset, but Dad told me not to worry. "You gotta have a thick skin," Dad reminded me before cleaning it off with the salt-water hose. "You can't survive out in the rings otherwise." On the other hand, you couldn't afford to annoy your neighbors too much. You might be relying on them to save your life in the next day or so.

We had a lot of prep work to do for the barbeque. Dad's lecture continued over shucking a few dozen ears of corn. "The threat of violence exists out here, but it was more of a social contract," he paused to light a cigarette. "You can only get away with so much before you receive a visit from someone asking you nicely to knock it off. If that doesn't work, the possibilities of reprisal were endless and everyone knows it. Weirdness that doesn't harm you directly is condoned. Real antisocial behavior is discouraged."

He looked thoughtful … like he was making a decision about something. Then he told me a really creepy story. "One time, a fisherman who had lived on the colony for almost six months, a recovering alcoholic, fell off the wagon and started assaulting his live-in girlfriend. None of the boats are soundproof and so of course, all of his neighbors heard it. So far no one has come forward to say anything so what happened next is pure speculation.

"The next morning, we get up and … the guy? He was just gone—clothes and personal effects were missing and his girlfriend was in the process of packing. She returned to the mainland later that day. The security team on the *Phoenix* did what they called a 'thorough investigation' but it went nowhere. The girlfriend refused to talk about it, threatened to sue them for not stopping the fisherman after her first complaint and just wanted to go home. They let her go, but they passed it off to cops on the mainland for follow-up. Either the guy committed suicide or he was dropped off the dock wrapped in anchor chain or he was simply put in a dingy pointed in the direction of the mainland and told 'Row … or die.'

Nobody knows for sure. Balance was restored to the Colony and things went back to normal."

"Except for the missing guy," I said. He shrugged.

"People still gossip about it. You'll hear a few 'Davy Jones Locker' jokes if you hang around long enough." He stood up and I could hear his knees crackle. "Let's get the dry rub together."

I had yet to see any violence from people in the Colony, but I saw a lot of weirdness. Since we were alone out here, people felt free to do whatever they felt like in their off hours. You had to accept the fact that life in the Colony was like a non-stop performance art piece. You were going to see things here that you'd never seen before and never would see anywhere else. In a fit of whimsy, someone hung hand-made street signs all over the colony. C Ring-1 was now "St. Charles Place," D-Ring-4 was "Illinois Avenue" and of course, the dock right in front of the *Phoenix* was called "Boardwalk."

It was like entire colony said "Yes, of course our docks should be named after the streets in Monopoly. Why wouldn't they?" I never got it.

The Colony seemed to immediately accept or discard weirdness or questionable behavior and I couldn't figure out where the line was drawn. Why *this* weirdness? Why was this little debacle tolerated and other ones were reason enough to bounce a person (or an entire boat) from the group? They let the street signs remain even though Pacific Fisheries refused to acknowledge use them in official memos. Sometimes I felt like I was in a weird movie where everyone was crazy except for me.

The "Children of the Black Rock City" were in the process of re-inventing themselves for The Big Fourth. They renamed themselves to "Tribe of the Burning Man," stenciled and spray-painted a Burning Man logo on the sides of their boats. Someone must have been going for a viral marketing thing because all of a sudden they started posting complex and ridiculous stories to their blogs to 'explain the mythology of their group.' Then they spammed up the community social pages with links to this trash. Riley started a backlash movement by posting the video he took of their 'parade' last year—a bunch of ugly, semi-naked people with paint all over playing marching songs and inviting other people to get naked and join in.

Rude pictures and videos started flying back and forth—it was only a matter of time before it got nasty.

I couldn't figure this place out and the questions were driving me crazy. I finally decided to ask Dad. "So what's your theory?"

"Huh?" he replied. We had mostly been silent for the last half-hour. Dad and I finished preparing the 'chili corn'—the ears would marinate overnight in a mixture of water, lime juice and hot sauce before going onto the grill. He set me to slicing a ton of vegetables for grilling while he put chicken, beef and pork into bags for marinating.

"Why is this place so weird? It can't just be about different cultures."

"The colony is like a boom town, Jim," Dad said to me. "The Colony has this 'kindred spirit' thing going on with the Gold Rush camps that grew overnight into cities of twenty thousand and then disappeared from the map just as quickly."

"Dad," I pleaded. "English … please."

"*Tal vez debería empezar a hablar en español para usted,*" Dad said suddenly.

"Huh?" I asked.

"Exactly," he grinned back. No explanation, no warning … sometimes Dad dropped a knowledge bomb on you to remind you that the world was bigger than you knew. Then he went on to tell me about how the Colony was the great-grandchild of certain eras throughout American history and it attracted a special branch of anthropology that wanted to study a boom town in progress. There hadn't been a legitimate occurrence of one in over a century and scholars nationwide did not want to lose the opportunity.

"They descended on us like a plague," he said darkly. "I blame Pac Fish for not doing more to discourage it. Grad students kept talking their way onto a boat for a few weeks or months to collect data for a thesis. At first, it was kind of cool, like we were all celebrities. But then it got old. The regulars, the lifers, started calling them 'the tourists.' You'd see a digital recorder and hear 'I just want to ask you a few questions'—you wanted to toss them overboard."

"What would they ask?" I wondered.

Dad snickered. "Dumb questions. They come up on this poor Mexican family, just trying to get enough fish to pay for a real boat and get out of the shakedown shack they were living in. 'Why are you living here? Why did you leave the mainland?' Why do you think?"

"Miguel was like, 'What are we, the Gorillas in the Mist? It's getting so they need to kick everyone with a college degree out of this place.'" Miguel knew about Dad's college years and liked to yank his chain over it every chance he got. "I was like, 'This ain't Utopia, babe.' People have done engineered towns and settlements before. Every single one of them had resulted in dismal failure. You can't legislate happiness, even when you have the resources to do so. This is a weird little place and it's constantly pushing against itself. Communities like that never last long."

"So why are you here?" I asked.

Dad shrugged. "I like the hours." We finished slicing veggies and putting things away in the fridge. Food prep had taken several hours, but it meant that Dad could get right to work on the grill tomorrow morning. We celebrated with a Coke for me and a beer for Dad.

Success had a lot to do with how you got along with other people. Getting along with people was based on a lot of factors. A lot of it had to do with the amount of time you'd been on board. The politics of the scammers, legal or illegal, that figured into it. How many times you'd helped out your neighbor fishermen versus how many times they had to pull your fat out of the fire. How much fun you were in a bad spot, how many times had you returned a tool or how many times had you stopped an act of unpleasantness? All of these little pieces were fed into a large, nebulous equation that everyone collectively knew and understood but never talked about. This gave you where you stood in the Colony.

The connections all ran deep and out of sight, like the massive crossbars that connected all of the docks together. The *Phoenix* was connected to the docks through the crossbars and all of the ships were tethered tightly to the docks. This was allowing the motion of the *Phoenix* to keep the Colony moving through the ocean and more or less stationary against the current of the sea. It was a common joke: if the *Phoenix* goes down, cut your lines or you'll go down with her. Every boat kept hatchet on deck for that reason and I had to learn about it pretty soon after I arrived. The connection of the *Phoenix* was unseen, but always there, like the connection of the community itself.

That night I was lugging garbage bags full of wrappers, corn husks and other junk down to the Garbage Barge when I came up on one of the Burning Man kids. It was just after nine o'clock … what was this kid doing outside? He was four or five, well past the age when kids were allowed to run around naked, yet here he was with a bare butt and chattering quietly to himself like a wolverine.

I approached him cautiously and tried to ask where his boat was. It is common courtesy to immediately return any lost child to his boat before he falls overboard or something. I got within five feet before he jumped up like a scared dog and ran away hooting and gibbering in a high-pitched voice. The sound was creepy and it echoed off the hulls of nearby ships. It was so weird … all I could do was stare after him, long after the wails had faded to the slap of water and cries of seagulls.

I thought the noise would attract someone. Maybe the boy was in trouble … being naked in public certainly violated the public nudity rule. Wasn't there something on the books about feral children? No one stirred, no one noticed. When I got back to the *Horner*, I told Dad about it.

"Told you those nouveau hippies were trouble," he grumbled. Then he told a similar story of encountering the Tribe at full howl when the moon was full. Everyone was either naked or scantily clothed in loincloths made out of red vinyl seat covers. "They said it was an ancient American Indian tradition—the Thunder Ceremony." Two more nights of this and the bare-skinned tribe had to beat a hasty retreat against random pepper-spraying.

We were supposed to relax and sleep in on The Big Fourth but when I woke up on Saturday, I could hear Dad thumping around in the galley. I dozed for another hour, but the sounds were getting louder. Dad was blasting some ancient dub music through the speakers to compete with the ranchero music next door. I tried to bury my head under like five blankets, but it was no use. The music drove me out of bed and I began to pull on some clothes.

I found Dad in the galley putting dry rub on some steaks. It was after nine in the morning – four hours later than our usual waking time. An uncomfortable thought had occurred to me and I needed to ask Dad about it. We didn't discuss it yet, but it was understood that the Colony was going on a bender. What would I do, being a kid who was Absolutely Not

Supposed to Drink or Take Drugs? Dad's answer was to leave me to do whatever on my own. "We're gonna be doing a lot of drinking," he said with his hands dusted in a layer of cayenne, salt and garlic powder. "You'll be okay, right?"

"Sure. of course," I replied. Why wouldn't I be? I'd been tending bar at the *Gun Range* and selling beers at the Grill. Although it was tempting to bum one or two, I managed to leave it alone and I was pretty proud of myself. I felt like the bad times were behind me and things would eventually get back to normal after I went back to the mainland.

I got invited to a party on Graham Cracker, a C-ring boat that raised crabs, lobsters and other shellfish. The larvae were incubated before being put out to sea to mature—it was a complex series of tanks and docks and it was a pain to maintain; very profitable though, for the Mormon family that lived on board. Mommy and Daddy Mormon didn't approve of the Big Fourth and used some vacation time to go back home to Oregon and see the folks. They entrusted boat-sitting duties to the teenager next door, one of the Children of the Tribe of the Burning Man.

Now, I would have that guy on principle. His sense of group dynamics was as dumb as the group he belonged to. However, the kid had access to the place and had scored some free booze and suddenly, the Graham Cracker was the party headquarters for every person under sixteen. Even if you weren't going to drink—you're your friends were going to be there and who wanted to sit this one out? Parents heard that their children were going to be on the Graham and didn't think much of it. Weren't Ray and Madison responsible people? It took a while for the truth to be told and by that time, the party itself had been going for 36 hours.

One of the kid scammers was there, providing booze and other supplies for a truly debauched teen party. At first I hung back, meeting people and generally chilling. The beer and cheap plastic-bottle vodka was flowing and I kept turning down Red Cups full of vodka and Red Bull. The third or fourth time a cocktail came by I said 'Why not?' and took a sip.

So ... if you asked me at that moment, I couldn't have been able to tell you why I decided to drink. It was just like diving off of the dock and into the water. One second you're dry, one second you're soaking wet—there's almost no space between. Now that I think about it, the fact that Mom blew off a chance to visit on the Big Fourth was part of it … I know I forgot to talk about that. It happened. Dad's constant do-as-I-say-not-as-I-do lifestyle was also getting under my skin. It wasn't a conscious thing. I didn't realize I was going to do it until I did it.

Still didn't get blitzed right then. I nursed the first couple. The party migrated here and there as the day stretched into the evening and then into the night and in the dark, no one was checking IDs. I didn't realize it, but Miguel had seen me with a cocktail around 9 o'clock, but assumed it was soda or water. A few hours later, midnight and the party was still raging— they were shooting a boatload of fireworks off of the back of the *Gun Range* and Miguel happened to catch me cruising by with a can of beer in my hand.

Things faded out after that. I don't remember how much I drank or if I had some pills along with it. It's kind of hazy. I didn't know that Miguel had seen me and that he was staring holes through my skull while I bounced from one party to another. It all faded to gray until the next morning and that's where Miguel found me: lying on the dock minus my shoes but with lipstick on my face.

If I were in his shoes, I probably would have done the same thing but I'll never admit that to him. He's grumpy even on the good days but at this point he was double-fisting plastic bags full of glass and metal and stepping over sleeping forms and puddles of vomit. Then he has to decide whether to bust me, ignore me or help me. The word 'patience' just wasn't in his vocabulary.

I was so out of it that I missed being dragged back to the *Barco de Arma*. I didn't wake up when Miguel rigged my feet to the block-and-tackle that hung off the davit on his foredeck. I just knew that something was wrong when my body left the dock and I suddenly realized I was hanging upside down and five feet from the floor.

Miguel had chosen his payback well. I was a complex pendulum on a moving ship: bad combination for anyone nursing a hangover. I harrumphed a few dry heaves. My head was pounding twice as bad as it was a minute ago and my eyes felt like they had been dipped in sand. I groaned and opened my eyes. Eventually, I could make out Miguel, regarding me calmly and sipping from a cup of hot coffee. I groaned again. "Let me down, man," I pleaded.

"Are you through drinking?" Miguel asked.

"Miguel …"

"Yes or no, Little Man." Miguel was angry. The difference between Miguel and Dad was that Dad would shout and bluster where Miguel was the cool bank-robber-type who would ask everyone to stay calm while holding a submachine gun. You didn't want to mess with either of them but somehow … somehow Miguel seemed a little more dangerous. I managed after a second to nod weakly.

"That's not the right answer," Miguel said. "You wanna swim back to your place? Want me to go get your Dad and let you explain it to him?" Miguel let a few moments of silence pass while I thought about that. "Right now, all I want to know is: are you through drinking?"

He stared two holes right through me. He was right; I didn't have a good reason for going on a bender like that. I was so ashamed that I wanted to cry. Miguel was treating me like a man and making me deal with it right then and right there. He knew about my probation and the 'no-drinking' part of it. One word to Dad and I'd be back to the mainland to spend the rest of my summer in YA. How could I have been so stupid? This wasn't a problem yesterday, but it was today. Why did I fall off of the wagon? Miguel wanted an answer and fast before he had me shipped back in handcuffs. I'd suffer through whatever this was and deal with the fuzzy questions later.

My current position and the hangover made it difficult to say, but the right answer finally came out. "Yeah … I'm through." Miguel nodded and untied the other end the rope, letting me down easily enough so that I didn't crack my throbbing skull on the resin-slatted docks. He was rough untying my feet but before he could send me on my way he grabbed me by my shoulders and pulled me close.

"*Tú eres mi hijo,*" he said tightly. "*No sea estúpido.*"

He cuffed me on the side of my head and released me. I walked barefooted back to the *Horner*, rubbing the spot where Miguel's knuckles had found me. I wanted to cry but was smart enough not to do it in public. Miguel had left a mark on me that ran deeper than almost anything else had since I got here. Miguel's words were lost on me—I don't speak Spanish—but I kind of got the gist. There still remained the question of what Dad was going to say when Miguel told him and I shivered about it for the rest of the Big Fourth.

I stayed off the party boats for the rest of the weekend. Other folks were also tired of the non-stop partying and so a few sections became designated quiet zones. As it turned out, I spent a lot of time with the guys of The Gloucester West. They never got over me taking three tries to understand what 'de south shoa' or 'wikked pissah' meant. I took a lot of crap over it, but it was a good-natured kind of thing.

The end of the Big Fourth wound down and everyone reached the natural limits of whatever they were on. You could only stay drunk so long, stay high so long or do whatever it was that you were doing before reality manifested itself. Pac Fish came swarming through the rings toward the end of the day and started busting kids for underage drinking. They took it seriously out here, they had said over and over. The punishment was heavy fines against the kid's boat. There were angry parents everywhere, or at least they would be when they sobered up. A few sleeping drunks were rousted with batons or the toe of a boot.

Dad came home from wherever he was partying at smelling of sour beer and cigarettes. The *Horner* party was done after the first day and Dad was gone after that … maybe something else had taken place but I never did ask. He just appeared in the lounge on Monday morning. I was under a blanket, eating cereal and watching cartoons. He barely acknowledged me before disappearing into his stateroom and shutting the door. I didn't see him for the rest of the day.

Later that afternoon, I took a walk through the Colony, looking at the aftermath. People were cursing as they hosed down the docks with saltwater. Broken glass was simply tossed overboard—it was going to sink so who cares? Solid bottles were given a home in the garbage barge and that was good enough for everyone. I eventually found myself at the *Gun Range* and decided to pay Miguel a call.

I saw as soon as I walked in that someone had let a sparkler off inside the *Gun Range*. A large burn mark on the carpet and the smell of gunpowder filled the air. Miguel was swearing as he scrubbed the burn mark; he would later cover it with a cheap rug that somebody's grandmother purled together one evening. I think he was angrier that someone had let off a sparkler in such close proximity to the real fireworks. All around the *Gun Range* lounge were big signs that said NO OPEN FLAME and DANGER—EXPLOSIVES. He looked up and saw me. He kicked the burn mark with his sandal and ducked under the counter. He continued swearing in Spanish under his breath and opened a beer. "What's up, kid?" he asked, sitting down on the rickety old barstool with a sigh.

"Just walking," I said. "Who did that?"

"When I find out, they'll disappear like that other guy," Miguel said ominously.

"What other guy?"

"Nothing." Miguel was silent, staring at the far bulkhead deep in thought. He looked over. "Want a beer?" I was startled. Was he serious? I decided that this was a test and told Miguel no. "Good man," Miguel said, smiling slightly.

"What did my Dad say?" I blurted out. I wanted to be more subtle but the suspense was killing me.

"About what?" Miguel asked, puzzled.

"When you told him."

"Told him about what?"

"About me ..." I couldn't bring myself to finish the sentence.

"What are you talking about?" Miguel demanded, sounding angry.

"About ... you finding me ..." I was confused. Why was Miguel making me spell everything out?

Miguel stared straight at me. "I didn't see you this entire weekend," he said. He continued staring a hole through me until I got the point. "I did find a drunk kid and we had a good time hanging him by his ankles, but it wasn't you," Miguel continued. "I have no idea where you were. You were here, staying out of trouble, right?"

At first I couldn't believe it. Miguel was handing me a golden-plated alibi after dragging me halfway around the Colony feet-first! Why was he doing this?

"Right?" Miguel demanded when I did not reply.

"Umm ... Right." This had to be a dream ... it was too good to be true. Before I could say anything else, Miguel quickly brought me back down to earth.

"Now ... you didn't see who brought the *maldito* sparkler into this boat, but you're working around the clock to find out. *Comprende?* That's what I'll tell your Dad and after you get me that, we're cool." He was using my bender as an opportunity to teach me a lesson and get something done—I had to admit, it was effective. Even if I thought it was unfair, I wasn't in a position to argue.

We started with the cleanup after breakfast—leftover beef and beans were made into huevos rancheros. The *Barco* was looking a little worse for wear as was the rest of the Colony. When I got back to the *Horner* that afternoon, Dad was out looking the fish over and he announced that Pen Patrol would recommence the following morning. He asked me whether or not Miguel had found out who almost blew the *Gun Range* up.

The Colony slowly put itself back together over the next several days. Pac Fish had a field day with the underage kids busted for drinking and it was the subject of a couple of Town Hall meetings later. Pac Fish stuck to their lines about 'obeying the law' and the boat folk hollered and crabbed about the heavy fines. The Children of the Burning Man went so far as to try and organize a benefit concert, but no one else was having it. They did set up a 'legal defense' fund that people kicked into and it helped pay off the fines for the affected boats. The sum total of everything that had happened to the Colony, before, during and after The Big Fourth was a big, fat zero.

Except for me.

Our current position is: 34°13'53.93"N 120°21'20.67"W

Chapter Five—Steeplechase

A COUPLE OF Saturdays after the Big Fourth, I woke up to the sound of a helicopter thumping overhead. I stumbled up to the flying bridge with a cup of coffee to see what was going on. A big white thing caught my eye. Out next to the *Phoenix* was an old white 'sternwheeler' river boat. It looked brand new. Was I seeing things? I called down the hatch for Dad to come and see.

"Nope," Dad said when he joined me a few moments later. "They bring her in to run the sportsbook for the Steeplechase. That's the *Dixie Star*."

"You told me they bet and stuff, but you didn't tell me about this," I said. "This is crazy … a whole paddlewheel boat out here on the ocean?"

"Yeah, they tow it down from up north somewhere," Dad replied. "They keep it there rather than trying to run a full-time casino. Actually, I'm trying to talk them into keeping it here after the Steeplechase is over."

Dad had explained the race to me before and I thought back to what explained before. "They call it the 'Steeplechase'," he had said.

"Why's that?"

"Because 'racing Jet skis all over the colony without getting killed' didn't have the same ring." Up until now, watching the girls practice in their bikinis was the high part of my week. The boat, however, was a bonus and I wanted to check it out after breakfast.

It was a nice warm day as I cruised through the rings toward the *Phoenix* and the riverboat. Everyone was in a party mood and Security was heightened to prevent the debauchery that went on during The Big Fourth. Some heavies had been imported from the main office of Pac Fish. Guys wearing khaki fatigues and carrying guns were patrolling the A-Ring where the *Phoenix* and the *Dixie Star* were tied up. An ID system had been set up to control access to the old river boat—teenage Colony kids were definitely not allowed. I would have to admire it from the railing of the *Phoenix*.

I could see people milling about on all three decks of the ship. I recognized some Colony folk but these people were working, not hanging out. Briefly, I saw Jeb Francis wearing a white coat and pushing a cart full of dishes somewhere inside. The others were unknown—mainlanders, I guess. The boat itself echoed with the noise of slot machines and I could see other games going through the windows of the first and second deck. *Nice work if you can get it*, I thought.

"Now you see," Dad's voice said right in my ear, making me jump. Maybe I was distracted by the noise and the lights but I should have heard him … he can be as quiet as a cat when he wants to. It irritated me.

He went on like he didn't notice my reaction. "This is a serious money-maker. I gotta find a way into this and then it's you and me and no more fishing."

"What's wrong with fishing?" I asked.

He looked at me with something between contempt and patience and said, "You tell me." He paused and put his hands in his pockets. "No better yet, don't tell me," he snapped. "Maybe you like getting up at the butt-crack of dawn and jumping into a cold ocean. I don't but maybe that makes me stupid."

"Gee, tell me how you really feel, Dad." He gave me a sour look. His quick-draw temper was always hard to get used to. I didn't say anything in response. Arguing with Dad was like running in quicksand, lots of effort and all you get is trouble up to your neck. I just didn't realize that he hated fishing so much, that's all I wanted to say. Whatever … I wasn't going to let him spoil my day.

Maybe he didn't want it to be ruined either because he suddenly blinked and then continued the discussion as though our little exchange never happened. "We're beyond the International Waters line and gambling is legal but Pac Fisheries refuses to let any casinos operate except for the

Dixie Star. Every once in a while, the Security team will make a raid and then it's either fines or fired-back-to-the-Mainland for some unlucky clown."

I listened to Dad and Miguel discuss the Colony's flirtation with gambling over late-night beers. It had nearly killed the place: Colony D was overrun with different Mexican gangs and East Coast Goombas. Finally, Pac Fish had had enough and exercised executive privilege (along with some pump-action shotguns) to remove them from the colony. Since then: no gambling.

Steeplechase was another matter and for that, they looked the other way. In the past twelve years since this Colony was commissioned, the Steeplechase has become the thing we're known for, even more than the fish. People come out from the Mainland and other Colonies to watch, bet and visit. It's a one-day thing and it helps generate a lot of income for individual members. Some boats make more in a day than they do in a month with Steeplechase.

"Pac Fish makes the most out of all of us," Miguel said bitterly. This is a source of conflict for a lot of people. "We do the work, we deal with the overhead of the tourists but *we* don't make that money, they do. Then they complain about 'overhead costs' and 'keeping admin expenses to a minimum'. It's very two-faced if you ask me." But no one does: they just quietly rake some cash in and make a few jokes about corporate behind their backs. If someone wants to dump a box of cash in your lap, why stop them, everyone seems to say.

Some of the tourists left the ship and went wandering—B and C ring were set up to sell food, souvenirs and crap. I checked out their stores and it was the same kind of snow-globes and corny t-shirts you find in Hollywood or Santa Monica. Kids from the Burning Man tribe got a begging scam going but it didn't last long. Security didn't want anyone to think dirty-faced kids were running around homeless on the Colony and shooed them out of sight.

Out on E-Ring, you could see the 'pit area' constructed for the different racing teams. The largest race was Jet skis or other personal watercraft, but they also had a build-your-own division. Different boats and 'skis were already in the water and drivers were milling around getting ready. I could see the girl from my first ride out, Jessica Cho—she was already a Steeplechase legend at 17. She usually finished first or second, but I didn't care about that. She was Asian, athletic and ran the race wearing nothing but a Speedo LZR suit ... serious sex appeal.

The race discouraged souped-up engines since you needed to navigate the course ... it wasn't just a flat-out run. There were minor tweaks but the 'racing commission', three drunken fisherman who took the job, personally inspected every boat.

The course was marked out only a few days ahead of time so that you couldn't practice it too much and it ran two laps around the E-Ring before entering the Maze. The Maze was the Colony itself, docks between C and E were re-configured to create a path that eventually let back out again. Boats had to be moved out of the way to make it work. To have the Racing Commission show up on your deck meant you had a headache on your hands, but it was reasonable: you could make money charging admission to watch the race.

They did have a flat-out competition: three laps around E-Ring and may the best man win. It was where they sent you if they saw you tweaked your motor too much or too often. No serious action on this race ... it was more of a warm-up to the real deal. Miguel was sponsoring one of those boats and the *Built by a Mexican* didn't have a prayer—but he plastered it with decals for the *Barco de Arma* and was hoping to win the 'ugliest boat' category. I found him on the *Barco*, hollering at someone on a phone in Spanish and writing bets down. He clicked off or hung up or whatever and grinned at me. "Welcome to Race Day," he said happily. "We're already up fifteen or sixteen large and the race hasn't even started."

"You're taking bets on that thing?" I said. "That's the fugliest boat I've ever seen. You're lucky it hasn't sunk yet."

"I'm not taking bets on that tub," he said. "If you think I'm stupid, why don't you just say so?"

"What are you doing then?"

"Getting some action from down south," he replied. "The guys who used to run the Casino over here still try to keep their fingers in and I run the middle."

"You're taking bets for the guys …" I said, maybe too loudly because Miguel suddenly shushed me and looked out to the docks. I turned and looked—a Security guy was walking the docks and looking in to see what was going on. The noise on the boats nearby suddenly dropped to zero; I guess we weren't the only ones who saw him.

It was weird how there were some things out here that everyone just *knew*, just immediately processed and responded to. Seeing a security goon out here where he shouldn't be fell into that category. I could see who it was: a guy named Marco that worked for Pac Fish. Ordinarily, he was pretty cool but we all knew what it was: he'd bust us if he saw anything he shouldn't. We weren't going to give him the chance.

By now, Marco could tell that we all knew he was there. Seeing his cover was blown, he didn't make more than a cursory check on the boats and waved to Miguel as he left. Appearances had to be maintained.

"I'm just providing a cutout for them," he said after Marco disappeared. "I take the risk from Pac Fish and I get ten percent. Simple." I was still pretty green but it sounded like a bad idea. Who wanted to get between a drug gang and their money? Miguel sounded crazy for taking it and I said so. He shrugged in response and changed the subject. I asked about the *Built by a Mexican* and he happily explained it was knocked together expressly for laughs. "Let's face it: any attention is good attention."

Dad somehow scored some seats on the *Dixie Star* for the race but I was barred from entering. He said he was sorry that I was locked out but that wasn't going to do me any good. I was supposed to find another place to watch the race while he tried selling the idea of keeping the *Dixie Star* here permanently. I was upset about missing out on the free food and punch. Nobody ever made punch out here and I missed it. Weird, right?

I was disappointed. I got on board the *Phoenix* and looked down from the rail to see everyone milling around on the top deck. I could see Mitch Cutter tending bar up there. Mitch was one of the few kids that were permanent residents of the Colony and at 16, he was also a die-hard scam artist. Dad didn't care much for him and after losing a bunch to him in a poker game one night, neither did I. Mitch hustled scams all day long but even he should have been too young to get on board the *Dixie Star*. So how did he manage that? I was seething at that point ... Dad was going to hear it from me when the day was over.

Riley and I ended up back on the *Horner* for the race. I had a cooler and a crappy lawn chair shaded by an ancient golf umbrella from the junk room below. Riley wandered in and then the races began. The inter-Colony speaker system started belting out a crackly version of the 'Star Spangled Banner' which we were supposed to stand up for. I didn't see anyone who did.

"*Welcome Race Fans,*" the speakers echoed over the water, "*to the 9th Annual Steeplechase and Regatta hosted by the Pacific Fisheries Colony D Complex located here on the beautiful Pacific Ocean.*" A big cheer started rising up from the Colony. It always gets the people going to know that they're on TV. There were now two helos flying around the colony, filming us. He started reading out a list of sponsors while they ran race highlights on a temporary Jumbotron over by the *Phoenix.*

While the highlights ran, you could hear the cheering start from one boat or another as someone came on that they recognized. The crowd was warming up and I started to get excited myself ... Dad never told me that it was this big. Then they changed it to a blooper reel and people started to fall silent.

Some of the accidents were no-harm, no-foul. Other ones were from times where people genuinely got injured. I could tell that this was Pac Fisheries way of putting their thumb on us. We might be the stars of the show but they could amuse themselves watching footage of our friends and family getting injured.

"Classy," Riley said at one point. The highlights eventually came to an end and the race was almost ready.

"Before we begin," the announcer said. "We'd like to review a few housekeeping rules to ensure everyone stays safe and we end the day happy." He started running down a list of rules that almost everyone had heard before. Who wanted to hear some rules from Pac Fish that they were only broadcasting for the benefit of the visitors? I heard the sound of hundreds of beer cans or bottles being opened simultaneously. It was a not-so-silent editorial.

The first race, the exhibition race, was a walk. There were three offshore racing boats that were entered: mainland people that we made a point of scorning. They thundered by maybe 50 meters from where we were and the sound from the engines rattled inside my chest. The girls hated those big race boats but we loved it—it's a total XY-thing. After that, a regatta of some of our nicer sail boats cruised by and we went to sleep for that. About half an hour after that, the tension was building and I knew the race was about to start.

I had taken a break during the Regatta to see how Dad was doing on the *Dixie*. I found him arguing with a guy in a suit on the B ring and kept my distance. The guy was Indian but he was dressed sharp: nice suit pants and a pair of brown loafers set him apart from our usual slacker-casual uniform. He was saying something to Dad and shaking his head and Dad's jaw was grinding tighter and tighter. He kept pointing at the *Dixie* and appealing to the guy but the guy wasn't having it. After a few minutes, the guy just threw his hands up and I could hear him say "forget it, Rick." He turned on his heel and walked away. Dad looked like he wanted to explode.

Mitch appeared from somewhere and stood next to me, watching it all happen. "Crash and burn," he said and snorted. He almost seemed happy to be seeing it and it made me angry.

"What's happening?" I asked, trying to hold my temper.

"Your old man is trying to talk Sahid into fronting him the cash to open up a Casino here," Mitch was chuckling. "Been three times he's tried this and he strikes out every time." Dad had never mentioned any of this to me—what made Mitch so well-informed?

"I was tending bar and listening to it," he said. "Just came out for a smoke and they're still at it." He looked at me with whatever passed for sympathy from Mitch. "Sorry, man ... guess you shouldn't be surprised." I considered taking a swing at him. But Mitch was larger and faster than I was and I didn't need him on my bad side. What kind of jackass insults a guy's Dad to his face?

He sauntered away and Dad was still standing there, staring at an empty space between boats. I didn't know what to say to him. His eyes were stormy and he looked, well ... lost is the word I would use. I came up to him slowly and said, "You okay?"

His eyes cleared and he was right back to his usual self—nothing was wrong, nothing could bother him. "Of course," he said quickly. "How are you?" He walked off, looking at nothing. I shook it off. If he didn't want to tell me what was going on, well … whatever. Just don't get upset when I'm not 'reacting to your mood' or something. *You can't have it both ways, Dad.*

The Regatta finished and the Steeplechase was almost underway. Back on the *Horner*, we took turns ogling Jessica Cho. Riley watched her through a naval telescope and kept a running commentary of all the things he'd love to do to her. The dirtier and grosser, the better, in his mind. I tried to ignore him while they rolled out a small cannon to be used as the starting gun.

I didn't hear the "Go!" but the cannon popped white smoke and everyone cheered at once. The racers exploded from the starting line and then, well, they were off. We had a pretty good field of view for the start but then they disappeared out of view around the far side of the colony. Riley cracked open a beer that he snagged from Jeb … I decided to pass but it wasn't easy. About seven or eight minutes later, they shouted and the racers passed in front of us again. Jessica was maintaining a small lead and it looked like she'd be crowned winner again.

"I'll give her the victory baton tonight," Riley said suddenly. I looked at him in disgust.

"Tell it to her," I said. "I don't wanna hear it."

"You'll hear it tonight when I'm giving it to her." I groaned … his comebacks were always worse.

"What's the matter with you, anyway?" I said. "Seriously."

"The doctors say it's genetic."

I shook my head and turned back to the race: Lap number two was down and soon they'd be heading into the Maze. With all the turns, it looked like something you'd trace out on a kid's menu while waiting for your burger and fries. Maybe that's how they put it together in the first place. Jessica had finished the last dog leg at the edge of B-Ring and was on her way out when disaster struck.

At the far end of the Maze, one of the Burning Man Tribe set up a rubber raft and was taking pictures or filming. He'd managed to plop down dead center in the middle of the Maze exit and was ignoring the oncoming

Jet skis as he caught pictures of the last riders making the entrance. People were screaming at him but he was too stupid, drunk or high to notice. She was slowing down to navigate around him but the guy behind her was coming up fast, trying to overtake her and didn't see the idiot in the raft.

He rear-ended Jessica Cho's Jet Ski and the impact knocked them both over the raft and into the water. The two Jet skis then hit the guy in the raft. I would find out later that the crash turned him into a paraplegic. Jessica was out cold and minus a life jacket. Jessica looked beautiful in that LZR suit she wore but it wasn't much for safety … she wouldn't be on top of the water for very long. The Jumbotron was nice and tight on the action and so of course you could see everything. We hit the deck shouting.

"Everyone, please stay calm while we get the medics onsite" the speakers droned. The race stopped and all the Jet skis that were on the race came to an undignified halt as they couldn't maneuver out of the lane and they couldn't get off, either. One of the racers was Jessica's brother: he jumped off of his Jet Ski and started clambering over everyone to get to her. He made it most of the way but fell off into the water. He eventually had to duck his head down and swam under the dock to where he could get out.

The medics were our guys and they expertly maneuvered her onto a backboard. While they moved her toward the dock the announcer kept getting in the way telling us what we were already seeing. People hated him for doing that: some suit from Pac Fish running his mouth while our girl, our crew, our *mate* might be dying out there. Even I knew that. "You just don't do that, man," I yelled in his direction. There was no way he could hear me but Riley nodded with approval.

Bottles started shattering against the bulkhead of the *Phoenix* and the announcer subsided. Jessica was being put onto the dock but it was a madhouse. Our people were pushing in to help just like we would on any other day. The official medics were shoving aside and blows were about to be exchanged. Guess where Dad decides to be during all of this?

I didn't bother to join the crowd down there; I decided to find Dad instead. I saw him on a phone on board the *Dixie Star*, talking heatedly to someone. It sounded like he was planning a military operation. I heard the words "chopper" and "extraction".

"Dad," I called into the boat. "What are you doing?"

Dad beckoned me on board—nobody was around to complain. He had his sly hustler grin going on. "They're calling a helo out from San Diego," he explained. "It'll take an hour." We were sitting at the bar on the first deck of the ship—he pulled out a cocktail napkin and started to sketch out a map.

"Normally," he said, "they have a medevac chopper standing by during the race. But ... the crew was called to respond to a problem on one of the offshore oil rigs near Santa Barbara. Even without the available crew, Pac Fish didn't want to disappoint everyone so they crossed their fingers and said 'okay'." His little map was of us, where the helo was coming from and where the hospital would be. It would take the chopper an hour each way ... Jessica could die before they got her to the hospital.

No major accidents had happened before so I guess I see their point. None of this would help Jessica—she was pretty banged up and a boat ride back to shore would take too long. "I can have one of those guys up there," he said, pointing up to one of the hovering whirlybirds, "pick her up and get her to Cedars in no time." Dad was cooking up another scam to make himself a hero.

So, pump the brakes: Dad seriously wanted a sports channel helicopter to *land* on the colony, pick up an injured person and then take off to take her to a hospital. Skip over the part where he wasn't her parent, wasn't involved and had no business trying to put something like this together.

At first I was like: this is nuts. But then I was like, why not? It also wasn't any weirder than anything else I'd seen here—who's to say Dad couldn't be a hero? He disappeared while all of this was processing but I knew where he was going. I turned and scampered off in the direction of the *Horner*. I found him throwing furniture out of the way on the flying deck. Some of it was light, rattan stuff and he gave it a hook shot onto the foredeck below. He stowed a folding table and had me help him move it into his stateroom. Going back upstairs, he picked up an old tire rim and considered it for a moment before dropping it overboard. Another bold move: if I had ever tossed something overboard into or near the fish pens, he would have thrown me in after it. Whatever ... his boat, he calls the shots. I just couldn't believe that we were going to have a helicopter land on the *Horner*!

Dad was on the phone again and I could hear the conversation better this time. "I have a spot open on my back deck, it's 60 yards from where she is," he said. "Yeah—just have him set down, I'll have her over here by the time he's down." Silence for a few seconds. "I don't know, you'll have to work it out with him … You think he's going to turn down a ride? I'm sure he'll be okay with it." He ended the call and was hurrying to where they were easing Jessica onto the docks. I could hear the chopper thumping away overhead.

The security team had everyone pushed back while Jessica was lying on the dock in a thick white cervical collar and covered with a blanket. I didn't realize how bad it was but she had gray skin and she looked … I guess bored is the word. Distant. Miguel told me later that she was in deep shock. Her mom and dad were people I knew from the colony and they were on their knees next to her, talking quietly. Dad was trying to get one of the medic's attention.

"What's the story on that chopper?" one of them called to the Pac Fish cop.

"On his way," he replied and resumed a conversation he was having on his headset. "ETA is about 45 minutes." The medic did a weird monkey-move from where he was on his knees and came quickly over.

"She needs to be moving now," he said urgently. "Deep shock and she's got some internal stuff that needs attention."

"What do you want me to do about it?" the Pac Fish guy said sarcastically. Man, what a dumb thing to say. Her parents probably overheard her and her Dad was some kind of knucklefighter from Asia.

He was already off of his feet and moving to do some damage when my Dad reached in and grabbed his shoulder. The guy was going to hurt someone and probably thought Dad was another goon reaching in to cool things off. He rolled his shoulder and shook Dad's hand off while pirouetting to give his other hand a chance to swing around and pulp Dad's nose. I didn't really put all of this together as it happened … it was just one big blur of motion.

Dad was faster. He managed to swing a paw up and slapped the hand away while shouting at Jessica's Dad. "I got a chopper!" he shouted, partly to explain or stop Mr. Cho from countering his clumsy block. Mr. Cho was still moving and had Dad in a hammerlock, face down on the deck before he could breathe. "I got a chopper!" Dad shouted again, his voice was muffled with his face pressed into the deck. The words finally got through.

Mr. Cho said the only dignified thing he could say under the circumstances. "What?"

"I got a chopper, man," Dad muffled. Alex let Dad's arm go and he painfully sat up, rubbing his shoulder. "One of those helos can take her to the mainland a lot faster than the Coast Guard." All of a sudden, everyone was shouting.

Mr. Cho was shouting and clapping Dad on the back, the Pac Fish cops were hollering to someone and the medics were shouting for some transport, whatever it was, to get Jessica in the air and on her way. It didn't take long for a suit from Pac Fish, wherever he was on the *Phoenix* or the *Dixie* to push his way in and lay down the law.

He appeared out of nowhere and pushed his way past the goon squad. "Who called ESPN and told them to pick someone up?" he shouted.

"I did," Dad said. "Coast Guard can't have a chopper—"

"I told you we had this handled, Rick," he shouted. "What in God's name are you thinking, telling that pilot to land?"

"Get the girl on board—"

"Is he *trained* to land on a moving deck?" the guy yelled. "Two casualties is bad enough you want to make it four or five?" The crowd fell silent at the argument but Dad wasn't giving up yet.

"Hey, this kid needs medical attention!" Dad yelled back. The crowd was murmuring their approval and if it weren't for the cops, this guy would have found himself in the water in a few seconds. The Pac Fish people were used to dealing with us, it seems and the guy stood his ground.

"I got a chopper diverted!" He said and there was no mistaking the scorn in his voice. "He'll be wheels up with Jessica and her parents in *8 minutes*, not farting around on little tub with a pilot who'll probably dunk the second he tries to leave." Dad was busted—the Pac Fish guy had it all under control. This wasn't what they led me to believe out here. They told me that the company guys were useless. The guy wasn't finished. He looked to the Pac Fish cops.

"Escort Rick back to his boat. I want to talk to him after this is over." He knelt beside Jessica and her parents. "You hang in there, kiddo," he said gently. He gripped Mr. Cho by the forearm. "We're gonna handle this, sir. You stay with her."

He stood back and started barking orders like a sergeant or a colonel or something. This wasn't a paper-pusher out for the day … This was one of the People in Charge. In that moment I realized that there is a big difference between a guy who is genuinely in control of the situation and someone who's trying to bluff.

Hint, hint Dad …

The line of Pac Fish cops moved everyone back so that the medics could move Jessica to the *Phoenix* where the Coast Guard medevac would pick her up. Dad was escorted back to the *Horner* by a couple of the goons. Nobody paid any attention to me.

I stayed to watch the helicopter land and then leave again. The Steeplechase was off, obviously, and everyone was standing around discussing the crash and a few people asked me what Dad had been up to. I didn't know anything, of course.

Dad was running a scam of some kind, told me very little about it and now that it had blown up in his face, he was under some kind of house arrest and I was out here, looking like an idiot just for being related to him. I was angry and sad for him—I saw his face when he realized his potential day-saving move was blowing up in his face. I sat on the dock for a few minutes with my head in my hands. What a mess.

I stayed away from the *Horner* until the Pac Fish guy and Dad finished their chat. I have no idea what they were saying but I knew it was going to be ugly. Riley found me on the dock and invited me home to the big Race Day dinner his mom had going. They lived on the A Ring, close to the *Phoenix*'s gangway. The dinner itself was amazing—she got hold of some fresh catch and started turning out equal amounts of Baja-style fish tacos and sushi. It was strange to see tortillas sharing space with sashimi and kelp wrap but it was so good you got hip to it. I forgot about Jessica and Dad for a while … it felt great check out mentally.

Jeb wasn't at the dinner for some reason. He appeared later, painters cap still on his head and his ever-present cigarette dangling from his lips.

He caught my eye and made a small motion for me to go outside. I found him outside, the firefly of his lit smoke bobbed and danced while he talked.

"You know about your Dad? About this deal he had going?"

"Which one?" I asked. It was a fair question … Dad had a number of things cooking at any given time. He didn't keep me up to date on all of them. Jeb flicked the butt off into the water and his face was lit briefly by the flare of his Zippo. I heard it clink shut and he was in darkness again.

"You're dad wants to run the gambling here on the Colony," he drawled. "I told him it was pointless but he had to try anyway. Sahid's the exec in charge of all gaming on the Colony and Rick thought he could sweet-talk him." *That made sense*, I thought, remembering the guy and Dad talking earlier today. Jeb continued: "It fell apart like I told him it would. You're dad has no sense for negotiation. He thought if it made enough sense to him, it should make sense to everyone else and Sahid wasn't convinced. I told him to sell it to Sahid but he didn't."

"Uh-huh." Why was Jeb telling me all of this? Back when I worked for him, he spoke maybe 20 words to me including the two words "you're fired". After that, he didn't acknowledge my presence and I did the same.

So now, Dad's in trouble—I'm not exactly sure what kind or how bad—and Jeb is telling me all kinds of stuff that my Dad never bothers to tell me.

This place is a floating nuthouse: people are trying to kill you, rob you or cheat you every minute of every hour of every day. Then they're having some kind of moment with you like someone should be making a flavored coffee to celebrate with! Is there any point where you're allowed to shout 'enough is enough'?

Apparently not.

"So anyway—your Dad's trying to impress Sahid as a 'fixer' of some kind. Some fix … he tried to bribe the ESPN chopper with a story and now they're all pissed off and trying to find the 'exec' who authorized them to land. Your dad faked it all—it'll be a massive stink before it blows over."

Jeb finished his second cigarette and turned to go inside. "Anyway, thought I should let you know what you're up against before you go home and he's drunk under the table."

Yeah … thanks a million. This whole thing made me weary and I suddenly felt very tired. I wanted to go home. I made some excuse to Jeb (who didn't deserve an excuse at all) and started walking for the *Horner.* I found Dad just as Jeb said I would, asleep and sitting on the floor leaning against our ratty lounge couch. He had an empty tumbler next to him and I could smell the peppery odor of tequila. I went to bed where I read for a couple of hours before my eyes were heavy enough to shut.

Dad did this to himself, I kept repeating. He keeps trying to get ahead somehow and all he gets for his trouble is more trouble. I don't know why he bothered … was fishing so bad? I was so angry for him and sad for us that I didn't know exactly how all of this was going to get better, if it ever did.

Mitch Cutter found me the next day, slipping my mask on and getting ready to snorkel it. Dad was still passed out in his stateroom and I wasn't going to waste my time trying to get him up. That meant that I didn't have a hose tender but so I was getting prepped to do what I could.

"Your *Dad* told ESPN that he was a Pacific Fisheries exec?" Mitch howled. "What's *wrong* with him?" Somehow, he got word about the conversations between Dad and Pacific Fisheries. Now he was here to gloat.

"I don't know, Mitch," I growled. "Is it any different than your Colony Cares crap?" The Colony Cares thing was a website he set up to accept donations for 'The Underprivileged Youth on Fishing Colonies'. What a load.

Mitch snapped some strategic pics of the colony, trying to impress people with the squalor we lived in. It was halfway convincing … he caught some of the Children of the Burning Man dressed only in red Naugahyde and it went from there. He shrugged.

"I'm just a kid trying to get by," Mitch said. "What's your Dad's excuse?" I swear he had no sense of tact, that guy. Meanwhile, I was trying not to throw myself at him fist-first. Show up to our boat and start throwing stuff around about my Dad? What was wrong with him, anyway?

"I guess he's trying to get by, too," I said. "Not all of us were blessed with your looks and charm."

"That's for sure," Mitch agreed. He managed to take a potshot from me and deflect it right back in my face. Classy.

"Anything else?" I asked.

"Nope ... heard the blowout between him and Rackenaur was a beaut." He looked at me with some kind of pity on his face. I despised him at that moment. "Why do you put up with him?"

I threw my mask down like a hockey player losing his mitts and flew at him. What a schmuck ... how long was I supposed to take it, anyway? It was kind of weird—I didn't even realize I was moving until I was moving, if that makes any sense. At first I was terrified, first time in a fight and this was with a kid bigger than me, but I was throwing my first punch before I could stop myself.

Mitch reacted quickly, getting his hands up and blocking the fist. At the same time, he grabbed my hair and got my face up. He backhanded me, hard, and sent me backward.

I flew for a few feet, almost into the water and stopped myself. I was sniffing back blood as I charged again. We both went to the deck, wrestling and trying to throw punches. A few kids started to crowd around, yelling stuff. A guy across the way saw us both and ran over—I didn't realize he was there until he was shoving us apart.

"Knock it off, the both of you," he shouted. "Mitch, get out of here." He gave us both a shove to keep us apart but we barely noticed. Our blood was still up and we were both looking for a way to get to each other. "Move, I said!"

"Not my fault your dad sucks," Mitch said from his corner. I lunged again but the guy from the other boat swung a beefy shoulder around and I bounced off. Not really graceful, I managed to land my tailbone hard on the decking, bruising it. The guy and Dad were cordial and he stuck a finger right in Mitch's face.

"One more word out of you and I'll hang you off my dock as bait," the guy snarled. "One more ... go ahead!" The violence in his eye made an impression on Mitch. He sniffed at me and sauntered away.

The crowd slowly dissolved and I got painfully to my feet. The fisherman turned toward me, no kindness in his eyes. "You got fish to feed," he said. "Get to 'em."

I finished my chores, avoiding talking to anyone that day. Dad appeared later and by some unspoken agreement, we did everything in total silence. He checked the pens over, saying nothing, just looking and nodding.

I was grateful for once not to have him in my face complaining about something. My clumsy end to the fight had gotten around the colony and so I stayed inside, not ready to laugh that one off. Dad disappeared somewhere later that evening … the *Gun Range*, I think. I fell asleep that night with the dull ache of my tailbone competing with the dull ache in my heart.

Our current position is: 34°18'10.70"N 120°23'45.29"W

Chapter Six—The Ensenada Run

IT WAS LATE in the summer when the Ensenada Run happened. I haven't thought about it much until now because it was so weird and terrifying that I didn't want to think about it. Those two nights in Ensenada were just one more clue, among all the others, that things weren't all right on the Big C.

Healthcare was something everyone thought about. We were pretty much left to our own devices out here. Accidents were handled by the ship's infirmary or you were taken on a 12 hour boat ride to shore. If you're hurt enough to need a medevac, Pac Fish will pay for it. But you'll find a way to repay them. They'll make sure of that.

Other stuff, like getting a prescription filled, that was a little different and slightly touchy. They didn't have a full pharmacy on board the *Phoenix* and some meds were still too expensive to justify getting one. Some members of the colony had set up a quiet business on the side going on the other side of the fence to Ensenada, where they'd pick up the drugs they needed and run them back.

I walked into the salon one morning and Dad had the flyer in his hand. "2 day trip to Mexico," he said. "Any takers?"

"We're going to leave the ship for 2 days?"

"We have to," Dad explained. "You're out of your meds." I guess the supply Mom sent with me was almost gone and something was preventing her from shipping a refill out from the mainland. "Pac Fish requires that a legal parent be here to take shipment." Uh-oh.

Dad had lost custody of us when he left us years ago. Mom spent a lot of money she couldn't afford to try and track him down. When that didn't work, she got his parents' rights suspended. Years later, when I was 12, Dad reappeared and spent a lot of time trying to rebuild our relationship. Although Mom tolerated his presence for our sake, she never got around to filing any paperwork.

"So you can ship me out to the middle of the ocean, but you can't ship my pills," I said.

"Pretty much," Dad replied. "I got Jeb and Riley to keep an eye on things. I like to get out of the house once in a while. Don't you?"

Sure, why not?

The boat was another pilothouse yacht like the *Horner*. We had to be there by 5 in the morning. I bundled up for the trip—Pacific or not, Mexico or not, the morning air out here is *cold*. I helped myself to some nuked breakfast burritos they had on board. Other than that, it was a pretty boring ride. You can only look at the sea so much when you live there to begin with.

Dad passed the time pointing out stuff like the rusting metal fence that marked the border. That really caught my attention. It stretches all the way out into the sand and I watched it, wondering just how many people tried to enter the country at that point.

We arrived in Ensenada around eight that evening—it was a longer trip than the ride out from Long Beach. The partiers on the boat disappeared and we took our time checking into a cheap place Dad knew about. The next day, we did a lot of window shopping with Dad keeping his whistle wet at almost every cantina we passed. Dad had been here before, his Spanish was okay and he knew a few good beach places. Me, on the other hand, it was my first trip down this far. Inwardly, I was so nervous about the trip I brought my passport and ID, just in case I needed to beat feet for the border. After a few hours, I relaxed and got into the spirit of being a *guero* tourist.

The trip wrapped up around three that afternoon and we were on our way back to the *Horner*. The skipper of our boat was a crusty old white guy named Greg. I didn't know him, but Dad did and spent most of the trip talking at him through the door of the wheelhouse. I tried to pass the time with the other kids on board, but we ran out of ideas about halfway through the trip. We were passing La Jolla around sundown when Dad snagged me. "Need you to do me a favor," he said quietly.

"What?"

"There's another boat from the colony on its way here," he said. "Something came up."

"And?"

"So the declaration was for two days only," he said. "They're gonna try to go back down with some of the same people. I can't go; I have to sit this one out. They want you to ride back and give the cops some story about losing your wallet."

Getting involved in the colony drug thing was the last thing I wanted to do, even on a dare. I hate to say it, but I wussed out. "Com'on, Dad," I whined. "I'm getting tired and stuff."

"I know," he replied. "This'll make us some brownie points that might come in handy later. Will you do it?"

I held out for a favor of my own. "I'm off pen patrol for 3 days," I said.

"One day," he countered.

"Two," I said. He hesitated—he really liked not having to do this.

"One day," he said.

"Aw, come on," I started to whine for real.

"One day," he said firmly. He leaned in close, "You might want to save my gratitude for something else that you need." He stayed leaned in that one spot, doing his little pin-you-to-the-wall-with-his-eyes thing. I was concerned, trying to think about what he might know.

I caved almost immediately. "Deal."

"Good, thanks. I'll let them know." He turned and disappeared back into the wheelhouse. The other boat was on its way and slid up next to us 20 minutes later. They were going to use the same boat for the trip since it was the one with authorization to go across the border. When the boat docked alongside, everyone not going back down south would transfer across.

I was scared and pissed. Dad's hokey schemes were usually harmless. Now he was asking me to involve myself in God-knows-what. I trusted Dad not to put me in harm's way but what about Greg the skipper?

Greg was a big wheel in this pill scam the Colony had going on. All of the different colonies in the LA area were in on this—it was huge. There were at least 3 boats on the colony that never fished; they just handled getting the drugs to the various colonies—sometimes they'd do an overnighter for emergencies. Dad tried to get in on the business and who could blame him? This was right in line with his 'no fishing anymore' plan.

I'm sure there was more to the story. I knew that the guys that did this were shipping more than prescription pills. It was kept quiet. We were out in International waters but were still under jurisdiction of the CG, the DEA and anyone else who wanted to come aboard and see if we were acting as a conduit of illegal activity.

I'm sorry if this sounds almost mobbed-up; it wasn't. The guys who did the run were pretty noble about making sure people could get drugs they could afford. The other stuff ... well, they seemed to keep it in its place.

When the other boat arrived there was a flurry of people transferring from one boat to the next. Packages and people were handed across and we aren't talking about water taxis. Everyone had to vault the rail. An older woman had to be eased gently across the rails and there were some tense moments as she teetered above the water between both boats. Then they added some fuel from a stack of gas cans that they brought up from below deck one at a time. Doing all of this took half an hour or so. Dad and Greg stood talking in the wheelhouse until the last packages were gone.

"Awright," Dad said, making ready to vault the rail. "Do what Greg says and you'll be fine." He grinned and rumpled my hair briefly. "This will help me out, pal. Thanks." He grabbed a handhold and was gone. Greg appeared in the wheelhouse door.

"Hold one," he said to Dad. He said to me: "Do you have your wallet with you?" I nodded. He held out his hand. "Gimme." I didn't want to, but handed it over without a word. He turned and spun it straight out at the boat—managing to neatly smack the cabin wall where it dropped to the deck.

"Rick! Keep an eye on that!" he called. Dad immediately grabbed the wallet before some of the kids had a chance to go through it. Then Rick was back inside the wheelhouse, gunning the engines. He scored a tight 180 on the water and we were heading south again in seconds. Within minutes, the boat for home was a small dot in the distance. I had not moved in all this time, holding onto the railing and staring at the going-home boat. I was hoping that somehow this was a joke. My hopes sank lower with every passing whitecap.

After a few minutes, Greg called to me. "Want some dinner?"

"I guess."

"They sent us a care package to tide us over," he explained. Hoisting a plastic grocery bag filled with paper take-out boxes, he handed it to me. "Warm these up in the galley and I'll join you in a few minutes—we don't have to change course for at least an hour."

I opened the bag to find that, when you were making an illegal run into Mexico for prescription pills or whatever, they fed you good. Viet Pho, noodles, chicken and vegetables were neatly organized in different packages. They even included some egg rolls and mustard.

Greg walked in as I pulled steaming plates from the microwave. "The simple pleasures," he commented. In an under-the-counter cooler, he pulled out a beer for himself and a soda for me. "Help yourself," he added. We sat and ate; Greg used old lacquer chopsticks while I stabbed pieces of meat with a kiddie-size plastic fork.

"Know what we're doing?" he asked, chewing a broccoli spear.

"No," I cautiously replied. This whole deal was twitchy and, frankly, I was too scared to ask.

"It's no big deal," he reassured me. "Last minute deal for some extra pills … cancer meds or something. Anyway … they asked us to come back for it and I said okay." He took a sip of his Pho, looking out to a vast horizon beyond the galley windows. "I'd just go back myself, but the cops know me. I can't just motor back into the harbor without a good reason."

"And so you need me to lose my wallet?" I asked.

"Exactly," he replied. "Actually, you really *did* lose your wallet because you're going to go to one of the places you visited today—a cop will be escorting you—and they'll hand you the wallet you misplaced. Now, the next part's tricky. The wallet will be empty and you're going to start a fight with the guy or girl who hands it to you. You need to make enough of a stink so that the cop believes you but not too much so that he feels like taking you into the station for a statement. Got it?"

I realized that Dad had buried me in something up to my neck ... exactly what I was afraid of. "I knew I should have held out for three days," I muttered.

"What?"

"Dad," I explained. "I told him I wanted three days off of pen patrol and he got me down to one day."

"Ha!" he laughed. "Rick puts you into this caper and all you get is one day off?"

"Yeah," I answered bitterly.

"Tell you what," he said. "You do this favor for me and I'll make it worth your while." We were both silent for a while—I was considering what Greg had in mind. I'd watched enough movies to know that the drug dealers would kill the guy who was doing the favor as often as they rewarded them. Would he try to hurt me?

Stuff like this that drove me crazy about Dad. How could he put me in this situation? I was angry and scared. Whenever Dad involved me in something, it was always at the last minute and always moving too quickly. It was like trying to dance but *whoops* they're doing a Salsa and you only know how to tango and *oops* you need to carry this refrigerator and *oh no!* you just remembered that you have some term paper you really should be working on and come on, come on ... why is everything *taking* you so long?!

We passed the next hour listening to the monotonous drone of the engines. I'd like to say we discussed the politics of the colony, thoughtfully discussed different methods of water desalinization and came up with a clever but thoughtful way to end violence in Palestine. I counted the beer mats he had thumb-tacked to the wall over the galley passthru. Greg disappeared into the wheelhouse to alter course and I thumbed through an old *Sports Illustrated* that he had lying around. The sky was reddening and the sun was almost to the horizon when he reappeared.

"We're pulling up in ten minutes," he said. "Remember what I said—make the cop believe you're mad but don't fill out a report." We tied off at the dock more or less in the 10 minutes he promised. At once, his attitude changed. He became snappish and withdrawn—if he said anything at all to me it was at a bark. "Don't drop the fender yet!" he hollered. Then he yelled even louder when I was late dropping it over the side. "Now, now! Do it now!" he almost screamed. Who *was* this maniac?

Holding me roughly by the arm, he marched me up the dock to the little shack the *Policia* kept. I didn't understand enough Spanish to catch what he said but got the gist from his gestures. He was all but screaming as he gestured to me and then to the town. Even the cops, who apparently knew him, were impressed. Finally, one took me by the arm and started off down the street.

"He says you lost your wallet, right kid?" the cop asked. I was surprised, thinking that no one besides me and Greg would be speaking English. So much for that.

"Yeah." I nodded.

"You were at *Los Perrito púrpura* today?"

I had to think about it. The *Perrito púrpura*? The Purple Puppy? Sounded like a head shop. I said, "Yeah" again and we started off with no more conversation. We arrived there less than a few minutes later—it wasn't a head shop.

The Purple Puppy was a bar—you could hear the music and noise from three blocks away; from a block away it was almost deafening. The place was a large, open-air cantina. The place was closed and shuttered in the daylight—now those shutters were open and it seemed like half of Ensenada was inside. In the middle of the place was a large oval bar manned by five or six people. White tourists were doing tequila shooters and a live mariachi band was going like it was Cinco de Mayo. The cop (his badge said 'Ruiz') and I went inside to the bartender, where he shouted to make himself understood to the bartender. This was the scariest part of the trip—what if the bartender wasn't in on it?

My heart sank when the bartender shrugged and shook his head. I didn't have to speak Spanish to understand that: I don't know what the kid is talking about. The cop looked back at me, trying to make up his mind about something and then asked another question. The bartender called up someone else—this smoking hot Mexican lady who was on the other side of the bar. She nodded immediately and disappeared behind the bar for a second before holding up a red Velcro wallet.

Officer Ruiz shouted something at me, but the brassy trumpet obscured it. I shouted "What?" and he yelled back. "Is it yours?" I nodded and screamed "Yeah!" He nodded his thanks to the bartenders and we headed off back to the dock. Home free ... or so I thought.

It was late and I had a hard time remembering all the twists and turns we'd just taken. This cop wasn't giving a tour ... he took the quickest route back to the cantina. I was completely lost and hoping he wouldn't simply drop me to find my way back to the dock. We were going down an alley that looked familiar when the cop caught me by the scruff of my neck and shoved me against the wall.

I banged loudly into loose sheet metal—the place was an old Quonset hut painted lime green. In a flash, he had his baton out and was shoving it into the base of my skull. He started frisking me roughly—did he think I had a gun?

"All right, kid," he hissed. "Let me see your real wallet." He continued frisking me, looking for anything in my pockets. "I know your fren' Greg. He's always up to something. Com'on—show me the real wallet." He continued searching ... started sticking his finger inside the waistline of my jeans. I felt like I was being strip-searched. Maybe that was next.

After a minute, not finding anything, he grabbed the wallet I got from the bar back and opened it, looking for something. The wallet had a few dollars in it and in his anger it flew open. A few paper dollars fluttered out onto the ground. Even though I was terrified, a small part of my brain said *someone will be happy when they find that tomorrow.*

"This is your wallet?" he said angrily. "This your wallet?" I was petrified, I could only nod dumbly. "Then where's your ID, kid?" In his anger, his accent was getting thicker. "ID" sounded like "Aye-Deeuh". "Where's your ID? All you American kids have an ID." Still being scared, all I could do was shake my head. This really pissed him off. He shoved me back into the corrugated sheet metal again and started searching all over again. He missed something in his first pass—his hand brushed something in my jacket pocket.

I could hear him almost gasp in surprise—he physically tore the passport right out of my jacket. It was a cheap windbreaker, but his rough treatment was so shocking that I almost burst into tears. The cops in the US had never treated me like this—even when I was at my worst, waking up hungover or coming down handcuffed to a hospital bed.

He stared at my passport for a long time—looking from the picture to my face. I stumbled onto the perfect solution by dumb luck. Of course I wouldn't have my ID—why else would I have brought a passport? He didn't even bother asking, just closed it quietly and handed it back to me. No apology, no explanation. He started forward, silently leading the way back to the boat.

Greg was reading from the old Sport's Illustrated as we walked down the gangplank. "Get your wallet, kid?" he asked as he stood. I nodded, afraid to say anything in front of the cop. Greg's eyes dropped to my torn jacket and it was all the explanation he needed.

He looked back up at the cop and something unspoken passed between them. All I could see was Greg's eyes, but they turned cold and hard. "Now that," he said, "was uncalled for. That wasn't nice at all." A few more seconds passed and then Greg looked toward me. "Let's go." I stepped aboard the boat; the engines were idling quietly and he had them humming in no time heading toward home.

I sat in the wheelhouse, my head back against the bulkhead, just processing what had just happened. Greg broke the silence first.

"I'm sorry," he said. He looked at me from gazing outside the front windows. "I'm real sorry." He told me how it shouldn't have happened—that the whole deal was *with* the cops and that the one who took me to the bar was the one who was gunning recently for a bigger chunk of the profit. He'd been turned down and was now looking for any excuse to bust Greg.

The boat trip back, all 15 hours of it, was done in silence. Greg tried to get some conversation going, but I was beyond talking. I sat in the wheelhouse, morosely staring out to sea. I was still trying to process everything that had just happened or what could have happened.

I couldn't defend what I did to get shipped out here and I wasn't proud of it. But everything I had done before I came out here seemed like a wet fart next to the dangerous crap Dad was into. What were they smuggling and why did it need our second trip? Why didn't they warn me about *El Capitan Loco*?

I felt like Dad should have warned me. He acts like he knows everything … was some advance warning out of line?

I had questions, but I didn't know who to ask. It seemed like the wrong time to start asking a guy like Greg. For all I knew, he was more dangerous than that cop. He gave up trying to talk. Maybe he felt bad about putting me into that situation. Maybe he didn't think about it at all. He didn't volunteer the information and I didn't ask.

I don't know if Greg called ahead, but it didn't really matter. When we docked, Dad wasn't there to meet us. It was a cold, dank morning just before eight and the walk back to the *Horner* was lonely and miserable. I could hear the bells of the marker buoys gently tolling and I felt like I was the only one awake, the only one alive, on the colony at that moment. The wind was blowing the fog over us and I could hear the fog signal begin to sound on the *Phoenix*.

Coming up to the *Horner*, a single light was on in the salon. I slipped inside to find Dad asleep on the couch, watching the feed. He had waited up for me but slept through me coming home. I didn't wake him, didn't cover him up or do anything … I just went to my bunk where I slipped off into a dreamless, exhausted sleep. The blowing wind moaned through the door leading to the rear deck. The perfect end to a perfect day for me.

Our current position is: 34°22'43.21"N 120°27'26.16"W

Chapter Seven—The Boys of Summer

I ENDED MY summer on the Colony with my arms wrapped around my knees and sitting with my back to the wall in a cracked vinyl chair. No, I wasn't in jail, but close. I was in the Greyhound station in Oxnard. A bus was leaving in 8 minutes, but I wouldn't be on it. Mom was driving up from West Covina to get me.

My stomach rumbled and I did my best to ignore it. There wasn't any money for food and I didn't want to deal with the creepy guy behind the counter any more than I already had. I had to borrow the phone to call my mother for a ride home and he had stared at me the entire time. Mom knew something was wrong when she heard my voice. All she said was "I'll be there in a few hours" after my 30-second explanation and then she hung up. With no money in my pockets, only my ID, I was about the saddest kid in town. What a way to end the summer.

After the Ensenada run and Steeplechase, the summer started to wind down. I don't know about you but summer vacation always starts dragging for me between the end of July and the middle of August.

There were a few interesting things that happened. Mitch Cutter came around again with some new scams he wanted me to get in on. Our Steeplechase fight was forgotten and he needed someone with the interest and talent for making old electronic gadgets work again. I was hosing off from pen patrol on a random Tuesday when he appeared, munching on an apple. "You do IT stuff, right?"

I turned around, surprised. No hello, no 'nice to see you.' One second Mitch wasn't there and the next he was. "Sure … sometimes."

"You're going back soon, right?"

"Yeah." Soon I'd be hoisting a sea-bag for another 12-hour ride back to shore. I didn't know how I was going to feel about it. Even Madison's emails from home, describing the trip to Disneyland and Vegas seemed washed-out and dull. I had spent my summer doing a man's work—hauling fish and living on the sea. Waving for the camera next to Goofy seemed corny and lame by comparison.

"So how about teaching me how to fix computers? I'll cut you in for a piece of whatever I make." Mitch carefully tossed his apple core into the water away from our nets. It made sense to me. If I wasn't there, my regular customers would go out and find the next kid who showed up.

"How will you pay me?" I asked.

"Through your Dad, through Miguel. Whatever you want."

Huh … sounded interesting. I was still cautious about Mitch, though. He was cheerful and friendly on the surface, but he had a mean streak. The bitter commentary about Dad and the Steeplechase debacle was one example. Some boats banned Mitch from their presence and spoke cautiously about me because of the association. Mitch was about commerce and as long as the deal was solid, there was no problem. If the deal went south, he wasn't above some payback. It was in everyone's interest to keep that from happening.

Above all, Mitch was a cusser. My mom had her moments and Dad certainly never held back. Mitch's parents were from the South and his dad had worked on an oil rig for 12 years. His dad swore like the Enduring Freedom vet he was and his down-home Bible Belt Fundamentalist mom reminded Mitch almost constantly that 'if he talked like his daddy he'd go to Hell.' The solution to the problem for Mitch was to swear out of his mother's earshot and life went on as normal. He developed a personal monologue called "The 20 Things Wrong With This World" that he recited for me on a number of occasions. I felt it was the most acute and articulate use of coarse language I'd ever listened to. Near the end of the summer, Mitch took delivery of some old junk. One of the lesser-known weirdos, Crazy Addie, had been collecting it for years. Addie was all set to toss it overboard one night and his neighbors were concerned. Just before violence ensued, Mitch slid up and declared his interest in selling and/or donating the junk after I'd fixed it and the problem was solved. He conned me into helping him haul what amounted to a truckload of random electronic parts out of Addie's boat. Then we sorted it for trash or repair. We were supposed to figure out what each thing was and whether it was worth anything. This is how we ended up being disk jockeys for a radio station on the Colony for about an hour.

The unit had an old battery and when I replaced it with a new 9-volt the power LED glowed. I tossed it onto the "Keep" pile. It had no label and I had to ask Crazy Addie what it was. "It's a broadcast unit," was the reply. "You can use it to transmit over FM." I immediately saw an opportunity and Mitch did as well. A radio station would be a moneymaker since the Colony was well out of range of any land-based FM stations.

Our first and last broadcast was a disaster. After several days of testing to determine the range of the radio transmitter, we pushed ahead with stapling and taping cheap fliers announcing the new station's existence. My wrist and fingers were sore from writing "104.5—COLONYVOICE" onto hundreds of 'borrowed' sheets of white paper. We stayed up all night creating music playlists and talking about what we would say. Privately, I was terrified from stage fright but Mitch seemed confident the whole thing would go perfectly.

It did not. Twenty minutes after six, when we had been talking for 20 minutes about nothing (I hadn't realized that radio patter required actual preparation and there were a lot of awkward silences during that time) that Mitch's stateroom door flew open. Mitch's mother entered the room, shouting incoherently. For those listening at that hour, they heard Mitch's mother screaming about 'devil music' and Mitch yelling for his mom to get out of his room. Mitch was so upset that his voice started cracking and I forgot to cut the microphones off. I took the first opportunity to leave the ship, but I could hear the argument echoing through random radio tuners as I returned to the *Horner*. More than a few groups of people were thoroughly enjoying Mitch's social implosion.

The radio station ended the same day it started and Mitch never mentioned it again. I was curious about the fate of the broadcast unit. Mitch said, "It was an experiment, it's gone" and that was that. We moved full-steam ahead into the 'computer guy' business. I spent a lot of time taking Mitch on calls and teaching him basic troubleshooting.

The last day of the summer finally arrived. I climbed out of the water that day and spat my regulator out for the last time. Dad and I were both quiet. No major chores, Dad and I spent the day together talking about what I'd be doing when I returned to the mainland and going back to school.

There was still a lot of talk about Jessica Cho: the bad news had finally arrived a week ago. A week in the ICU, another month doing physical therapy later and the prognosis came back. She wouldn't be doing any walking, anytime soon. What's worse, while her parents were at her bedside they went into default on a couple of mortgages. The Cho Family quietly packed their things and returned to the mainland. The boat itself returned to the possession of Pacific Fisheries and would probably be used to break in newcomers.

I noticed something weird happened, just as they were leaving. The boat was leaving from the *Phoenix* and had to make its way through the Maze. The original Steeplechase route was gone now and the route had been moved back to normal. Ignacio, the boat skipper who first brought me out to the Colony was giving them a lift back home, free of charge. As the vessel swung around in a neat little circle to point the way it had come in, people were lining the docks and waving their good-byes.

It was kind of touching. The route of the Maze was lined with people who wanted to wanted to see them off. Maybe it was like when you grew up in a neighborhood and they all came out to shake your hand when you moved away, I don't know.

"It's not right," I said, watching the Chos depart. Dad let some time pass and all we could hear was the grumbly diesel farting its way out of the Maze and into the open ocean.

"No," Dad replied. "No, it isn't. They're going to turn the boat into a shakedown shack. Worst part of it is: no insurance and no help from Pac Fish."

"What do you mean?" I asked.

"Pac Fish makes them all sign waivers before the Steeplechase," Dad said. "They get hurt, it's on them. They know it, too. The amount of money coming back from the race is worth the risk and others just do it for pride." He cracked a can of beer open and took a pull before continuing. "I heard they gave Alex a token payment for his trouble. Maybe four or five grand—it wouldn't even cover a day of what it costs to have that little girl in a hospital bed." Dad snorted bitterly.

Insurance and health care were things that I didn't think very much about. You get hurt, you need a checkup, Mom or Dad take you to the doctor and all you have to do is be brave and take that lollipop they give you. Dad was talking about money and doctors and waivers—it was all over my head. "Don't you guys have insurance out here?"

"You do," Dad replied. "Courtesy your mom and step-dad. Me, I pay into their little scheme and hope I don't get a disease they don't cover." I turned to go back inside where Dad prepared two man-sized steaks for the grill as our last dinner. Steak was rare in the Colony where everyone just ate what they were growing. Dad skipped the culture-grown stuff and had gone to the trouble of getting an on-the-hoof steak from shore. He took fussy care in mixing a grill rub and making some fresh guacamole. Our last meal together was nicer than anything else Dad had done for me. He even cleaned up the top deck and set out a real table with a cloth and non-plastic silverware. "No dishes for you tonight, boyo," Dad said. The dinner was great and I could see why people liked my dad despite his weirdness.

I was running some last minute computer calls for people on the Colony who knew I was going home that night. Little things came up that could probably wait but I wanted to get it out of the way until Mitch was fully functional. After that, I was packing up back at the *Horner* when Miguel stopped by with something interesting to tell us. As I entered the lounge, both Dad and Miguel were standing over a ratty old map of the California coastline. "What's up?" I asked.

"Buried treasure," Dad said, grinning.

Buried treasure? Images of pirates and gold doubloons danced in my head.

"Not quite," Miguel said. He tapped a point on the map and made the paper rattle. "The kids have a scam they asked us for help on. They want to take you with them as part of the deal."

"Which kids?" I asked.

"Your friend, Mitch," Dad replied. I was surprised: Mitch hadn't said a word to me about this. "He and a buddy are making a trip to drop some electronics off."

"He wants me to go?"

"Sure. Says he wants to run you back to the mainland as part of the deal. I thought it'd get me out of having to pay for a trip," Dad explained. "What do you think?" None of this smelled right to me—why didn't Mitch say anything about this before? Plus, I knew him: he's always one step ahead of everyone else. For him to offer to do something like run I back to shore, well ... there had to be a catch. Right?

I didn't get much of a chance to think it over. Mitch had appeared and was knocking at salon door. Dad let him in. "Did they tell you?" he asked me. "I got some electronics coming in and Miguel loaned me my boat. I'm going to clean up on this one—maybe open a video arcade out here."

Mitch was really amped up talking about the deal. Someone was unloading a bunch of old game machines and other junk. He had finally hit the big time ... maybe I picked the wrong time to leave.

I never did get to sleep. Dad and Miguel were up late discussing the scam, I had to finish packing and we were set to leave around midnight. I promised myself that I would be visiting the Colony again next summer. I cleaned my stateroom and I even left most of my clothes, the semi-clean ones, in a drawer next to my bed. The rest of my stuff was tossed into an ancient sea bag that Dad had given me. As a finishing touch, I left a note on the door: "Don't change anything—this is my room now." I smiled thinking about what Dad was going to do when he saw that.

Still, I had to admit: The plan was fuzzy. Miguel had loaned his boat and Mitch was bringing in a bunch of 'electronics.' He had conned his 'friend' into driving. The pickup was some beach by a Naval Air Station and I was going to ride along. Additionally, the boat that Miguel donated was one of his secret projects. You couldn't haul big bulky stuff in it ... Mitch had to know that. There was a lot he wasn't saying.

I put it out of my mind. Riding in Miguel's boat was worth the trip by itself. It looked like an old wakeboarding or ski boat, but Miguel had made some modifications. It was fitted out with extra-large fuel tanks, sonar, an illegally tuned radar mast and a supercharger on the old Chevy marine V8.

It was a smuggler's boat—built for fast runs along the coast and away from the Coast Guard, shallow enough to go where their big cutters couldn't follow.

I had been shown all the features during a lazy afternoon while Miguel spun tales about working marine salvage down in Key West with some guy named Fisher. Until now, the boat had remained under wraps at the Cho's empty boat garage. "I have to find a new place for it," Miguel said before leaving. "This'll help me pay for a new berth."

I was happy, though. This would end my summer in style. A fast run to the coast in a hot ship to pick up illicit cargo. Who would even consider doing something like that in this day and age? Dozens of happy thoughts ran through my head. My 'How I Spent My Summer Vacation' essay would blow the doors off of any other entry—how could I lose?

Like I said, I never slept. I guess Dad didn't either. He was up when I yanked the sea bag up from my room to the salon where Dad was enjoying a beer and a cigarette while reading a Mickey Spillane novel. We sat together on the couch in the Salon, watching the feed and waiting for the other person to speak.

Dad finally broke the ice. "It'll be quiet around here." He didn't say anything about whether he'd miss me or how much he enjoyed having me around. If he felt anything at all, it was news to me.

"I had fun," I said cautiously. I never get straight answers out of my Dad about how he feels. I didn't know if I deserved one, but it might be nice to hear my dad say *something*, right? It wasn't going to happen today.

Dad stood, finished his beer and carefully placed his butt into the can. "Well," he said, holding his hand out like I was a long-time roommate off to a new place. "Take care of yourself. Gimme a call when you arrive."

Maybe that's as good as I was ever going to get from him. I decided to not to make a big deal out of it. "Sure thing, Dad." He smiled and swatted me lightly on my head.

"Don't get all stupid once you get back on shore," he said. "I know where you live." I grinned, hoping we could get out of this before it got mushy. Dad apparently had the same idea. "You gonna stand there all day? Get moving!" That had been my rallying cry when we were working on something on the boat. It meant 'do what you were supposed to be doing' or maybe 'wherever you're supposed to be, here isn't it.' I used it to make a clean break, running for the *Barco de Arma* and Mitch's treasure run.

This weird guy, Yusef, was sitting on the couch in the lounge when I arrived. I had seen him from time to time. He was a dark, silent man who sold fish larvae on the A Ring. Mitch never talked about him and until last night I didn't realize they were in business together. Before now, they never acknowledged each other's presence. Mitch was at the bar working the controls on a handheld GPS and sipping chai from a large steel mug. Miguel still asleep, I guess ... I didn't get a chance to say good-bye. We exited the *Gun Range* from the back deck where Miguel's boat was tied up. I noticed that he finally added a name on the back: *RumRunner*.

"Cute," I commented to Mitch, who was settling in at the console. He saw the named and grinned. Yusef glanced around briefly and then cranked the engine into life. We cast off and he started moving away from the dock. He kept the motor throttled back to keep the noise and wake levels to a minimum. Until the quarter-mile mark was reached, that is. When we reached it, Yusef throttled up the engine and we were off.

The trip was fun and I enjoyed it—the engine had a nasty growl and it was making 40 knots without a problem. We might have gone faster, but the choppy seas prevented it. They were heading north to some pick-up point and I would help them unload.

They were vague on when I'd be dropped back at the pier in Long Beach. I was supposed to call Mom when we were on our way. I wasn't too worried about it, though. They had the whole thing worked out with Dad, right? We continued far out to sea for over two hours, before turning slightly toward land. I was getting kind of nervous—I had never been this far out to sea before.

"Relax," Mitch said, not taking his eyes off of the radar screen. "The pickup is at a place called Point Mugu and we're just loading up from the truck. After that, I'll get you back to your mom." I knew that Mugu was up by Malibu so I guess that made some kind of sense. Still, Mitch sounded kind of snotty about it and I realized suddenly why I didn't like him: He took every opportunity to bust my balls.

"Actually, we're not going to Mugu," Yusef suddenly said. It was the first time he said anything around me and I jumped a little. "Mugu is a naval air station. Not exactly where you want to be picking up a bunch of stolen merchandise." He smiled at his own joke. "There's a piece of the old highway out on the road and we'll be landing there. Shouldn't take longer than 20 or 30 minutes." He made a slight course correction and looked closely at Mitch's GPS unit. "We should be there in another hour so try and get some rest now."

That killed conversation until we were within sight of the drop-off point. It was Mugu Rock, created when the highway department carved a route for the PCH out of the hillside. The highway used to go around it and the last crumbly pieces of roadbed were still visible like a freeway for ghosts. This was what they were using as a 'rendezvous point.' It was a dank and gloomy night. Wind and fog were driving the cold straight into my bones. Yusef spoke quietly to Mitch as approached the shoreline, asking for position checks and readings on the depth finder every few seconds. He spun the wheel and tweaked the throttle to keep us away from hidden dangers under the water. I started freaking out because I couldn't really tell what was going on. On either side of us, I could see waves breaking over rocks and shoals. What if we ran aground and I had to swim for it?

Yusef must have been thinking the same thing. After ten minutes of trying to figure out how to tie up to the rocks in the dark without bashing into them, he suddenly gunned the motor in reverse and pulled us away. "I'm an idiot for not thinking of it," he shouted. "We'll beach on that point over there." He pointed to a small beach just to the north and pulled out his cell phone. He told their contact about the change but whoever it was, wasn't happy about it. Yusef had to argue with him in some language until we reached the shore.

Finally, he hung up and said, "He's on his way. Let's take her in." Yusef killed the motor and allowed the waves to take us in. I could hear the sand hiss under the boat hull when we touched the shore. Nobody made a move to get out. We sat in the darkness listening to the waves chuckle and push us into the sand.

Within a few minutes, I saw some headlights stabbing the fog. A panel van pulled into the parking lot about 50 yards away from us. The contact guy was an old Portuguese guy and he was pretty grumpy about changing what he called his 'contact position.' Yusef shrugged and gestured for us to get started.

The 'merchandise' everyone was so weird about turned out to be a bunch of rotting cardboard boxes. The same kind of trash I had just finished going through for Crazy Addie. I was glad I didn't have to inventory and fix this truckload. Let Mitch do it—he needs the experience.

The entire van was stacked full of junk. Box after box of old circuit boards and dusty plastic left over from when TRON, the first one, was a big hit. I took about twenty trips with large, sagging boxes of junk across the sand to where Yusef was stacking them on board the *RumRunner*. I was getting exhausted. Walking in sand takes a lot out of you.

I stumbled with one box and dropped it. I swore under my breath and started picking things up. Then I thought I saw something strange. I had a small flashlight … Dad had given it to me at some point and I stuck it in a pocket last night so it wouldn't get lost. I twisted it to life so I could see what I was doing. It didn't feel like metal and plastic. Neat, double-freezer bags full of blue pills. A few other ones had white, pink or red capsules. There were no labels, but I didn't need them. What a shock: Mitch's 'buried treasure' scam was nothing more than a badly disguised drug run.

This place never gets better. It only gets worse, I thought. Mitch had borrowed Miguel's boat to run drugs to the Colony. I had nothing to do with it but I knew no one would believe that … not even my probation officer. The other boxes were probably full of drugs, too. I was suddenly terrified at what I had gotten myself into.

Did Dad know? Probably not … I mean, hopefully not. Especially not after that run down to Ensenada. He swore to me that stuff like that would never happen again but here I was, up to my neck again in trouble. I wasn't among friends and I was a long way from home. What was I going to do?

The decision was about to be made for me. The old guy had noticed the light and walked over. "What are you doing?" he demanded. He snatched up the light and hurled it into the breakers where it shorted and died immediately. *Guess it wasn't waterproof.* He grabbed me by my shirtfront and hurled me backward to the sand six feet away. He was yelling at me while picking up the stuff that had fallen out. Mitch and Yusef had seen the commotion and came running up.

"What's going on?" Yusef asked harshly.

"Snoopy here … Probably wanted some for himself." Yusef didn't bother to ask my side of the story and he went off on me and Dad.

Yusef and the old guy took turns screaming while they finished loading up the boat. Mitch turned to stone. I looked several times in his direction hoping that he would do something, defend me or put a call in to Dad. All he did was sit in the pilots chair and ignore what was happening five feet away. I had no idea what I should do at that point so I finally sat down on the sand a few yards away and waited for it to be over.

Every time I think I've seen it all, these bums managed to outdo themselves. It's really amazing. The weirdness dipped into dangerous, borderline psychotic, behavior on a regular basis. Everyone just accepts it on the Colony and I guess that's how they deal with life on land, too. The gray, foggy sky had lightened—dawn was approaching and they needed to be on their way. I just wanted to get back to my mom and forget this night ever happened.

They were heaving against the boat, trying to get it deep enough to use the motor and off the sandy beach. Yusef waved me over to give them a hand and with all three of us pushing while Mitch worked the throttle, we managed to get it deep enough to where he could put the prop down and pull the boat free.

Yusef heaved it into deeper water and pulled himself up over the lip of the bow to land on a few boxes. I was ankle-deep in the wash and wondering how I could get aboard without getting soaked. It turns out that they already had an answer for that.

The engine was growling and the boat pulling further into the surf. At first, I was confused—were they going to make me swim out to it? Was that their idea of fun? There wasn't a dock in sight … it's the beach after all. The boat began to nose around to head for deeper water. I was running into the small breakers and shouting for them with my heart sinking—this wasn't going to be pretty.

"Sorry, kid," Yusef yelled to me. "I guess we're too heavy to take you back. Emil will take you back to your mom." Emil, I guessed, was the angry old man who had just broken a million laws with the cargo he just delivered. I'd rather ride with an angry wolverine. "What about my mom?" Yusef's answer was to shrug.

"You guys were supposed to take me back," I hollered.

"I was supposed to, and then you started poking your nose in where it didn't belong. That was right about the time I realized we were too heavy to take you."

The subtlety wasn't lost on me—Yusef was pissed because I figured out what was going on and this was his way of pointing it out. It was a rotten thing to do. Maybe Mitch didn't agree with it but he wasn't saying anything. I could barely see him over the dash of the boat, but he was looking out to sea like there was absolutely nothing more fascinating than a gray, foggy sky at 5:30 in the morning.

So there I was, standing in cold salt water up to my knees and screaming for a ride. I never felt more pathetic or lost in my life. What kind of a jackass takes a kid for a boat ride, promising his Dad to deliver him home safely and then leaves him on a beach somewhere?

The other thing that made it so surreal for me, now that I think about it, is this. When you're thirteen or fourteen, you have no idea what to do when the adults you're with suddenly turn on you. That moment of 'it's-gonna-be-okay' that suddenly turns into 'Oh-my-God-no-it's-not'. It's awful. "What am I supposed to do?" I screamed.

"I guess you'll figure something out," Yusef shouted. "Good luck." The boat was pulling out into the water and I had to strain to hear the last thing he said to me. "Hurry up, kid. I think Emil's leaving."

I turned around to see the insult added to the injury: Emil's headlights were on and he was slowly backing out of the parking space. I splashed out of the water and made a run for Emil, who was preparing to leave 75 yards away in the predawn darkness. My sneakers were squishing with water and sand was sugaring my feet and wet pants. Just as I reached the broken asphalt edge of the parking area, Emil was pulling out into the traffic of the PCH.

"Wait! Wait!" I screamed and it was debatable whether Emil heard me or not. Maybe he did hear and decided to leave anyway. The kind of guy he was, it makes more sense. I was panicking, running after the van that was speeding away and my breaths began to sob in my chest as I realized that yes, this was happening and yes, I was stuck in some godforsaken stretch of road in the middle of nowhere with no one to contact and no way to get home.

I was sobbing as I stopped to catch my breath. I took a page from Mitch and started screaming a bunch of oaths standing there on the side of the road. It was the kind of cursing that the good people at the Naval Air Station nearby would have applauded. My voice was cracking and my face was red from crying and running—I thundered violent epithets with all the emotion of a preacher in a church tent revival. It made no difference at the moment, but it made I feel better for some reason.

The taillights of Emil's van disappeared around a bend in the distance and eventually I ran out of things to scream. My breath rasped in my throat and, looking to my right, Mugu Rock loomed overhead in the gloom.

I had to hike back down to the beach where they had dropped my sea bag. It was right at the water line and a few waves had reached it. I opened it up to find that all my clothes had been soaked. All my electronics would have been ruined, if I hadn't packed them in little Ziploc sandwich baggies.

Suddenly, I realized that my phone had been mortally wounded. I moaned when I saw that the the bag had been punctured and my phone was sitting in two inches of sandy salt water. I don't think the warranty was going to cover that one. I stayed there on the beach, crying for a while. Why not? On the ocean, no one can hear you bawl.

Part of me died in the sand there. I know that sounds sad, but I think it happens for everyone. There are little moments in life that kill whatever illusion of safety you have. The adults have abandoned you, nobody's going to help you. If you're going to keep breathing, you're going to have to suck it up and take care of yourself.

No one should have to learn it the way that I did, but I didn't have any choice in the matter. After a while, I thought about getting out of here. Behind me, back at the parking lot, an RV that had camped there overnight had lights dimly glowing inside. I picked up the bag and walked toward them.

Early risers, I thought, wondering what time it was. I wiped my face on a damp sleeve and tried to blow the snot out of my nose without getting too much on my hands. The orange glow behind the curtains looked friendly and as I approached the rear door, I could smell the coffee brewing. "Hope they have a phone," I muttered under my breath.

I was about to raise my hand to knock at the door politely when I heard the *schkk-shckk* of a pump-action shotgun being racked. Something hard poked me in the ribs while an elderly Midwestern voice commanded: "You hold it right'chere,"

I instantly raised my hands and froze, dropping my sea bag next to my feet. I'd never had a gun pointed at me, but I knew what the appropriate response was. Now what?

I finally risked a turn of my head to see who it was. A wiry old man with a bristly, white mustache wearing nothing but an old Western shirt with fake pearl buttons, faded blue boxers and a pair of battered cowboy boots was holding a pump-action shotgun on me. "I was watching the whole thing. I've called the police. They should be here directly."

"What a night," I muttered. Did this ever end? The comedy of errors that this evening started out with just kept getting better and better. Now I was at the scene of a drug shipment, with the cops on the way, no phone, no ride and no money. If this were happening to anyone else, I'd have laughed my butt off. All I wanted to do right now was cry. I can't believe this is happening to me.

"You with Al-Qaeda?" the old man asked suddenly. I should have seen this coming.

"What?" I asked, carefully.

"What?" the old man repeated sarcastically. He stepped forward aggressively, putting the muzzle of the shotgun into my face. "Are you a terrorist? Are you with Al-Qaeda?" Before I could respond, the muzzle was pushed almost into my eyeball. "Don't you lie to me, boy!" the old man shouted furiously.

I couldn't keep up with all of this crap. Mitch and Yusef. The botched 'electronics run' that was nothing more than a badly disguised drug shipment. Left at the shore to fend for myself … we all know how good I am at that. Now there's an old man in his underpants with pointing a gun at me, interrogating me about terrorism! All I could do was stand silently and hope the old man was smart enough not to pull the trigger.

"I saw you come outta the water with them other boys," he drawled. "I saw you carry them boxes fulla junk. You makin' bombs? Who's your contact?" The geezer grabbed me by my shirt and threw me against the vinyl wall of the RV. "What did they give you to betray your flag, son?" he shouted. The old man raised the shotgun up to chest-high and it seemed like he was going to try and run me through with the muzzle.

"Stand down, Bob," a voice from my right said wearily. A female voice, older and also from the Midwest. She was thickly built with red hair that had rusted from age and wispy with bedhead. She put her hand out gently to Bob and his shotgun. "Put it down." Bob suddenly looked confused and embarrassed, holding the weapon and walking around outside in his unmentionables.

"Grace?" he asked, bewildered.

"It's okay, Bob," she said. "Go on inside." Bob looked confused, like a lost child, suddenly looking from the gun to me. His face crumpled slightly and he looked like he might burst into tears. Bob lowered the gun and leaned against the RV, trying to pull himself together. "I'm sorry about that. Are you all right?"

"Yeah," I said, wondering what had just happened. Bob walked away like a man carrying a heavy load and disappeared around the backside of the RV. I could hear the scrape of his boots as he walked around to get into the vehicle from the driver-side door. "Um …" I began, trying to say something by way of explanation but since that seemed to be impossible, I just repeated himself. "Yeah."

"I'm very sorry," she said. "Bob's still dealing with it. Gets up and thinks someone is about to attack us. The gun wasn't loaded." She took in my appearance or the first time. "Are you okay?"

I looked down at myself. My pants were soaked and I was covered in sand. The dark windbreaker I was wearing was half-off of my shoulders, my eyes were red from crying and screaming at Emil. I wasn't sure who the weirdo in this picture was, this old guy Bob or me. *Maybe this place brings out the weirdness in everyone,* I thought to myself.

"My friends were fishing," I explained. "They had a problem and I had to get off." The woman took this in and I could tell she knew I was lying. I took a second stab at it. "The boat was overweight and they needed to make it lighter."

"Are they coming back?" she asked.

"I think so ... I just need to use the phone."

"Oh, of course," she said, hurrying to get inside and get a phone for me. She passed it to me and I tried to dial Dad's cell number but got only voicemail. I tried it a few more times and then tried Mom. Same result.

I tried for an hour, but I wasn't able to reach either of them. While we waited the woman, Grace, told me that she and her husband Bob were retirees. They traveled all over the country. She turned out to be quite hospitable given the circumstances. Thank God they didn't ask any more questions about my story because I sure didn't have any answers.

"We're heading north on Highway One," she explained. "We can't drive you to West Covina but we can take you into Oxnard to the bus station, no problem." I could get Mom to buy a bus ticket and I'd be on my way home.

That sounded like a solution to me. After a couple of cold pieces of Danish and a hot cup of coffee that tasted absolutely wonderful, they grumbled north into Oxnard and dropped me off at the Greyhound station on Fourth. I had to borrow a phone to call Mom and I finally got through. I also had to ignore the creep behind the counter. He was being unusually helpful and after I had hung up I saw the look in his eyes.

Oh, gross, I thought. Disgusting. No real surprise after what I had gone through and would probably endure when my mother arrived. The entire trip was such a mess and I couldn't imagine explaining this it to Dad, much less Mom.

Why had Mitch lied about what the trip was ... or did he not know? Did Dad or Miguel know? Why didn't they tell me to be more careful with the cargo? Was dropping me off part of the plan or did Yusef decide to improvise? What should I say to my Mom? The questions just kept spinning farther and farther from center ... it didn't make sense no matter how hard I tried.

I was exhausted, but this wasn't the kind of place to fall asleep in. A headache was throbbing behind my right ear and the pain traveled across the top of my head stop just behind my eye. Miserable, exhausted and in pain—this is how I ended my first summer on the Colony.

I was taking my first steps on the road to adulthood in that waiting room. Doing *something* that was real, something that was important and even a little dangerous felt better to me than getting baked and sleeping until 2PM.

I wasn't afraid of a man's job and I had survived the previous day's nonsense. Getting high and partying all the time … that wasn't who or what I wanted to be. Whenever I was hung over or coming down, I knew that I wanted something else out of life. I just had no idea what it was I wanted or how I would get it. I really thought spending the summer with Dad would help me figure everything out.

Until now.

This little adventure poured a bucket of water over everything. I felt like I was back at square one. I was stuck in this bus station and Mitch was probably back home by now, telling Dad whatever he felt like. Then there was Yusef and Emil, who knew what they were capable of? I felt like I was waiting for another shoe to drop.

I dozed in the nasty black chair all that morning waiting for her to show up. The Greyhound Rent-a-cop hassled me a few times, but I kept repeating that my Mom would be there. Please God, let it be true. Mom finally showed up around noon and looked about as sour as I had ever seen her. It was the same kind of look she gave me him I got probation and my heart sank again. I'd left home under a cloud of trouble and that was exactly how I came home.

At least, that's what I thought. Her face was sour and at first, I thought she was angry about me. It turns out that she was violently angry at whoever left her boy to hitchhike into the Greyhound station from some cold, dangerous beach on the coast.

When she opened the door to let me into the car, her face melted and she pulled me close. In seconds, we were both in tears. I was home again and realized with a rush of emotion how much I had missed it. It was the first hug she gave me since I left almost three months ago.

Our current position is: 34°29'31.63"N 120°33'28.95"W

Chapter Eight—Intermezzo

IT TOOK A while for everything to calm down after my ride back to the mainland. My mom was livid pissed; that's a direct quote. She screamed at Dad when she finally got him on the phone later that day. I had slept on the ride home and woke up when we pulled into the driveway. Madison and Marty were on the lawn and the house looked weird after not being there for the entire summer.

You know that feeling you get after you leave your house for a week or two and then you get home and it feels like you're visiting for the first time? Imagine how it feels after three months. It made my flesh crawl.

After I had unpacked, I took a shower. It was the most luxurious thing I'd ever felt. Hot water that didn't go cold after thirty seconds … an entire shower that lasted longer than four and a half minutes. I stayed in there until my hands turned wrinkled and plump. The bath towel felt like something out of a hotel after a summer of line-dried castoffs. My room, my real room, was larger than the salon on the *Horner* and my bed felt almost too wide after all that time sleeping in a bunk.

All Mom wanted to know how it was that I ended up in Oxnard while she was waiting for me on the docks in Long Beach. I told her the entire thing was a big misunderstanding and they had gotten lost on their way. She didn't buy it.

"They got lost up in Oxnard?"

"Yeah … kind of," I said.

"What's that mean?"

"It means they got turned around and then they ran out of gas," I was making this crap up and she knew it. She was dropping my wet and sandy clothes into the washing machine but paused to give me her full attention.

I started babbling—I hate when I do it, but I couldn't help it. When I was lit or high, I could talk my way out of anything. I can't really do it when I'm sober and the more I talked, the worse it got. "They borrowed some to get home but it wasn't enough to get me back to LA and they didn't to be asking you for gas money when they arrived." Blah, blah blah ... so much crap. I finally ran out of words and prayed that she wouldn't give me the third degree this time.

She stared at me for a long time, months it felt like. Then all of a sudden, she took a deep breath and said, "Okay. I believe you." My mouth almost fell open, but I clamped shut before it could. "I'm just glad you're okay, Jim." She turned her attention back to the laundry and before I could slink away she said, "I hope you ride with people who are more responsible this time." Trust Mom not to see a belt without trying to hit below it.

My first day back just felt strange. I'd say it felt like a hangover, but I hadn't had a drop in 2 months. It just felt weird. Everything was out of place. Any place I sat felt way too comfortable, anything I looked at was way too clean. It that made me feel unsettled. We sat down to dinner that night and I regaled them with tales of my crazy summer. Madison had been collecting the pictures I sent home and I did a little slide show of everything. Mom had probably looked at the pictures every day, but she made a big show of listening to my stories.

I went to sleep that night in a bed that wasn't gently rocking on the water. The lack of motion felt strange and I kept jumping awake again at the street sounds of the neighborhood outside. Cars swishing by weren't the same as boats in the early morning. A cat knocked a garbage can over and I almost fell out of bed. My body clock had changed and I had to work hard to go back to sleep after I awoke at 4:30. It took a while and mostly I just listened to the silence of the house and smelled the warm, clean smell of a home as opposed to the wet, fishy smell of the *Horner*.

I finally heard from Dad. He laid low after he heard from Mom, but I got his mail, telling me to call, about a week later. It was the day before school started. When he picked up, I could hear that he was at the *Gun Range*.

"Hey, sport!" he shouted into the bad connection. I could hear the tinny pop of guns behind him. "Are you okay?"

"I'm okay now," I yelled back. "You know what happened?"

"Yeah. I'm so sorry, Jim," he yelled. Imagine that, I thought—Dad apologizing for something. "Mitch and Yusef are banned from using the boats ever again. I had them go back out there to find you as soon as they told me what happened."

Dad knew that something was up when they arrived back so early. He threatened them with the 'anchor chain party' unless they got back out there to take me home.

"What's an 'anchor chain party,' Dad?"

"Never mind," he answered ominously. I thought back to that guy who disappeared around the Big Fourth. "Let me finish."

Dad forced them back on board and they immediately headed out to the beach to see where I was. I was gone by then and Dad was near frantic trying to find out what had happened. Mitch and Yusef were no help, Emil was gone. Bob and Grace were dropping me off at the Greyhound station by that time. Dad was convinced that those knuckleheads had done something to me and was getting ready to waterboard Yusef to get the truth out of him.

"Your mom's phone call got put through before anything happened that couldn't be undone," he reported. Dad couldn't stop apologizing, swearing that those two were 'on his list' and 'he would make things right … eventually.' He sounded relieved to hear that I wasn't angry with him. He was wrong about that. Not that I really want to get into it, but how bad do you have to screw up to lose your son? I mean, seriously? I couldn't believe that Yusef was still breathing after that.

No, I wasn't over it but I didn't let on when Dad called. We kept it light and cheerful and he kept making a big deal about 'the good memories we made' out there. I was depressed for the rest of the day without really knowing why.

Then I got an email from Riley. He told me that not much had come of Mitch's electronics run and as far as Dad was concerned, all was forgiven. I couldn't talk about any of this with Mom. I didn't tell her about the drugs or about Dad.

My probation officer was pleased to see me. "I've been keeping track of your progress this summer, Jim—you're doing very well. Keep it up." She showed me a few of Dad's emails. I had to stifle a laugh because his mails were almost total fiction with a few pictures thrown in for good measure. She had no idea what went on out here ... why would she? Dad took advantage of this fact. I wasn't going to challenge it, though. I wanted to be done with probation.

School started a week later and I did the rounds as The Colony Kid. The part that sucked was having the kids I had been hanging with yawn over everything that I told them. They spent the summer drunk or high or getting laid and I couldn't relate. I mean bully for them, right? It was a big ol' thorn in my pride that I didn't have anything to top that. I did ... sort of ... but sex tends to trump anything else, especially when you're 14.

My English teacher was politely interested but wasn't assigning a "How I Spent My Summer" paper so there went any potential A+ papers for me. Schoolwork has always been kind of a walk for me but they never get tired of telling me that I'm not living up to my true potential. I found myself thinking back to everything that had happened back out there.

As the months of fall passed by, my grades started slipping again and the kids who were previously unimpressed with all my experiences started coming around to hang out with me. My mom was nervous about it ... what a shocker. Other than saying "remember what happened last summer" she left it more or less alone. That was weird, having her do that. Before she'd be on me like our dog, Molly, on a piece of steak that falls off your plate. You couldn't get a chance to move because she was there stopping you before you even realized you were thinking about it. Things were a little different now.

So my friends and I hung out for a while but my heart really wasn't into it. The work of the Colony, the weirdness, the hijinks ... the danger. How was getting baked and sitting on your friend's couch all afternoon going to compare with that?

I'd tell them stories about it and they were bored. Who cared about Tribe of the Burning Man doing primal scream rituals at dawn while the

Gloucester West fisherman chucked empties of Steel Reserve in their general direction? We saw each other less and less.

Before the final kiss-off, I did down a couple of beers with them on one afternoon. A brownie got passed my way and, well, it probably had pot in it. I didn't check. When I got home that night Mom, Madison and Marty were eating dinner like a normal family in the dining room and ignoring me. I was lit and feeling pretty gross, anyway.

It really got to me how happy they seemed. It reminded me of something they said during rehab about the rest of the family working to be as normal and happy as possible. What was I going to do, pick a fight because they didn't wait for me? I blew them off to go hang with my friends. I suddenly hated myself … hated the partying and hated getting drunk or high. It was a moment of clarity and I took advantage of it.

It wasn't easy to say no the next time, but I couldn't hang with the Party Kids anymore. There was some unpleasantness when I told them that I wasn't interested. I ended up cutting a few days with a fake note from Mom so I could avoid some drama. It was the last time I partied with my old crew.

It's hard to tell people the truth about the Colony. I could explain as much as I wanted, but people just didn't get what a weird, wild place the Colony was. I don't think I was the only person with that problem, though. I saw this quote painted on the side of someone's boat and it stuck with me— *'What should I care if they single me out for sneers and laughter? I never truckled, I never lied. I told the truth.'*

I stared at it for a while, trying to figure out what 'truckled' meant and said without realizing it, "I wonder where it's from." Not loud, really—just under my breath.

Out of nowhere, a voice shouted "Frank Norris." I turned in surprise, but the nearby docks were deserted. I never did figure out who was close enough to hear me and cared enough to shout an answer back. Now that I think about it, it gives me the creeps … who was that guy?

People's eyes would glaze over whenever I started telling them stories about doing pen patrol or running a scam. Or they would start telling me stories 'they heard' about the drugs, the weirdos and the crime. Other would simply change the subject at the first opportunity. I could never understand that.

Life on land was becoming tedious and stupid to me. It didn't have the same edge, the same rush that Colony life did. Living at home with Mom was comfortable but I felt like whatever toughness I developed out there was starting to leach out of me. I got a kick out of watching my arms and legs develop that swimmers' tone and it was a shock to get out of bed one morning and see the familiar cording of my arms beginning to blur under skin and fat.

Thanksgiving was over and we were into the Christmas season. I was looking forward to some snowboarding with Marty and Mom in Lake Arrowhead when an email from Dad arrived. The Winter Catch was coming up and he was looking for some extra hands. Mom immediately said 'yes' when I asked to go out to see Dad during Winter Break.

My Winter Break visit was a nice break from the noise back home. I thought I had sea legs before … but I was wrong. I was queasy for the first week last summer but then I got over it. I even made jokes about seasickness and laughed at the people wearing the patch or taking a pill. I'm sure you can guess where this is going.

Going down to the dock this time, I was actually looking forward to the trip. I had the process down, joked with the guys at the dock and gave Ignacio a wave when I saw him pull up. I wouldn't go as far as saying Ignacio was glad to see me, but he was less mean to me. I guess he saw me as less of an idiot.

There were other people on board the boat this time: a family of three and of course, the groceries. I really felt like an old sea dog … finding some potatoes or rice that wouldn't crush under my weight and sat down before Ignacio could say anything. It was near the rear hatch which turned out to be a good thing. Exiting the breakwater and the 5 MPH zone, Ignacio turned the tiller hard to starboard, pointed the boat toward the horizon and gunned the motor.

When the boat topped its first big swell, my stomach suddenly put in an appearance. This isn't right, I thought, feeling the first blast of nausea. Maybe Ignacio was doing it as a prank for the newbies? I glanced up to see him holding the tiller and throttle tightly but otherwise was ignoring his passengers. Okay … maybe not a prank. The swells increased in strength as they left the coast and our forward speed was maybe half of what it might have been in a calm sea. My stomach leaped higher and higher into my throat, partly out of seasickness and partly out of fear. Would the boat hold under this kind of abuse?

I studied the passengers to take my mind off of my rebelling stomach. A man and woman, younger than Dad, but not by much. The other one was a teenage girl. I wasn't sick enough to ignore my hormones yet. The way she was bundled up I couldn't really see what she looked like, anyway. The weather turned colder, rain and spray started to splatter against the port.

"You guys new?" I asked, pitching my voice over the engines. My voice cracked a little on 'new' and it made me blush.

"Yeah," the guy yelled back. "We wanted to come out to give it a try—someone said it was easier in the winter."

"The trip out isn't," I replied and the man laughed and nodded. I jammed my fists under my armpits and tried to stay as stable as I could. My stomach was getting worse and worse. I tried to ignore it and practiced standard Colony etiquette: You introduce yourself by giving your name and the name of your ship. They mentioned the boat they were using, some shake-down shack that I hadn't heard of. Ignacio started talking as well and we managed to pass the day pretty well in conversation. At the end of the day we made the trip intact and the colony was in sight. I felt like the worst was over when the girl finally spoke up.

"I like them," she nodded toward my Ramones shirt, "the Ramones. Do you like Green Day, too?"

"Green Day?" the man said—her dad, obviously. "What do you know about Green Day?" She scowled at him and he laughed.

"I like them, but I'm still going through all my Dad's old rock albums," I said. "In fact, I—" my stomach wrenched suddenly and I had to suddenly jump up and start for the back door.

"Turn the knob up!" Ignacio roared, immediately grasping what was wrong. The knob mercifully turned suddenly and I was able to make it to the back rail before heaving my guts out.

The rain had gotten heavier and my coat was in the bag on the cabin floor. I was soaked in seconds just standing out there. My teeth were chattering from cold and from barfing, all I could do was hold on and try to get my guts under control. Ignacio was less than sympathetic, his only move was to release the wheel long enough to close the door on and then return to steering.

Smooth ... real smooth, Ace. First girl I tried to have any serious conversation within months—becoming violently ill is a deal-breaker. I came back to the cabin after about ten minutes, dripping wet and sick. Whatever game I thought I had totally destroyed. Ignacio refused to let me near the groceries again and instead had me drive the boat. "It'll keep you busy," he said. They were sympathetic but left me alone and made conversation with Ignacio instead. They didn't even say good-bye when we arrived and I was stuck pulling cargo duty. *Just like old times.*

"Who's Stacy?" Dad asked two days later.

"I have no idea," I said, around a mouthful of cornflakes.

"Girl about your age," Dad began. "Said you met on the ride over."

"Oh! Yeah—I didn't know her name."

"Too busy throwing up to get her name?" I guess Dad heard about the Technicolor Yawn from Ignacio. I responded as only a 14-year-old can.

"Daaad!" I pulled it out into three or four syllables.

Dad grinned and shrugged. "Hey, none of my business. She came looking for you. Said to come see her."

He handed me a slip of paper with female writing on it: *'Swing by. Seas of Cheese. D-Ring.'* That was the start of our relationship—puke and a note.

It got even more awkward when I saw what boat she was talking about. It was the Cho's boat ... the one they were on until Jessica got hurt. Pacific Fisheries was indeed using it as a 'shakedown shack' as Dad had predicted.

"Shakedown shacks are boats that Pac Fisheries uses to introduce newcomers to the Colony. If they have no boat or skill, they get brought on for 2-week trial periods. If they last, they can move on to a better spot ... as soon as one opens up. It cuts down on the riff-raff. Some people come onto the colony thinking that it's going to be one way, find out that it's different and then whine about it. Reminds me of some people I know."

"What's that supposed to mean?" I demanded.

"Nothing," Dad replied innocently. "I was talking about this family that came on the colony not too long ago."

"Who?"

"No one." Dad refused to explain any further. Happily, Stacy and her mom and dad—graduate students working on her dad's thesis in anthropology—weren't the 'riff-raff' that Dad was complaining about. They were hard workers, one of the first crews up every morning to check their fish, even in the rotten winter weather we were having. None of this scored points with Dad though.

Stacy's mom and Dad decided to take up the colony life while they traded off work time on their doctorates. I think Dad was threatened by them even though he was nice to Stacy.

"Don't get used to it, Jim. Nobody on the *Seas of Cheese* stays long enough to make friends." He gave me a lengthy lecture on the subject of colony life and then stumbled off to his room with a bottle of Bacardi white. He wanted to avoid being asked why anyone would choose the life he had just got done describing. As his door shut, he mumbled something about 'yuppie fags from the Left Coast.' I realized that Dad's problems with Stacy's folks lay elsewhere.

We got together because we were two kids of the same age stuck in an unpleasant situation by our families. Over time, I discovered that Stacy was a great kisser, thought I was cute (no other girl had told me that, before) and provided a fairly calm oasis when Dad got on the warpath over something.

"You guys must have done it," Riley proclaimed on Thursday afternoon.

"Of course," I lied. We ended up making out that evening, so it wasn't entirely untrue. Stacy's parents had a sense of humor about our relationship, but that came to an abrupt end one night. I was sitting on their fishing porch when Ethan, her dad, walked onto the back deck with a large machete and buried it into the wood with a *thunk* next to where I was sitting. Stacy had let it slip that we were getting physical and I guess he was concerned.

Ethan squatted on his haunches and murmured into my ear. "I like you, Jim ... that's why you're getting a warning. Just remember," he said, pointing straight at my crotch. "If you value your *cajones* ... not even once." He retrieved the machete and disappeared just as though he'd never been there. I never tried to get past second base after that.

We moved into what Riley referred to as 'the friend zone.' Lots of talk and IM'ing—no texting service out here. I only had two weeks to establish some kind of relationship that would continue after I got back to shore. Ethan gradually won Dad's respect and they discussed different topics not related to fishing.

Dad and Ethan spent a Monday evening debating aspects of anthropology and the Colony over a bottle of cheap red wine. Their arguments got more passionate after the second or third glass, but they parted on friendly terms. I tried to listen, but the entire discussion was way over my head. Dad could be incredibly intellectual when the mood struck him ... he never behaved that way with me. Why was he so nice to Ethan? "I thought you hated them."

"When did I say that?" Dad asked, looking confused.

"You never say anything nice about them."

"I'm not a fan, kid, but it's been a while since anyone got me warmed up on the sociology of the colony." He lit a cigarette and blew smoke at the ceiling. "You'll never catch the rest of these knuckleheads cracking a book. Ethan's a nice change."

I was due back on Saturday. The day before, Dad and I were working cold weather pen patrol ... this was a change for me. In the cold weather, you swapped off pens and spent double the amount of time warming up. Dad wasn't demanding that I do the work ... he even offered to swap me for his heated dry suit, but that creeped me out. I didn't want to wear Dad's suit, you might as well be trading underwear. Dad shrugged and commenced pulling neoprene over his head. He also went to the extra trouble of brewing a large pot of hot coffee and boiling water for hot chocolate. Some of these preparations ought to have flagged me that something was up, but I was distracted with an email from someone at school.

Dad poured himself a large cup of the coffee. "Okay, sport. Let's roll." We went out into the fishing porch while Dad finalized his dry suit prep. It was cold out here, but my wetsuit was keeping me warm. Dad took the first pen and left me out there on the dock as line tender. No big deal. I felt myself moving into the same familiar routine of holding Dad's line and listening to the regulator for any weird noises. Dad moved quickly through the pen. Practice makes perfect. He climbed out, spitting his regulator out and groaning as he pulled himself up on the ladder.

"So cold I almost turned into a woman," Dad said through his chattering teeth and I laughed … Guy humor. I was anxious to get back at it again, but Dad stopped me as I was pulling my mask and fins on. "It's colder than I thought. Let me do it." How cute, Dad was worried about me.

"Nah, I got it, Dad," I said. I did this for over two months during the summer—what was the problem? I bit onto the regulator and waved bye-bye to Dad as I stepped off the dock and into Pen 2.

The cold water was bad, it turned out. As soon as I jumped into the green world again, I started to hyperventilate. This was cold, colder than anything else I'd ever felt out here. I slowly got my breathing under control and tried to swim. The cold water drove spikes into my head and swimming took more air, more effort and more time than I ever remembered it taking. Was I that out of shape? No … it's just cold. I pulled myself out of Pen 2 with a groan and slumped over on the dock, gasping for air.

"Com'on, ya big baby," Dad said, pulling his face mask back on. He tried to warn me and I didn't listen. I wasn't getting sympathy from him. I groaned again and finally caught enough breath to say: "My nuts ache, Dad." I was horrified to hear a female snicker on the docks behind me.

Stacy had decided to drop by and say 'good-bye' before I left tomorrow. I was so cold that I didn't notice her when I first climbed out of the water! The teenage years of anyone's life seems to be populated with epic stories of embarrassment and shame. With a little time and distance, you can laugh about it, but when they happen, the world manages to skip a beat. My unrecoverable gaff was there for all to see and enjoy. *Epic Fail.*

My earlier problems were nothing more than a distant memory. I was frozen, unable to turn or raise my head. My heart started doing crazy palpitations while I cast about frantically, trying to explain why I was refusing to get up off of the wet and cold dock. Dad was unaware of all of this and when he turned around from where he was finalizing his prep, he saw me lying frozen on the dock like road kill. "Get up, Jim!" he ordered.

I wanted to commit suicide right there. Since there were no swords to fall on, well, the only thing I could think of was: Leave. Bolting upright, I walked away from both Stacy and Dad and disappeared into the *Horner*. Dad was left standing on the deck open-mouthed and confused.

I didn't come out of my stateroom for hours and when I did, Dad was quietly looking over some inventory sheets that had to do with how large his catch was, which was shortly being turned over to Pac Fisheries. He didn't say anything and neither did I. Don't ask me if I want to talk about it.

God help me if Riley ever found out. We shared a last dinner together of canned tomato soup and grilled cheese sandwiches. We talked about the catch, about Madison, about school and I just kept chattering to keep the conversation steered away from me and my huevos.

I returned to the mainland the next day without a word to Stacy. Give it one or two days, tops and I'll have a new nickname: Ice Cold Nuts or something. I refused to meet anyone's eye when I boarded Ignacio's boat for shore. When I got back, I didn't bother telling anyone about Stacy. There was no way I would hear from her ever again.

This made the mail from her about a week later a nice surprise. She wrote to ask how the trip was and told me how Dad and Ethan were continuing to hammer away at each other with their 'differing world views.' She had met Hector, Mitch Cutter and Jeb Francis, who she said "kept staring at her in a really disgusting way." I surprised himself with a lot of manly talk about 'taking care of Jeb' or other nonsense. If Ethan was comfortable about using a machete on me then he could handle anything Jeb might dish out. This was my first serious relationship … I was falling for her hard. I had all the classic symptoms.

Our current position is: 34°36'13.03"N 120°40'1.51"W

Chapter Nine—The Welcome Mat

FRIGGING RILEY. HE IM's me late in March while I'm discussing my return to the Colony and asks "Has Stacy told you about Mitch?" That was all he needed to say. I was completely paranoid about Stacy breaking up with me and hooking up with Mitch. Like I didn't hate him enough already. I fantasized about the perfect method: tied to the flukes of that antique anchor on the *Gun Range* and dropped off the side—no muss, no fuss.

I don't think anyone would miss Mitch much, but I think Miguel would miss the anchor. He dropped this drama bomb on me one night when I was chatting with the both of them. She's going on about something over on one window and Riley's telling me she's secretly cheating on me in another. What I did next was very ill-advised:

ME: ARE YOU CHEATING!
STACY: What?
ME: Are
ME: You
ME: CHEATING ON ME!???
ME: ARE YOU CHEATING ON ME!!!!!11!!!????????/?
S: No, Jim, I am not cheating on you. Who told you that?
M: It doesn't matter. When was the last time you saw Mitch?
S: Riley told you I was seeing Mitch, didn't he?
M: When did you see him!?

M: That jerk—I will kill him—you better kiss him good-bye
    because he's dead tonight, DO YOU HEAR ME!?
M: I WILL HAVE HIM GONE—ONE PHONE CALL.
S: Jim, calm down.
M: ONE PHONE CALL—I'M DIALING RIGHT NOW

Blah, blah, blah. Can you imagine a 14-year-old talking like this? I
think I got it from a movie. I might have sounded really tough except my
voice was cracking and I sounded like Mickey Mouse.

I go on like this for a few hours with Stacy. We start arguing back and
forth, we suddenly bring up all kinds of relationship crap and we almost
break up over this. Riley disappears on me in IM after 'promising to keep
an eye on Stacy'—idiot. Now I have all kinds of questions and he drops out
on me! I wasn't sure who I was more pissed off at, him or Stacy. Either
way, the entire thing makes me absolutely crazy and I lose it. She reacts by
getting pissed herself (and I can't blame her, I was a real ass) and our
relationship almost ends right there.

About 9 o'clock that night I'm in my bedroom, still fuming, when the
phone rings. It's Riley and he's laughing his butt off. "Hey baby," he says
laughing.

"Where have you been all day? I've been trying to get more info out of
you and she's denying everything!" I was ready to reach through the phone
and throttle him.

"Of course she's denying everything, what do you expect?" He was
still laughing.

"Whattaya mean?"

"I made it up."

His laughing and my current state of mind made me a little slow. The
sentence took a few seconds to register. "What?"

"I made it up. I was yanking your chain."

I went mad … seriously. Completely insane. He hung up on me, still
laughing as I screamed at him like I did at Emil at the good ol' Mugu Rock.
Marty and Mom ran into my room convinced I caught my balls in a light
socket or something. I tried to get Stacy back on chat but she was offline
and Mom wouldn't spring for a phone call. "It's too expensive.

Emergencies only," she said. Relationship emergencies didn't count, I found out. I was frantic; I sent an email to Dad late that night. He got back to me the next morning.

Sounds like you screwed up, his email read. *Let me see what I can do.*

I had to wait for several days on pins and needles. Dad decided in his infinite wisdom to cut me a break and explain the whole thing to Ethan, who in turn explained it all to Stacy. Imagine a father sticking up for his daughter's boyfriend. It doesn't often happen but in the end they both went to bat for me. Now that I think about it, this was a huge favor. Stacy and I spent a lot of time making up and inventing steamy scenarios via instant messenger and email for 'makeup time' when I got back out there. We had a relationship to mend.

But what to do about Riley? Great prank but I was still pissed that he'd pulled it on me and I wanted some payback. I asked Dad and all he said was "Hey, I just saved your relationship." Miguel? I didn't bother asking. It was necessary to get Riley. In fact, it was a moral imperative.

A gay kid in my English class was offended when I asked him what I wanted but then he decided it was funny after all. He gave me a picture of himself with his digits on the back and I mailed it off to Riley, courtesy the Pac Fish offices that accepted mail for all colony residents. The first picture he ignored, the third or fourth, I got an email from Riley. All he wrote was "IS THIS YOU?"

I had forgotten the prank and replied back "What?" Then he breaks open with this story about a rapist sending him pictures and planning to 'do something.' He sounded genuinely freaked out and it was all I could do not to give the game away. I stayed with my "I know nothing" line. I took a picture I had of Riley and started putting his face on a variety of beefcake pictures to email them. I started getting updates from Stacy when his mom heard and freaked completely out.

She had the IT staff at Pac Fish trace the mails and demanded they run it down as a potential terrorist threat. The gay kid used a fake address and they never traced it farther than a high school library computer. He didn't know what high school I went to so it was a perfect cover.

Probation ended, finally. I had my last visit with my probation officer, a last urine test and that was that. Mom was happy, but she still got on me about school and Stacy. The tone of the conversation was the same except for Instead of 'slacking through high school because of your hoodlum friends,' I was 'slacking through high school sending emails to your girlfriend,' We fought about once a day over something and the whole house was on edge because of us.

As luck would have it, I got stuck one night about three weeks before the end of the school year. Marty and Madison were out at the store and I was up in my room playing video games while Mom had her friends over for cocktails. I stopped for a biology break between rounds and on my way to the bathroom I caught part of a conversation that sounded like it had something to do with me. I stuck around for a listen. It's always jolting to hear your parents discussing you like a kid you barely know. She was answering someone's question.

Mom sounded a little buzzed when she said "Who knows?" Another muffled voice said something I couldn't make out and Mom responded. "Some girl he met out there. I swear the only reason I sent him out there was because it was either that or county jail. In county, he'd have been the girlfriend instead of having one!" The girls broke up laughing at that one. Glad you think rape is funny, Mom.

"It's just that ... I don't know where he's going these days," she confessed to the wall. "He was such a sweet boy when he was younger and then, he was drinking and getting arrested every month. He turned around after the last summer, working on the boat with his dad but now he's starting to go back the other way again!"

The conversation went downhill from there and I was burning at every word. The fact that Mom just dumped my business out there like that in front of a bunch of old cows—man ... it just blows my mind sometimes. I felt like more than betrayed. She was betraying me, and taking things to a level I'd never even consider! She was my mother, I'd never do this to her ... how could she talk like this about me? I stood there, listening to them and getting nauseous from rage. Finally, I just went back to my room.

I never told her that I had heard what she said. She always had my problems chambered for whenever she was in a corner she didn't like. "I may not be the world's best mother," she'd yell shrilly, "but I was there to get you out of jail!" What else could I say after that? Stacy was sympathetic but she was over a hundred miles out to sea and there's only so much anyone can say or do in that situation.

I had another "Big Fourth" moment the next day. Mom and Marty busted me for drinking some of Mom's cheap tequila while they were at some RV & Boat Show. Madison was at a friend's house and I had the place to myself. Normally, that's a chance to kick back in my boxers and watch some movies on the big TV. I was looking for something to eat when I saw the bottles on the top shelf of the pantry. Mom and Marty had some margaritas from the night before and she bore some grains of salt. I wanted to see if I could handle it now, and took a half-shot while I was standing pants-less in the kitchen.

If you haven't had some in a while, the peppery taste of cheap tequila tastes like the expensive stuff. I had that half-shot and before I could say "that was good" I was pouring myself two more. I carried the tumbler back out to the living room and nursed it through two old sitcoms—"I Love Lucy" and "The Brady Bunch," I think. Took another two and balanced a tower of crackers on top of a plastic tub of hummus to carry back to the television. By the time I was done, the half-bottle was down to a quarter and I was caroming off of the furniture to get back and try and add enough water so that it looked like none was missing. What did they care? It's not like you can taste the difference if you mix it.

Well, they did taste it. Marty noticed that the Sauza had turned a weird color during their absence. He took a small taste and his eyes narrowed. Mom had a sip and there wasn't anything else to say. I just imagined that this is what happened, actually, because I was sleeping it off in my room when they burst in.

Of course, they smelled it on me. I was under the covers and sweating—I practically reeked of booze. Marty was pissed and called an immediate Family Meeting. I'm a mean drunk and a sloppy one, it turns out. I slumped into the couch as Mom and Marty both sat down and said, "Boy, we haven't had one of these in a while. Who's knocking over the trash cans this time?"

"Still the weisenheimer, Jim?" Mom asked. She slapped me, hard, across my face. I was still buzzed and it didn't really hurt.

"I didn't raise you to be trash," she hissed. "I didn't work to put myself through college while Madison was doing chemotherapy, I didn't re-marry, we didn't make this home so you could get blitzed and turn into the loser you so obviously want to become!" She reached out, grabbed me by the collar and gave me this little Alpha Shake. Marty reached out to stop her, but it was over before he could move. "What's gotten into you? Why do you want to do this to yourself?"

That actually was a great question. I hadn't the slightest idea and I wished someone would tell me. Why did I want to drink? I knew what it did to me—knew what a hangover felt like. I knew that every time, every time, I'd come out of it going 'This is the last time I do this.' So why do it again? I was 14 at the time and the concept of addiction was fuzzy to me. I was sort of hungover when they discussed it in health class.

Before I could answer, Marty stepped in. He's a slight man, but with powerful shoulders and he works out a lot. I never took him for a tough guy, but he was both pissed and concerned. That brought the toughness out.

"Here's what it is," he said. "Ala-Teen. 30 meetings in 30 days." My head was buzzing and I wasn't exactly sure what he was saying. This was all so confusing. Why couldn't they let me sleep? "You have a problem, Jim, and we need to know how to deal with it."

I was furious. AA? They wanted me to go to AA? Man, all I did was slip a little after months ... *months* of keeping it together! This makes me an alcoholic? I was ready to give them all of this information but the tequila was keeping me from putting it together. All I got out was "justhadafewdrinks ..."

"Enough is enough, Jim," Marty answered. "You're 14, you shouldn't be drinking at all. If this is where you are at 14, I don't know where you'll be when you're 18 or 25." When he stood they both seemed to be standing very far away from me. "Anyway, this is out of your hands. We're going tonight and you'll go every other night until you leave for your Dad's place."

I started swearing at the both of them. Swearing like that little girl in 'The Exorcist.' I even surprised myself. For a few seconds, I thought maybe it was a trick, like someone was doing an impression of me, but then I realized the truth. I couldn't believe I was saying stuff like this, but I was. Mean, vicious insults that started with 'you're not my real Dad' and ended with 'I know why Dad left you'.

When I want to be an ass—I really outdo myself.

I ran out of words, finally, and waited for the killing stroke. Mom and Marty received what I said in silence. Marty's face was wooden and Mom looked like she wanted to cry. Marty broke the silence.

"You're a mean drunk, Jim," was all he said. "This is a really ugly side of you." That's something we all could agree on.

It took an effort on Mom's part not to take the top of my head off, but she managed. "I'm ashamed of you," Mom said and then stalked off to the kitchen.

Marty didn't move … he was staring me down. He didn't look so much angry as hurt and disappointed. All my anger and meanness came down 'Mom was here and Dad was out there.' Dad was out on the ocean because he couldn't get it together to live here on the land. Me and Madison couldn't make up a single, normal family out of the pieces we had to work with. Mom vents a bunch of crap to her friends and it made me feel like she didn't care about me at all. I needed a month to process all of this but right at the moment, however, I was a drunken teenager sitting there on the couch, wrecked and in my underpants. The room was spinning violently, instead of just pleasantly rocking. It was the hallmark of oncoming puke instead of just a standard buzz.

I've been drinking so much that I know the difference now. Maybe I do need help.

I was sullen and silent as we drove to my first AA session. Not Ala-Teen for some reason, I guess that was on a different night or too far away. Marty changed his evening plans and we ate early. We showed up at the meeting in Pamona just in time to hear the opening introductions. Marty didn't pressure me to do or say anything and I just spent the time listening to what some of these guys and gals had gone through to get to whatever got them here. The coffee was pretty good.

I still wanted to get out of going to any other meetings. I came up with stomachaches. I sprang homework assignments on them. Marty shrugged and pointed to the car. Gee, you think he was on to me?

I'm not saying that what I heard in those meetings had any impact on me. I heard some truly horrific stories and it made me realize what a whiner I had been. I didn't let this onto Marty, though. I kept finding ways to make each trip as irritating and time-consuming as possible. He never took the bait, he just made sure my butt was in the chair every time and that I was to listen politely.

I tried to smuggle my headphones into one meeting—he snapped them up and pocketed them. I never saw my headphones again. I tried to ask for them back, but he gave me this violent look. I shut up after that.

So no big moral here … they got me to the AA meetings. I didn't have much of a choice and I went. I didn't get much out of them and still no closer to why I liked to drink. The shame of it made me depressed and those last few weeks at home before I shipped out again were pretty tense.

Mom came to my room the night before I left and shut the door behind her. I was packing my stuff into my sea bag from the Winter Break trip. We hadn't had much to say to each other this whole time and now I was bracing myself for The Big Speech. It was going to be painful for the both of us.

"I guess we're saying good-bye the way we did last year," she said hesitantly. When I didn't reply, she added, "That's pretty sad, Jim."

"I know."

"You're too young to be this messed up. I asked you a question last year … do you remember?"

"Not really."

"You don't remember what I asked you in the Denny's last year before I dropped you off and you went away from me for three months?"

"No," I lied. I did remember the question. I remember breaking down and crying in public and feeling like such a wuss afterward. Some things, you just want to forget. Who, me? Drink? No, I don't like to drink. Cry in public with your mom? You must be trippin', dude. I don't do stuff like that … I'm a tough guy.

There were times, lying in my bunk and dog-tired, that I'd remember those moments. Or I would simply be feeling low about how things were going, about how hard the job was, and my thoughts would return to that painful moment. My dad would see the look on my face. "Your sins are weighing heavy on you tonight," he'd say and then stay out of my way.

I hated guys like Mitch, who didn't live with the same guilt that I felt, the shame I felt, for screwing up what should have been an otherwise perfect life. Doing my probation, I'd look at the other kids around me who weren't thinking about anything beyond grades or clothes or getting laid or high or whatever. Kid things, not adult things. They certainly were not worried about getting their records expunged when they turned 18 or getting violated on their probation because they were in the wrong place at the wrong time. Even if I didn't drink before, I'd start because keeping everything straight in this world is a gift beyond anyone's ability to give.

Even me.

So I lied to my mom and told her that I didn't know. It was so much crap. She could see on my face that I knew exactly what she was talking about. This time, she wasn't content to just leave it for Dad and the Colony to straighten out.

"I asked you why, Jim," she said. "Why do you drink?"

"I don't kno—"

"Don't know doesn't count this time," she snapped. "*Everything.* Everything you've been through and you're still drinking."

"I drank once!" I fumed. I toed the line, didn't she see that?

"You were passed out, you idiot!" she flared. She called me a knucklehead or an idiot when she wanted to say something worse but censored herself out of parental duty. "You drank until you passed out and you're almost 15 years old. You seriously think half of a bottle of tequila isn't a problem?"

"No, but ..." I just gave up. She wouldn't understand it. She'd lecture me like this and then she'd be back with her hen party on Friday or Saturday, boozed up and 'venting'. They would understand her, but no one would take the time to understand me. That's why I drank ... but it was more than I could put into words for her. I really wanted this conversation to be over, but we weren't done yet.

"But what?"

"... nothing."

"So what's up? Why do you drink?"

"I don't know."

"How can you not know, Jim?" she yelled suddenly and I jumped. "If you don't know, who does? I've known you for your entire life and now I feel like I don't know you at all!"

We stood there, staring at each other, for seconds and then minutes. I had no response and I eventually started staring at the floor. Mom had a way of breaking me down until all I could do was stand there and take it.

"Something's wrong, Jim—this isn't acceptable. You know that, right?" The evening air was filled with the hum of street noises and I had no choice but to nod. "This has to end. Somehow, some way—you're going to figure out why you drink and stop doing it or this is going to ruin you." Seconds passed while I processed this. She turned and left the room without another word.

The next morning, Marty drove me to the dock and we made the entire 90-minute drive in complete silence. I felt like my life was irrevocably broken with Mom and Marty. Our lives were a house that had just burned to the ground. I had no idea what tomorrow would bring.

It was a clear, hot day when I arrived back on the Big C. Another trip out in Ignacio's fishing boat and I spent most of the trip in the pulpit at the nose of the ship, just enjoying the breeze and letting the dip of the boat be my little extreme-sport diversion for the trip. Ignacio, for his part, had about as much to say to me as he ever did. The rolling didn't bother me like it did back in December.

Actually, I enjoyed it—it was like going back out to your favorite vacation spot. You relish those little details that you didn't realize that you missed. When he spun the wheel to head into the Maze, the old Asian lady who I saw when I first arrived here waved to me and I waved back. Her name was Greta Lee and she was friendly. I knew that. I felt like an old sea dog because I knew that.

I noticed that the *Dixie Star* was back. I was surprised—we a couple months away from Steeplechase. Ignacio tied up and I actually enjoyed helping him with the usual cargo chores. As the last bag of rice hit the dock, I heard a sharp whistle—Riley was leaning over the railing of the *Phoenix*, grinning evilly. He flipped me the bird and I grinned while flipping one right back at him.

"Welcome home, loser," he called. "How's your love life?"

I laughed and called back, "How's yours?" He stopped laughing and scowled at me. I stuck my tongue out in response. All the stuff with my Mom disappeared. That was a mainland problem. I was back out here with my people and that trash could wait.

People waved when they saw I returned and that felt great. They were surly to outsiders but once they accept you, you're in for life. I soaked it all up—this was a welcome change from life on shore. I was talking to someone right next to the *Phoenix* gangway when my dad appeared from out of nowhere to say hello.

"Well, there's the big man," he said happily, and stuck out a hand to shake. I grabbed it, my first man-to-man handshake with my Pop and then he yanked me close, giving me a bear hug. "Nice to have you back."

"Nice to be back," I said, nodding to the big white structure just to our right. "What's that thing doing here?"

"Oh, that?" he looked up, carelessly at it. "I run it." I was about to pick up my bag when I realized what he said.

"You what?"

"I run it. I was gonna tell you, but I wanted to surprise you." He looked at me, not able to hide the sly smile at being able to pull one over. "Surprised?"

"Oh, my God," I almost shouted. "You did it. You actually did it!" We both yelled and shouted—Dad had pulled off the scam to end all scams and was running the *Dixie Star* as he promised he would.

I started to see him a little more clearly. He was wearing a pair of clean chinos and a freshly-pressed cabana shirt. His normal three-days-worth of beard was missing and he smelled faintly of aftershave. All of this was a far cry from the usual look and feel. Dad was running a casino. He had a steady job on the colony. He was finally out of the fishing business, just like he wanted.

I was very happy for Dad. But still—I was a bit distracted. There was a certain someone that I came out to the Colony to see. She wasn't there when we arrived on the *Horner* but after I had dropped my bag in my room, Dad beckoned me out to the fishing porch. "Observe," he commanded. A ship was cruising by, a stripped-down and modified houseboat, by the look of it. As I looked closer, I suddenly saw what it was. "Heck," I said. "It's a fruit stand!"

Dad was smiling happily. "Another one of our deals—Miguel bought an old houseboat, fixed it up and ships out fresh produce from somewhere to sell it here."

"Doesn't Pac Fish know?"

"Know? They're partners!" he beamed. "They get a piece of it and we get to sell to all the different colonies. It's perfect!" I was impressed—Dad had put together several very successful scams in a very short amount of time. Why didn't he tell me?

I re-checked all my emails to be sure, but nobody had breathed a word about any of this to me. Not Riley, Miguel, Stacy or her parents—it was all a complete smokescreen. But who cares, right? I mean, this is seriously amazing what Dad has managed to create. I've never been so proud of him in my life.

I should have seen it coming.

Our current position is: 34°45'23.45"N 120°41'28.20"W

Chapter Ten—The Brief and Unsuccessful Voyage of the Cooger & Dark

BACK AT THE *Gun Range*, Miguel was grilling some flap steak while they filled me in on the fruit stand and everything else that had been going on. They had been experimenting with importing groceries to the Colony. Miguel's brother was some kind of manager at a grocery store in Glendale and they worked out a way to run milk and cookies out here on a modest profit.

They even gave Stacy a job. She was actually working on something as a surprise for me. I wasn't allowed to see the boat yet. Waiting to see her in these next few minutes would be more difficult than the previous 5 months. It was all I could do to not yell "I want to see my girlfriend!" at Dad. They said it was her idea so I choked down my complaint and sat down to lunch. They had a lot to tell me.

"It's a rough gig, though," Miguel said. "Other guys do it and we're all trying to keep our prices as low as possible." He said something bitter in Spanish. All I caught was *'pendejo.'* Wordlessly, I looked to Dad for a translation.

"He's talking about the Children of the Burning Man," he explained. "They were selling their groceries under cost. They were losing money, but we were going out of business." Their profits were sinking lower and lower with each grocery run. Pretty soon Miguel put a halt to it, judging that their next order wouldn't even cover the gas it took to bring the groceries out.

"I might as well pay Ignacio to do it," he complained. Running food and other staples out in the rain, you dealt with leaks and packages that weren't adequately wrapped. You ate the cost when you couldn't sell the food and Dad ended up eating a lot of dinners made out of half-ruined bags of rice and dried pinto beans.

It was a pretty dark time for Dad. Without the groceries, he was back to pen patrol in the wintertime. Even with a dry suit, it's still cold, wet and miserable. Around the middle of February, Dad was fighting a cold and had been eating Fisherman's Friend more often than hot meals.

"We were keeping our distance at the moment. The grocery deals had cratered and we were both pretty stressed about that," Dad related. "My cold was getting worse and I was skipping Pen Patrol to try and recover. We started losing fish."

"On top of this," he continued, "some payday loans and capital investments made by Pac Fish were starting to come due." Dad went on to outline how he took a loan out to buy the *Horner* when he first arrived at the Colony. He had refinanced those loans every single year he had been out here—seven, and counting—and then he got a nice little note from the AP department of Pacific Fisheries. "Due to changed policy the outstanding loan could not be refinanced or extended and I should make plans to repay Pacific Fisheries within the next 8 months." He was still bitter about it. That letter could brought Dad's time on the Colony to an end.

"But then, two guys from the Children of the Burning Man showed up. They were able to bring out groceries at prices that were even cheaper than Miguel. They wanted me to deal with the customers and be the storefront."

"How did they get the groceries so cheap?" I wondered. Dad and Miguel snorted simultaneously.

"Stolen, no doubt," Dad replied. "I was broke. I didn't ask questions."

Dad liked that they didn't approach him as a flunky, he said. They saw him as a valuable asset, hearing stories about his previous experience running orders in from shore. The older guy, Stan, was a total burn-out, but he was still sharp enough to talk numbers when he wasn't maundering endlessly about 'how it all could have been.' The younger one named Chris seemed to be positioning himself as a leader. He had the ideas, creating a bulletproof shipping empire and he left the details to his older counterpart. They wanted to hire Dad and pay him a salary. Much better than trying to collect on each grocery sale.

"They had the moxie and they had the money," Dad said. "Anyway, I was out of time. It's worked well so far. Shipments and money started coming in … I've started to make traction on the loans. Plus, the winter catch paid off well."

Oh, right—the catch. My experience with the cold water of the Pacific made me forget that Dad had been able to sell off his fish. All three pens had been sold at the same time. Just a hair less than five thousand pounds of tilapia. They were paying four dollars a pound for tilapia this year, so it make for a pretty tidy sum for Dad.

With the money, Dad started making some things nicer on the *Horner*. He got one of the left-over race boats from last year and named it *Horner C Minor*. Yes, I know it isn't a real musical term. Deal with it. He got a new flatscreen for the salon with satellite TV coming in. He also got himself some new breathing gear and a new wetsuit.

"I started making new deals with people again," Dad continued. "Greg from the Ensenada trip started buying groceries and so did a lot of other people who blew me off before. Between the prices and the fact that it was me, not the hippie freaks, we started doing pretty well." Dad wasn't content, though. He still had his sights on one really big score: Getting the *Dixie Star* back to Colony D … permanently.

"He never shut up about it," Miguel said—transferring the meat to a cracked china plate. The *Dixie Star* was docked and shuttered up north at another colony—C or B up around Santa Barbara—when it wasn't here. "He was working a deal to get it down here on a trial basis and then I realized that the *pendejos* weren't selling fresh fruit and vegetables."

"So?" I asked.

Miguel shrugged. "So I went to work." Within a week, he located a burned-out ship that he could recondition. With Dad's help, they towed the wreck back to the Colony and gutted the wreckage to begin the process of rebuilding the ship without a dry dock or any heavy lifting equipment. Dad invested money to purchase equipment and materials out of his growing funds. The burned parts of the ship were removed and they built it up as an open space that would accommodate shelves and bins and cash registers. Someone installed a decent lighting scheme that you might see in an upscale grocery store and figured out how to run it all using a floating solar power array. They stocked the shelves with some on-shore groceries and fresh produce from local hydroponic gardens.

"I was planning a 'launch party' flyer for the 'Farmers Market Boat' when an email arrived from Pac Fish," Dad said. "They were interested in our ideas for running the *Dixie Star* year-round on the Colony and wanted a meeting. We got permission to bring the *Dixie* back and dock her next to the *Phoenix*." He grinned and ruffled my hair. "You were coming in a few weeks … I wanted to surprise you.

"So we got the deal for the *Dixie Star* signed and a week after that, we were in business." They had a decent restaurant set up on the Promenade deck and put together some great gourmet seafood dishes. I would have thought the place was out of the price range of the Colony but it was jammed every night. It was a nice change from the usual rough-and-crusty lifestyle.

"The slots and table games filling up the place when this other thing happened," Miguel said and Dad nodded sourly. The Asian members of the community were concerned about the kind of attention the *Dixie* would bring and perhaps criminal elements. They were vocal about it, enough so that everyone had to have a sit-down in the Executive suite on board the *Phoenix*. For an entire afternoon, Rick and Miguel had to endure squabbling from Pac Fish, the citizens and other hangers-on.

"So what do you recommend? Should we close the *Dixie Star*?" the Pac Fish suit asked their spokesman.

"Not at all … we welcome the income the *Dixie* generates." The spokesman was a tough old gent named Le Cheung. He spoke English with a British accent and his arthritis forced him to limp along with a carved rosewood cane. He lived with his family, or what he called his family: poor expats from Macau and Taiwan. "We think the gaming facilities would benefit from some Asian influence and balance out the clientele."

They wanted to install games like Pai Gow and mahjong, Cheung explained. Dad was totally against it but Miguel wanted him to give it a chance. The main thing, according to Dad, was that Le Cheung wanted to take it over, not share it. "We give them this and next week they're back for something else. Maybe a bigger piece of the action," Dad had complained.

"I said that I didn't think so," Miguel grinned. "For one, they know there are more round-eyes and brown people on this boat than Asians. They kick us out, there's a big hole in the water where the *Dixie* used to be before morning. The *Dixie* is big enough that nobody wants it to go away."

"Yea, but I was right about our share of the profit going down."

"We're still making money, pal," Miguel said mildly. "A smaller piece of the pie is better than no pie at all." The whole thing started out crazy and was moving too quickly to have any control over. Dad still saw a million problems with it but decided to along with it. Like Miguel said … they really didn't have a choice.

Dad finally stopped his story long enough to take a bite of Miguel's flap steak. I haven't mentioned it up until this point but he does make some of the best steak you'll ever taste. It's amazing.

"The details of setting up the *Dixie* kept us going 24 hours a day," Miguel said. "Who knew that people would eat so much bread at a restaurant? We went through 90 of those sourdough rounds in the first night and we thought that would last us a week." Getting bread out here was difficult, too, forget fresh bread. They had to run around getting a bakery set up and ironing out any 'quality control issues'.

"I was still upset about the games," Dad continued. "I said to Miguel, 'You seriously see no problem having them along for the ride like this? I mean … pai gow? I don't know pai gow—I've only seen people play mahjong. We're supposed to be running this casino and I don't know half the games we offer.'"

"Yeah, and I was like 'So?'" Miguel laughed.

"So I was like, 'what happens when we have to step in? What if there's a problem? How would we know if the customers were getting cheated?'"

"Just like I told him, we didn't need to," Miguel explained. "It doesn't matter if we know the game as long as the customers do. Look," he put a beer down and began to gesture, a move that meant Miguel felt passionate about something. "They can't run a dirty game—they'd be out of business in a week if people stopped playing. They'll have to run clean games or at least look so clean no one can tell the difference. Meanwhile, the white guy and the brown guy—they run the rest of the show and everyone knows we're just looking for an excuse to throw the tables overboard."

"Are we going to throw the tables overboard?" I asked.

"No. It doesn't matter what we're going to do—it only matters what they think we're going to do."

"Huh?" I was lost.

"Miguel's logic is layered." Dad explained. "Sound familiar?" Ugh … layered logic again. This was one of Dad's favorite things to beat me over the head with last summer. I was not going there with him now.

The way they saw it, *Dixie* was a huge success. On the first night, half of the Colony was trying to get in the door. Poor folks who had been living on their start-up loans were trying to get in and Rick had those folks bounced before they got a chance to sit down at a table. On one issue, Pacific Fisheries had been absolutely adamant and Dad was determined to meet it: keep the trash out. Sure, it sounded harsh but there was a moral to this story—you couldn't afford to let the guys who owned you money get into even deeper debt. Even if they were positive they could win enough to pay off their loans, you didn't let them in.

"The fishing, the *Dixie* and the scams were a beast to keep organized but man, was it paying off!" Dad was smiling … happier than I'd ever seen him. He had been through a lot these past few years, working and scraping to find a comfortable spot here. Along with rebuilding his life in some semblance of order, he wanted to build his relationship with us. I have to say that it was great to see that after all his talk, he was getting there. Dad took some time away from the casino to work on the Farmers Market boat. There were still tons of details they had to work out.

"Then he comes up with this name for the boat," Miguel said. He sounded like it was irritating and amusing at the same time.

"What name?" I asked.

"The *Cooger & Dark*."

"What's that?"

"Literary reference," Dad replied. "From a book. See, it's from an old Ray Bradbury novel and—"

"Never mind."

"Everyone likes the name," Dad complained. "Nobody wants to hear about where it comes from." The burned out hulk had new paint and welded-steel structure, new vinyl and paint. It looked like a custom job you might have spent your 401K on, the one where you docked it in Lake Arrowhead or Lake Mead and never went anywhere else.

We finished our late lunch and spent a few minutes trying out a new .223 rifle that Miguel had purchased. I was very happy … this summer would be perfect. "When can we go see the boat?" I asked.

"Right now," Dad grinned. "We need to take a spin around the colony and show off the sign anyway."

We strolled over to where the boat was docked, halfway between the *Horner* and the *Gun Range* on E-ring. People were still welcoming me back and it took a few minutes to work my way over to the *Cooger & Dark*. It's hard to be polite when all you want is to see your girlfriend and get to all the making out we discussed. Don't worry—I'm going to be a gentleman: I still remembered Ethan and his machete.

It was really supposed to be a perfect moment for me. I think Dad wanted it, too. I landed at the Colony and he's pulling out surprise after surprise. The *Dixie Star*, the floating farmer's market … I'm getting hugs and handshakes from everyone I run across. The Land of the Weird is welcoming home one of their own and now … now my Dad is no longer a screw-up. He's hit the jackpot and I'm going to be spending the summer basking in the glow of it all. It makes what happens next almost hilarious.

The trouble started somewhere underneath. The original engine had been gone over by someone, not Miguel obviously, and a fuel leak had been missed. The boat was idling before its trip around the Colony with new banners advertising a 'Farmers Market Experience' merrily flapping in the breeze. We were watching and waiting to board Dad's most recent accomplishment, another milepost in the journey away from being 'Rick the

Ocean-going Loser'. It was at this point that the fumes got heavy enough to ignite.

My first view of Stacy in five months was her running in from the back screaming "Fire!" What do they say about the best-laid plans? Never mind.

Stacy lands in my arms, screaming about the fire. Flames were already popping out from somewhere to the rear. Dad and Miguel immediately charged aft holding extinguishers while Stacy and I watched from the dock. People came running, including one guy holding a salt-water fire hose, but it turned out to be unnecessary. Miguel emptied his extinguisher down the small porthole in the engine bay and ended the emergency. Of course, now the boat and the produce were smoke-damaged. Of course, no one wants a tomato that smells like burnt plastic but that was only the beginning.

After demanding they be reimbursed for the now-unsellable produce, the hydroponic farmers decided they would rather work together and create a small storefront that 'wasn't so stuck-up'. In less than 20 minutes, Dad had lost his boat and most of his vendors. Then the Pac Fish Rescue Team arrived … they wanted an accident report on the operation they were part owners of. According to Pac Fish, if you set your own boat on fire, they give it a shrug and maybe a funeral. If something that belongs to them happens to burn, then it becomes a Loss Management issue.

They asked questions about the boat itself, how 'it arrived on Colony D when the accident investigation was still more or less in progress on Colony B.' Like that was our fault … Miguel got permission to take the thing from some admin guy he knew on Colony B. But wait, it gets better.

It turns out that the boat was involved in a wrongful-death lawsuit filed against Pacific Fisheries because someone died of smoke inhalation trying to put the fire out. Their attorneys wanted to haul the scow into shore for an inch-by-inch investigation on how the fire started.

When the boat became the *Cooger & Dark*, any evidence they were planning to use disappeared and they were screaming 'cover-up!' Pac Fish was very unhappy that a key piece of evidence was now unavailable to be used to help their case.

Their unhappiness landed like a rotting whale carcass in the office of the Asset Manager on Colony B, who had given it to Miguel. That person was afraid for his job and was burning up the air between Colonies B and D demanding that Dad and Miguel help get him out of this mess. Dad wanted to spend the afternoon with me, but instead I was stuck farting around on the *Horner*. Dad and Miguel returned around seven or eight that evening. Dad immediately poured a drink for each of them. A double-shot of tequila each … the meeting had not been pleasant. Dad tossed his back and grunted as the alcohol hit him. "Those guys are a cross between a CPA, a lawyer and a cop," he said darkly.

"What's a CPA?" That was a new one, to me.

"An accountant." There was a brief, ominous pause.

"What's an accountant?" Give me a break, I'm 14.

"Look it up!" Dad suddenly roared. Over by the console, I could see Miguel hiding his mile by ducking his head and massaging the bridge of his nose. This should have been funny to me. Under normal circumstances, I would have been cracking up at this little sitcom. Instead, I was depressed. It was just as crazy here as it was at Mom's house … maybe more so. I didn't know it at that the time but it was about to get a lot worse.

Our current position is: 34°55'16.74"N 120°42'26.90"W

Chapter Eleven—A Cane-Sugar Coke and the Trash Man

THE NEXT DAY, I was stuck having to restocking the cold case with water, beer and soda at the *Gun Range*. I wouldn't have minded, but I had to listen to yet another conference call between Dad, Miguel and the admin guy on Colony B. The *Cooger & Dark* was a smoky and sour-smelling hulk tied to the fishing porch. If I had a choice I would have gladly been elsewhere.

"What about all the remodeling we've done?" Dad complained.

The asset manager was aghast. "You remodeled it?"

"Of course," Dad sounded puzzled, no surprise there. What did Pac Fish think they were going to do with it, set up a floating 'don't play with matches' museum?

"So now the boat can't be investigated because all the original wood, flooring and paint have been removed." The manager's question wasn't really a question at all … more of a statement.

"Uh … I guess." Dad still sounded bewildered. Since when was this an issue, much less their issue? I heard the manager sigh and it sounded like a weak fart on the speakerphone line.

"Do you idiots have any idea what you've done?" the manager asked.

Miguel suddenly straightened up. "No, what have we done?" he asked, sounding concerned.

"You guys just cost this company a million-two in a legal settlement. Those idiots are gonna walk off with the store and you helped them do it." The sheer audacity of the man was something new to me. I'm 14 years old and even I know how it works; Dad and Miguel weren't in the wrong—this guy was. There was no way they could pin it on Miguel or his Dad.

Unfortunately—Dad didn't see it that way. "How did we help them do it?" he asked and I winced, hearing the wheedling in Dad's voice.

You don't have to be an adult to know that a career middle-manager like that takes anything that sounds like weakness as a signal to go for the throat. I don't know how I knew that … instinct, I guess. I just wish that it was somehow instinctive for my father, too. He had somehow missed that lesson. Fortunately, Miguel was there to catch it and he handled it neatly.

The distortion of the manager's shout into the phone made it difficult to hear. "You idiots just destroyed the one piece of evidence we could have used to prove that it was their fault!"

"After you gave it to us." Miguel was calm, almost icy. It reminded me of that day on the dock when Miguel was asking me whether I was 'through drinking'. I braced myself.

"I didn't give you permission to tamper with evidence!"

"No, you just gave it to us—you relinquished your control over whatever happened to the boat after that."

"But not to remodel it!"

"Says who?" Miguel wanted to know. "I have a 'Release of Ownership' signed by you and I'll be happy to show it to anyone who wants to see it."

"You think anyone's going to care about that after I tell them that you remodeled the boat? They'll just hear 'one point two million dollars … lost … by you knuckleheads on the water out there' and that's all they will need to know!"

I was stunned—what a jackass! Did he seriously think he could screw Dad and Miguel like this? When people sounded so certain it automatically made me wonder what they knew that I did not. I tended to believe, by default, that they probably knew more than I did. But this is why it's nice to have a guy like Miguel around.

Not even blinking, he replied "What makes you think they don't already know about the release?"

"Well—" the line went silent and I thought they lost the call. I could still hear the hissing of the connection and so I knew he was thinking. Pac Fish staff frequently got it into their heads that the Colony folk were dependent on them for any communication with the homeland offices and it made them arrogant.

Pac Fish employees tend throw their weight around with us. The more ignorant citizens get messed with in ways that make me ill. Miguel had learned early and often that it paid to have his own listening ears. Fortunately for us, Miguel had already used them.

"Why don't you call Sally over in Loss Management and talk with her about it, Bob," Miguel said. Now I had a name to go with the voice.

Bob was one of the guys on Colony B that had built a reputation for efficiency and sleaziness that translated over to us. Dad introduced us last summer on the *Phoenix* but he didn't make much of an impression on me. Bob had his uses ... in fact, he was one of Dad's silent partners on a few scams. He was also was slimy enough to put all that to the side when things hit the fan. When it suited his purpose, he'd throw us under the bus. We were nothing but Colony trash to him. I never liked the guy.

"You guys better get ready," Bob sputtered angrily but I could hear the difference in his voice. The fight was out of him. I had to smile as Miguel calmly explained the situation to Bob: that they were ready for anything Bob wanted to try. If that wasn't enough, they were comfortable solving this in the unofficial way if official channels were not sympathetic. The *Cooger & Dark* was hauled back to shore to be 'investigated' a day later. I never heard a word about it after that.

Life started to settle back into the pattern I started last year. There were a few differences, though. At first, everyone was cheerful and friendly. It slowly started to be replaced with something silent and tense. People were nice to your face but they avoided the *Horner* if they could help it. Dad went back to being snappish and reclusive again, just like last summer.

It bothered me but I didn't want to signal anything to Madison when I called home. I bored her silly with stories about the crazy stuff we did out here and she was campaigning Mom to come out here.

Whenever I talked to Mom or Marty I kept it simple. Everything was fine, Mom ... I'm not having any trouble staying sober. *No wino soccer moms out here,* I wanted to say. Dad told me about a small group that did AA and NA stuff out here but I never got around to going. I was staying out of trouble, why waste my time?

If I have one piece of advice about Pen Patrol, it's this: *Don't take a break.* My first day back was absolutely miserable. I thought at first that I was reacting to the cold—I felt my arms and chest getting tired and starting to burn. The ache continued to build when I was halfway through Pen 2 and by the time I jumped into Pen 3, I was feeling like a drowned rat. I took a lot of breaks and Dad started yelling at me like it was my first day on the job.

"Get that skinny butt moving!" he shouted so loud I could hear him through the water. I could see him gesturing at me from the docks, arms moving like an angry Italian grandmother. I didn't bother coming up to straighten things out. Knowing Dad, the best course was to get things done as quickly as possible. Down at the bottom of Pen 2, I could see old repairs I performed last year. Dad had really let the nets go while I was gone.

"Com'on, com'on!" I heard faintly. *Nothing ever changes* … you'd think he'd just be happy to see me again. It took over a week for the soreness to subside and then I was diving like a pro once again. I was pleased to see the flab I'd built up over the winter come melting off again. I was back to eating whatever I wanted to. I saw a lot less of Dad with his job on the *Dixie* and I was getting creeped out with some of what I was seeing around here. Where did he get the money for the *Horner C Minor*, anyway?

One morning I was out hauling a couple of sacks of trash over to the Trash Man. They got rid of the garbage barge and put in a complicated recycling system. Whatever you couldn't recycle, you were supposed to take to the Trash Man and let him take care of it. He rolled a large-wheeled cart around all day long. An old white dude, flowing white hair covered with a greasy trucker's cap … faded blue flannel shirt, jeans and old work boots. He was enjoying a cigarette in the morning breeze when I came up with the bags.

"Got two more," I grunted.

"You're Rick's kid, right?"

"Yeah." I never spoke to him but I guess he was a friend of Dad's.

He smiled, like we were old buddies. "Rick's kid," he said cheerfully. "Now that almost makes us family. Smoke?" He held out the butt to me, offering it.

"No, no thanks," I said, grossed out by the thought of sharing a cigarette, especially with this guy. Whatever … just another nut in the bin.

"You're Dad and me were doing some business," he said. "Know where I can find him?"

"He's back on the boat."

"I mean when he wants to do business." He peered intently at me.

"Business?" I was puzzled. What was up with this floating funny farm? Couldn't people make sense?

"Never mind," he said quickly. "I'll catch up with you later." He picked up the handles of the cart and started moving off down the docks, whistling something. I turned to see Dad watching us both quietly.

"What did he want?" Dad said stiffly.

"Nothing," I said. "He was asking for you."

"Nothing?" he asked. "You sure?"

"Uh … yeah," I said. That guy was weird but Dad's reaction was even stranger. Too much going on that I didn't know about—I didn't want to get sucked into it.

"Stay away from that guy, Jim," he said. "I mean it. He's trouble." Dad didn't explain more until we were back inside, but had a lot to say about people running scams that cut him out of business and how things had become a lot more stressful since my last visit. That was saying something … I thought things were full-on crazy the first time I visited. I hadn't seen anything yet.

The actual fishing being done by the Colony had dropped off considerably. People were still busy but they were running their own scams instead of raising fish. Pac Fish Admin had a bunch of memos out there complaining that 'the metrics had fallen' and the Security teams were making daily trips out here to crack down on the 'non-mariculture-related businesses.' The Trash Man was around more often. After our little chat, I started seeing him almost every day. He was always near our side of the Colony even though he was supposed to be taking care of everyone.

Riley summed it up this way: "Yeah, it's different. But it isn't bad." We were delivering produce for Grandma Alice and Marie—it gave us a chance to catch up. Little by little, I started learning more about the changes that had taken place since Christmas.

"You know that Mitch is dealing, right?"

"Yup," I replied. No real shock there, after that run last year.

We stopped down at the new 'Restaurant Row' that had appeared on C-Ring. Some boats had taken a page from the *Dixie Star* and opened a pho place, a taco stand and a grill. Pac Fish tolerated it and the food was good … I started swinging by for some fish tacos at lunch every day. The Phoenix Grill was still around, but Jeb was busy with his job on the *Dixie Star* and someone else was running it.

"There's a lot more going on but it's cool," Riley explained. "Let's face it, this place was always weird."

Maybe from Riley's perspective, that was true. For me, there was weird, there was Colony weird and then there was *this*. It really was getting more dangerous out here. Not everything had changed, though. Miguel and the *Gun Range* were still a popular destination and I resumed my duties as counter jockey / range master. Julian the sniper was still out there practicing with the two rifles—they didn't bother me as much as they used to.

Then there was Stacy. We had that little reunion on the dock while the *Cooger & Dark* almost burned down but it was a bit distracting, what with the fire and screaming. I planned to get to all that catching up we planned on over email and chat but then it seemed like she got too busy with everything her parents were working on. If I got to spend an hour with her, it was a good day … the rest of the time I had to wait for her to finish helping Ethan with Pen Patrol or run an errand.

Pen Patrol got more difficult. New people had moved in next to us, on the other side of the *Key West Forever*. They were die-hard partiers that kept a scene going 24/7 on their boat. I'm serious: nonstop partying … it slowed down around sunrise but then started back up again in the early afternoon. It sounds awesome but when you have to get up at five and jump into freezing cold water to do your job, you want some peace and quiet. I wasn't going to find it with nonstop noise, boozing and clouds of pot smoke going on next door. Dad tried hollering at them a few times but gave up and advised me to invest in some ear plugs.

"Why didn't you tell me about all this?" I finally asked Stacy one afternoon. We were on the top deck of the *Seas of Cheese* and watching her dad snorkel through pen chores. She shrugged and continued working on the toenail she was painting. She finished one foot and set it in my lap to dry while she worked on the other one. Stacy was wearing a pair of short-shorts and a green bikini top that matched her nail polish. She looked hotter every day—my hormones were slowly overcoming my fear of her dad and his machete.

"It's always been weird, Jim," she said. "You told me that on my first day." This was true, I had to admit. *It's weird, but in a good way*, I had told her. I took her around and made the introductions to people I thought she'd like to know. Partly out of courtesy and partly because I wanted guys like Mitch and Riley to know she was with me and therefore 'hands off'.

"There's weird and then there's weird," I said, splitting my attention from her green toenails and the rest of her. Stacy reached behind her to readjust her bikini strap, giving me this *amazing* view of her cleavage. A small moan escaped my throat unconciously. Do girls *know* what that does to guys? I looked up to see her watching me with a mysterious smile. Yeah, they probably did. "It wasn't always like this," I squeaked, managing to stay on topic.

"That was before the accident," Stacy said.

"Accident?"

"Yeah, a couple of guys got killed on the other side of the colony," she explained. "My friend Ricky says they were killed at the *Gun Range*."

I was shocked … Dad had never mentioned this. "Killed at the *Gun Range*?"

"Yeah," she replied, so matter-of-fact that it scared me. "It's a dangerous place, right?"

"I know, but …" I said. Then something else clicked with me. "Who's Ricky?"

"No one," she said in a sing-song. People dying … random guys around my girlfriend? *Girls*, I thought darkly.

So I guess people died at the *Gun Range*. Nice of Dad and Miguel to tell me. Following that, people started acting like hooligans and shattered the calm that we all worked to preserve last summer. How do you get from there to here in only a few months?

I wanted to tell Mom about all of this but we were barely on speaking terms. Madison was dead set on coming out here and I could only drop so many hints. When she did get permission to visit, Dad started going crazy 'getting things ready for his baby girl.' Madison would be coming to join me for a few weeks and then we would be going back ashore together at the end of the summer. Dad had me running around cleaning up and fixing minor problems.

I don't want to complain too much about it but it did bump me to have Dad act like that toward Madison. When I showed up all I got was a nasty, damp blanket and half of a bunk. Now Dad's making sure that everything is perfect for Madison. What about me?

During the next day, I was working pen patrol … alone again. Dad had been there for the first three minutes and then disappeared somewhere with 'stuff he had to do'. Was it too much to ask that someone stay here in case I got into trouble? Sometimes sharks broke into pens … it wasn't unheard of. We had a modified pole spear as part of our dock equipment for that reason. Whatever. It was lonely doing pen patrol like this. I was wishing for someone to show up and keep me company. I got my wish but it wasn't what I expected.

As I neared the ladder for Pen 3—I saw a pair of hairy legs dangling into the water. They didn't look familiar and I felt a flash of anger. Trespassers received a dim welcome, especially when they put their grubby feet in our cash crop. I climbed out, ready to read someone the riot act. It was the Trash Man … just sitting there and smoking a cigarette, gazing out toward the horizon like he had nothing better to do.

"What're you doing here?" I asked, somewhat harshly.

"Nothing," he said. "Your dad left and I thought you could use the help."

"So what, you're watching us?"

"I have my eyes open, Jim-Bob," he said. "I don't have to watch, I just have to see." I hated that about adults … all they had to do was open their mouths and they were saying things that knocked the wind out of my argument sails.

"Good for you, I guess," I said. "See anything interesting?"

"Maybe. Question is … how deep into it are you?"

"I don't know what you're talking about," I said firmly. It was the truth. This guy thinks my Dad is doing something wrong and he isn't so it's like, leave us alone. If anyone knew anything about drugs, it had to be Trash Man. He sounded like he was hopped up on some goofballs. I was standing on the dock, opposite him, holding a towel and going through the motions of drying off. I was hoping to look busy so he'd leave.

He shrugged. "Maybe you don't. But you should." Without another word, he walked down the dock and disappeared. The whole scene would have been weird enough but Dad had returned from wherever he went and saw us talking.

"You come after my kid?" he asked sharply. I'd never heard him talk in that tone of voice and there was something vicious about it.

"Rick, don't do this," the Trash Man said. "I'm not coming after him but you know they will." Dad's expression changed and he grabbed Trash's shirt front like he was going to hit him. "We can help you."

Dad didn't hit him but he almost threw him overboard. Grabbing the Trash Man's meaty shoulder, he shoved him … hard. "Next time I see you or even think that I see you, you better know that it's on," he said. The Trash Man staggered a little but recovered and grinned at us both. It wasn't a pretty sight.

"You're in over your head, swabbie," he said. "Better think it over." Without waiting to see what Dad might throw at him, he turned and shuffled off down the dock. He picked a turn and then disappeared. Dad was glaring after the Trash Man so hard that he burned a hole in the air. I came up behind him—partly to ask what it was all about and partly to see if he was okay.

"Dad—" I began but before I could do anything else he whipped around and stalked back to the *Horner*. He didn't look around, look to see what I was about to say—anything. The cabin door on the *Horner* slammed … I didn't bother checking to see if he locked it. That was the second time he took off and left me hanging today. I walked to the *Gun Range*, still dressed in my wet suit.

Miguel rustled up some spare clothes at the *Gun Range* and I changed in the head. He didn't say anything after I told him the story, though. He just sat at the counter with his elbows making grooves in the old wooden bar. A jai alai match was in progress from Puerto Rico.

"Is my Dad okay?" I asked. Miguel smiled sadly

"When is Madison getting here?"

"She's leaving the dock tomorrow and she gets in tomorrow night. The thing is ... I'm not sure she should be coming out anymore."

"Oh ... that's too bad," he said. "I'm really excited about meeting her."

I reached into the cooler and brought up a cane-sugar Coke; the kind they only sell down in Mexico. Madison would be on her way in the morning. I wanted to put a call into Mom and tell her to skip the trip with Madison and then book a boat ride for me back to shore. I asked Miguel if I could make a phone call.

He looked at me, still smiling sadly. "Phone's broke, amigo," he said. "Who you want to call, anyway?"

"My mom."

"Why j'you wanna call her?"

"To tell her to not send Madison," I said.

"Nah, you don't wanna do that," Miguel said. He started talking about some new fishing business that was partnering with Pac Fisheries. I wanted to scream at him about how my dad and some weird garbage man were about to have a gunfight right there on the dock and Miguel was calmly explaining the economics of the fishing industry. It was beyond surreal.

Did this just happen? I asked myself that question several times. What really happened, anyway? Dad just had a disagreement with some nut on the colony. It's happened before; some of the weirdos needed more than a gentle reminder to keep their distance. Any other time this happened, I filed it under "Colony Loony Tunes" and forgot about it. Was I overreacting?

I hung out at the range for a long while, hoping to give Dad some time to not be there when I got back. The sun was dipping toward the horizon when I heard a loud alarm go off. It wasn't far away and I think it was coming from the *Phoenix*. Immediately, the alarm was followed by the Ah-HOO-gah sound of an old-time ship's klaxon from the Colony-wide speaker system. The effect on Miguel was immediate—he left his bar stool and ran back to climb to the upper deck.

I followed Miguel up to the top to see what he was looking at. He was scanning the horizon anxiously. The Colony PA system crackled and a voice started speaking—we normally didn't hear from this thing outside of

Steeplechase Day. They were cheap low-fidelity speakers, it was like listening to a drive through but these guys weren't selling Whoppers. "*Now all hands,*" the PA boomed. "*The colony is being approached. Keep all families indoors. Repeat, keep all families indoors. Colony Patrol, man your stations. Repeat: Colony Patrol, man your stations.*" The klaxon stopped but then another alarm started, some electronic thing that sounded more modern and annoying.

I looked back toward the colony and was surprised at how quickly the docks had emptied. Every boat or ship was closed tight with shades drawn. The smell of cook fires and barbeque was still there, but the breeze would blow it all away in a few minutes. The usual waterfall of a hundred stereos and a thousand conversations had disappeared to be replaced by the wind and cries of a few seagulls.

When I looked back again, Miguel had disappeared. He hollered from below: "Jim, get in here!" I went below to see him at the gun cabinet.

He had it hauled out here from shore at some point—a light oak cabinet with feathered glass windows and a lighting system that he never used. 8 feet wide and covered with green felt inside, it held all the guns we rented and it was locked up when they weren't in use. We checked guns in and out of this thing all day, it was really nice. Watching Miguel, I suddenly saw that there was more to the cabinet than I'd realized.

He fished a key out of his jeans and unlocked a small keyhole I'd never really noticed before. He swung the back panel of the cabinet open and inside was an entirely separate section of green felt. It was also full of guns, but not just rifles. He grunted as he pulled a large monster of a machine gun out and set it on the bar. Something with a skeletal shoulder stock and belt-fed ammo coming from the green metal box it had mounted underneath.

I heard someone enter the cabin and looked up to see Julian. He was out of breath from running and he was carrying both of his rifle cases. He nodded briefly and then he was outside and climbing to the top deck. "They're coming in from the south," he said over his shoulder.

Miguel reached into the hidden compartment again and pulled out an ammo box. He swept up the machine gun and gestured to the ammo box. "Grab that and come with me," he commanded. I reached down to pick it up but it weighed a ton. It took two hands to hold while I crab-walked to the back deck.

"Com'on, com'on!" Miguel yelled impatiently. He helped me climb up to the top with the ultra-heavy canister. I could hear boats approaching—was that what everyone was yelling about? It sounded like a bunch of fishing boats … nothing to get excited about. As I set the ammo box down, I had a hand grip me by the arm and pull me down to the deck. The move scraped the heck out of my leg and I yelled.

No sympathy, a hand came down to slap me on my forehead. "Shut *up*," Miguel hissed.

"Everyone's got their panties in a wad," I said, still gritting my teeth from the pain.

Julian lay in a prone position with his heavy rifle like he always does. Not even taking his eyes of the horizon, he snaked an arm out to rap me pretty hard on the head with his knuckles. "He said 'quiet'," he whispered harshly. "Now shut up."

"We're in a lot of trouble here, Jim," Miguel said—maybe he was sorry for scraping my leg and then hitting me, but right there he just looked scared and that's something I had never seen before. "Those aren't just boats, pal. Those are pirates!"

Pirates? In this day and age, we've got pirates off the coast of Los Angeles? He had to be joking and I wanted to laugh in his face. Miguel pulled the bolt back on that monster gun and the sound of it shut my mouth. Heavy metal parts were clicking together with all the seriousness of a jail cell or a bank vault. It all sounds different when it's happening right in front of you. Behind all these sounds continued the rising and falling wail of the ship alarm. It felt like a dream and I suddenly wanted to wake up.

The PA system spoke again, "*Colony Patrol: man your stations. This is not a drill, repeat, not a drill. Bogies approaching. We are signaling proximity. Proximity signaling is now.*" The pitch of the alarm changed to something else, the up-down-up-down of a ship's collision alarm that Dad had told me about. You couldn't miss it and it made my ears hurt after a minute.

Miguel nodded toward the front of the boat. "Get down back there and plug your ears, Jim." I crawled on my belly to the little bar area he had set up there. I never noticed it before, but the top deck railings were kind of a weird two-layer setup. The original outer layer of steel railing had an inner cage system that was backed with chicken wire. In between the two were old bags. I reached out and tapped one … they were filled with sand—all of them. Funny, I'd never noticed that before.

The boats sounded closer now and I could see Julian and Miguel's feet as they lay side by side facing out. The railing that's usually there was folded down and they were quiet, not paying any attention to me. Miguel had put the machine gun aside and was looking out of a small pair of binoculars. Julian had said to me once that 'this wasn't the same as a spotter but better than nothing'.

"*Colony Patrol, hold your fire,*" the voice boomed again.

That's when I knew this wasn't a movie. Somewhere on the colony, at some point when I wasn't there, they actually sat down and discussed shooting at people. Not only that, they had it all worked out like a fire drill. Hear the bell, grab a gun and prepare to kill someone. This wasn't Afghanistan, this was the United States! Didn't we have the Navy for this kind of thing?

"*Hold your fire, please. Do not engage unless you receive fire.*" The warning echoed throughout the colony, the sound of human beings going to war.

It didn't hit me until later that night, when I was banging awake at the slightest sound, how quickly the world had changed. One minute, Dad and his buddies are being weird for the sake of weird. The next minute, one of the steadiest guys I know is looking through a rifle scope.

Is this real? Is this the Colony? Is this me, is this my life?

At that moment, hunkered down and holding my ears, my needs were very simple. I wanted the land, I wanted my Mom and I wanted to never see the colony again—not necessarily in that order. Coming out here, I had stepped across an invisible line that I didn't know was there. Now I was in the most dangerous place I had ever been to in my entire life.

I could hear the boats … they were maybe 300 yards away. I couldn't see them, I could only hear them … engines echoing in the little bowl of the back deck. Grumbly diesels and a lot more gas-powered motors. A few high-pitched PWC engines. It sounded like a convoy, nothing special, something I'd heard a few thousand times since coming here. That's what I couldn't get over: it was all so normal.

It took forever for the sound of the engines to leave us. I stayed down there, my legs cramping and then going to sleep. I guess they buzzed the colony before turning around and heading back south again. It probably took twenty minutes but it felt more like 20 years. The entire time, Miguel and Julian were like stone. They didn't move at all. The alarm changed in pitch and the klaxon went away.

My legs were cramped and I had to pee. I didn't dare move until Miguel turned to look back toward me. "You okay?" I nodded and he smiled grimly. "You're a man today, boy." He looked back toward the horizon and it was quiet for a minute, nothing to hear but the wind and the ship's alarm. The wailing alarm eventually went silent and an eerie calm set in.

"*Stand down, stand down,*" the fuzzy voice said. "*First, let me say: well done. Patrol captains report to the wardroom for a debrief … no later than 1730. Thank you for your cooperation—the alarm is now over.*"

The echo rolled through the colony and it fell flat around my ears. The alarm was over. People were no longer trying to kill us. Life was normal. *Adults are such* liars. I wanted to piss myself and puke simultaneously. I could hear people slowly start to come outside again. Miguel hauled himself off the deck wearily, rolling his neck so that I could hear individual vertebrae pop. Julian rolled to a sitting position and picked up the rifle so he could cradle it in his lap.

"Come on out," he said, not looking at me. I stood carefully, looking at the horizon, still trying to process what had just happened.

"No worries," Miguel said. "They just buzzed us. They do that sometimes."

"Buzzed us?" I said. "You guys had guns!"

"So did they. We have more."

"Guns? Pirates?" I started to hyperventilate, like I did that day in the winter.

"Calm down, bud," Julian said. "They've just stepped up their stuff in the last few months. We've all had to get used to it." He explained how the colony was a pit stop for drugs and illegal aliens. Pac Fisheries was turning itself inside out to remove it but it hadn't cleaned house yet.

"Why didn't you guys tell me about this?" I asked. "Does my Dad know?" They shared a look and Julian busied himself putting the gun back in its case. Miguel disappeared below to re-lock the gun cabinet. No one ever answered my question.

I returned to the lounge. The gun cabinet looked like nothing had touched it and I saw why I hadn't noticed the lock before—it was covered by a tiny circle of felt. You really had to look in order to see it. Miguel was wiping the counter with a rag and I asked him to use his ship-to-shore cell phone. Mine was still on the *Horner* and I didn't want Mom to scream about the bill.

"Who you wanna call?" he asked again.

"My mom." What a dumb question …

"You don't wanna call her, Jim," he said, smiling sadly.

"Why not?"

"Because."

"Because why?" I finally screamed. "I want to go home! I want my sister to stay home. I want to catch the first boat or plane back to the mainland!"

Miguel's reply scared me more than anything else that had happened today. "You'd never make it," he shrugged.

"What do you mean, 'never make it'," I demanded.

"Just that," he said. "They watch who leaves. You especially."

"Me?" He just nodded. "Why me?" I was just a kid … who would spend that much time watching me, even if I was on a boat heading for shore? Why was I so important? The answer hit me and I was afraid to ask Miguel the next question.

"Miguel." He looked up at me, smiling with a pained expression on his face. "What's my Dad up to?"

Our current position is: 35° 5'54.83"N 120°40'11.77"W

Chapter Twelve—T-Minus 30

SO LET ME tell you a story. It'll help you understand the rest of what I'm about to say.

When my sister was 2 and I was 6, I asked my mom to shave my head so I could be like my little sister. Madison was diagnosed two months after her second birthday with a rare form of cancer, Ewing's Sarcoma. The radiation therapy and other treatments meant that she lost her hair. My sole contribution to her recovery was asking to shave my head.

At the time, we three were living with my grandparents while Mom went to school and paid for it by doing nights at a video store over in Sunland. She was gunning for an MBA and finishing her third year and she was on track to graduate early when the doctor drops the atom bomb on us. Madison had bone cancer and she might lose her leg.

Nobody told me what was going on—I was six, after all. All the adults started acting weird: Mom and Grandma were crying and Grandpa was out in the back yard. Rather than let us see him cry, he was viciously attacking the lemon tree with an old pair of hedge clippers.

Mom had to quit her job and we spent days in different offices filing paperwork so that she could get her daughter treatment for her cancer. When you're poor and you're on state assistance, getting any kind of medical is difficult and when it's cancer, it is impossible.

But don't tell Mom that.

She attacked the problem like everything else in her life: she made it her full-time job. Paperwork, calling offices, sending letters and even threatening to call every TV station in LA—she made sure that they didn't let Madison down when it came to getting any kind of decent care. Mom became rabid on the topic and it's something I've never forgotten. I remember that look in her eye when she reached across the counter and grabbed an oncologist by the front of his shirt. I have no idea what she said to the man, I saw all this happen through the glass in the door of his office, but it got him to switch out Madison's meds.

As Madison's treatment started and she was miserable, cranky and tired all the time—it really threw our house into a mess. Her little curls started falling out and she cried because it hurts to lose your hair. I was a pill myself because all I really understood was that my younger sibling was getting 100% of the attention and all I could manage was what was left over when she fell asleep and just before someone would collapse in a weary heap on a bed or couch. I threw tantrums, I started acting up; I just wanted someone to pay attention to me.

Mom, Grandpa and Grandma all realized that I needed some more information about what Madison was going through. They told me that she was sick and every sniffle or stomachache would have me running to Mom, "Mom—do I have what Madison has?" They got a few books for kids about being sick, but I didn't make the connection until the sixth or seventh time through one about kids and cancer. It finally dawned on me what was going on and I asked Grandpa, who was reading to me: "Does Madison have cancer?" Grandpa's eyes welled up and he was unable to answer.

Not one of my prouder moments.

Anyway, now I understood that my little sister had a serious, possibly life-threatening disease. I had no reference for this and the problem went from "Mom doesn't love me anymore" to balloon into some big, huge issue that I couldn't wrap my little head around. At this age, though, kids have marvelous coping mechanisms. I asked Mom one day, 'could I shave my head?' and she looked at me oddly: why did I want to do that? I just shrugged and said "I dunno … make Madison feel less weird, I guess." Her eyes filled with tears and she pulled me close. She kissed the top of my head and sent me to Grandpa.

I thought he might be upset at the request; he's been cutting my hair out on the back porch every month for several years. For some reason, though, he just smiled and said "Sure, sport." Grandpa drew on the old bed sheet that was my barber apron for the longest time and then took the guard off of his old Wahl clippers. In the warm evening air with the smell of lemon blossoms all around us, he shaved my little head back to a fuzzy cue ball. Mom and Grandma laughed and cried at the same time—I held Madison up and we took a picture of the both of us chrome-domes. Mom keeps the picture in a scrapbook somewhere.

I'm just telling you this so that later on, when you ask why I'm freaking out because the Colony just turned into the Wild West, I can say "I love my little sister" and you'll understand what I mean. I guess I love her. As much as anyone can … Madison can be kind of a pain.

Where was I?

The last 24 hours sent me into a complete panic when I suddenly realized how dangerous the Colony had become. Pirates, guns, drugs … that crazy Trash Man … somehow it was all connected and it was all bad. Now my sister was walking into this thinking she was going to spend her summer making fun of the Children of the Burning Man and scoring free sodas off of me at the Phoenix Grill.

I had another one of those moments where the problems go completely sideways and you have no context for it. Just like when I realized my sister had a disease that might kill her when I was six. This time, however, I didn't have someone around to laugh and cry at the same time or read a book to me that explained what was going on. I was in over my head and now I was bringing one of the most important people in my world to be a part of it.

To the phone.

After the pirates had paid the Colony a visit, I spent the rest of the day going from boat to boat trying to beg a phone call. Any of my customers that might have some minutes they felt like lending, anyone who had a phone for emergency purposes—I paid them all a visit. I didn't want Dad to know what I was up to and he liked to sniff my cell bill for calls to the mainland he didn't feel like paying for. Either way, nobody wanted to let me call.

I felt like I was on the Bizzaro Colony by the way everyone blew me off. Nobody could help me. Every single person I asked either had no minutes or no phone or both or was just unavailable. What was going on?

Even if I had no phone, I could send email to her phone and catch her on her way to deliver Madison out to the dock in Long Beach. I sent emails to her and to everyone else I could think of who could call her and tell her to get back to me ASAP. Dad saw me running around frantically and was suspicious. He cornered me and asked what was going on but I spun a story about asking Mom to send my new camera out. "What new camera?"

"My *new* one, Dad," I said, exasperated and pitched to make it sound like there was nothing else going on. "I got a new one for my birthday— Auntie Sue gave it to me."

"First I heard of it," he grumbled. "Whatever. Your sister arrives in a few hours and I want the place to look nice. Get cracking." He was still surly about the Trash Man and was hiding out on the *Dixie* rather than being in a place where I might feel free to ask embarrassing questions. He disappeared again into the docks and I was left fuming: how was I supposed to make the phone call when I had a boat to clean? I decided to take my chances and put the phone call through on my cell. Rushing back to the boat, I started looking for it. I stashed it here in my stateroom, plugged in and charging, before I left in the wintertime. Dad never came in here anymore (the words "disgusting" and "barnyard" kept coming up) and I figured it would be ready for me when I returned. I grabbed it and punched the power stud.

No power …

I let out a little scream of frustration and then started tossing my room for the DC-inverter. It was an old beast, leftover from the Mitch Cutter Discount Electronics Emporium. No juice, it refused to light up when I plugged it in. I threw it at the wall in frustration but it rebounded to land painfully across the top of my right foot. This day just wasn't getting any better.

A few minutes of swearing and massaging my foot went by and I kept trying to think the problem through. I couldn't stop my sister from jumping straight into this hellhole. I was out of options to try and stop her from coming. Only thing I could do was watch out for her and hope that Dad would be more protective of her than he was of me.

I rushed through the cleaning job in record time. Dad spent so little time here so he wouldn't notice the difference. With his hours on the *Dixie*, he was rarely home before midnight. He'd get up again in the morning and disappear just after breakfast. There was one other option I wanted to try.

"You're worried about nothing," Miguel said, after I asked him to let us stow away on a grocery run.

"What're you talking about," I tried not to whine but I couldn't help it. "You guys had machine guns out!"

"So?"

"So? So? That's all you can say?" Was I going crazy? Miguel did understand that this was no place for kids, much less 11-year-old cancer survivors, right? "She's 11!"

"It's a little crazy, I'll admit," he said. "Those guys are just getting their ya-yas off by acting tough. Nobody's gonna do anything to your sister."

I decided to take comfort in what he was saying. What choice did I have? I muttered a "yeah … thanks" and disappeared back to the *Horner* where I had just enough time to spot check and make sure Dad wouldn't find anything wrong. Everything looked fine … unless he broke character and really started looking around.

They would leave the docks at about 7 and it would take eleven or twelve hours to get here. Around 6, I picked a spot on the *Phoenix* and waited for Maddy to arrive. Dad wanted me to tell him when she was getting close so he could keep working on the *Dixie* as long as he could. The 'Viewing Deck' up on the second deck was deserted at this hour. No one would hassle me while I watched and waited. The sun was dipping low toward the horizon when I finally spotted a small speck on the horizon. That speck slowly turned into Ignacio's old scow and long before it entered the maze Dad and I were down at the receiving dock to meet it. Ignacio was taking his sweet time getting up to the dock and I could see a small face in the pilothouse window with an ear-to-ear grin.

"Daddy! Jimmy!" She was waving and laughing and so were we. The three of us had a nice little reunion hugging like we were shrink-wrapped together down there on the dock. She kissed Dad about a hundred times and even deigned to give her older brother a small peck on the cheek. Ignacio eventually started complaining that I was making him late delivering groceries.

I didn't mind … I halfway figured he was going to do this to me. Dad had to get back to the *Dixie* but he promised to bring home some dinner.

We had the place to ourselves and I helped her unpack and settle in. Madison spent the time bringing me up to speed.

She started talking about what life was like after I'd left in June to come out here. A few fights about how Marty had handled my 'treatment' but then things calmed down and life returned to normal. Mom didn't talk about me for about two weeks and then she suddenly started discussing letting Madison come out to visit like nothing had ever happened.

That was weird and upsetting. Mom deals with being upset with me by getting buzzed on cheap boxed wine with her friends. She blows up at me in private because all that Mommy talk had focused her frustration.

I swear I could go from zero to hero in a week, join the Marines and win a Nobel Prize but I'd never hear anything but "Good, you got it together ... finally" from her. I put it out of my mind and decided to just be happy for Maddy ... first night aboard is weird for anyone and I was determined to make it much easier for her than Dad did for me. That's what big brothers do, right?

Dinner that night was some take-out from the *Dixie*. Dad actually went to the trouble of ordering dinner and bringing it home in those expensive foam containers I never got to use. Whenever he brought leftovers home for us he would use oversized freezer bags that are a nightmare to scoop anything out of. Still—I understood what was going on: Dad's little girl was here and nothing was too good for her.

Dad being Dad, he noticed that the house was a mess and it took him all of a half-hour to boil over. "You were supposed to clean this place up!" he hissed at me at one point while she was in the head.

"I did," I shot back.

"Oh, yeah? What's this?" he asked, bringing up a handful of Cheeto dust, candy bar wrappers and an old sweat sock out of the depths between the sofa cushions.

"That wasn't there an hour ago!" I protested and he shot me a look.

"Give me a break," he said, his tone was dripping with contempt. "Your old socks magically spawn inside couches?"

"Say that three times fast!" I suddenly said. It was like grabbing the cheese off of the mouse trap before it snaps your fingers. He suddenly choked with laughter, snorted and he had to hold back some loud '*haw-*

haws. Dad's lecture hour was over before it started. When Madison returned, we were all talking and laughing together. It was one of the best family dinners I think the three of us ever had.

Over the next several days, we put Madison through a boot camp on mariculture and seasteading. Whatever passes as boot camp for an 11-year-old girl, that is. She sat watch on pen patrol while Dad or I snorkeled our way through shimmering clouds of fish. She tried snorkeling exactly once … she choked on the hookah rig and went on strike. Dad didn't force her and made her the permanent line tender. Aside from Pen Patrol, Mad was a good sailor. She didn't mind helping me swab the decks, haul fish feed or keeping the *Horner* together. Stacy came by, introduced herself, and three minutes later it was like Maddy was her long-lost little sister.

My only complaint was the cooking. Madison's started experimenting with different recipes when she was bored. I would come in from pen patrol dead tired and panting … there she was chopping up some of the last of the *Cooger & Dark* produce. I immediately flipped … Dad was known to be cranky about a lot of things but he was positively rabid about preserving any fresh produce we got. She was making a salad and actually had put together some kind of dressing out of some ancient vinegar and oil that I didn't even know Dad had.

This produce thing wasn't a joke, either. I was hungry one afternoon and decided to have a carrot or two instead of waiting for dinner. We have all kinds of snacks and cheap bowls of ramen … I just grabbed the carrots instead making a healthy snack choice for probably the only time during my adolescence. Dad came home later, found the carrots he was going to make as part of dinner and flipped. I got the ramen I was supposed to have for lunch for dinner while he enjoyed the tri-tip sandwiches he'd brought home from the *Dixie*. It was a pretty twisted thing to do to me but then I guess I had it coming. Whatever.

So anyway, back to Madison's salad. Well … I was concerned. That's another way of saying that I was freaked out. I was running around trying to figure out how to replace the vegetables and hide the evidence when Dad walked in. He was supposed to be on the *Dixie* until much later but he decided (without telling anyone, I might add) to take the afternoon off.

Dad was wearing a pair of oil-soaked dungarees … maybe someone needed an extra pair of hands for engine work. My heart sank and I was trying to figure out a way to take the blame when Madison marches up and asks Dad to try her 'salad dressing'. Dad dips a finger in and tastes it. I winced and waited for the explosion.

All Dad did was grunt with approval. "Nice work, kiddo. Guess that'll go well with the pasta I'm bringing home. I'll be back in an hour—be ready to eat when I get here." He disappeared into his room to change for something on the *Dixie* and I heard him ask me from behind the door: "Why don't you do stuff like this, Jim?" My jaw fell to my ankles and I looked at Madison. She gave me one of those evil little-sister grins in response. This kid could get away with murder, I swear …

Back on the *Horner*, where there was plenty of legitimate work to do after I was done running scams or errands for Dad, I would see her with some of the Children of the Burning Man or the Gloucester kids. She always made friends easily. I'm not going to lie … it made me a little jealous.

Somehow, Jeb got the Grill concession back on the *Phoenix* and Riley wanted me to come along for the ride. He appeared late one morning and said "Mom says you can have your old job back. Interested?" I was surprised—I thought I was banned for life after the Streaking Incident. While it didn't earn me the notoriety I was hoping for I got an endless string of grief from the older women who giggled and whispered when I was around. I got some attention, just not what I was hoping for. Cougars … yeek.

"So what do you say?" Riley asked. He was attempting a one-cheek sneak but stopped when I gave him a stony look.

"I'll think about it," I replied. "Get outta here before you cause a biological disaster."

"I'm fine!"

"Whatever."

"So you'll do it?"

"Sure … now go!"

"I'm fine," he said. "I gotta—" he stopped and his face suddenly changed. Standing quickly, he said: "I gotta go."

"Dude …"

"I'm okay, I just—"

"That's nasty!"

"I didn't do nothing!"

"Get outta here!" I was laughing my head off. His face was the deepest shade of red … almost purple. Riley leaped through the door and was running faster than I'd ever seen him go, disappearing back toward home for a change of underwear. In one single move, he topped my most-embarrassing moment of last summer. Bravo!

Riley never busted my balls after that. I had a juicy (no pun intended) piece of gossip that topped any stupid thing I ever did. Dad refused to let Mad go to work with us—no work permits out here—but she hung around a lot. I didn't want Riley to start messing with her the way he did with pretty much anyone else. He stopped making lewd comments about the female side of the Colony folk whenever Maddy was around and I think our productivity shot up as a result. Riley's mom was so happy, in fact, that it made him miserable.

Why? Because her response was to give us more hours. Now we were working there almost 8 hours every day. Riley's response was probably at an inverse proportion to what his mother expected: he started actively looking to get fired. His theory was that he was a kid and at some point, there wasn't enough money to justify spending your life working a cash register while your friends goofed off. I had to admit it—he had a point.

Anyway, Riley started showing up late and leaving early for starters … not easy when you sleep 10 feet from the boss. He'd leave the at the right time, but he'd take such a long time getting there that we might have been open for 2-3 hours before he finally strolled up. I'd yell, threaten to call his mom and he'd just shrug, only to leave maybe a couple hours later and I'd have to handle closing up. Charming.

"Why don't you just quit?"

"She'd never let me," he said, constructing something evil out of a bucket of grill goo, rotting meat and a flat Coke. "She says I need to use my time effectively. Be a productive member of society."

"What's with the bucket?"

"Nothing … just my pink slip," he said happily. He disappeared maybe twenty minutes later and in another fifteen minutes I started hearing screams.

Eventually, he made his way back and I found out that Riley was painting the words "EAT AT THE PHOENIX GRILL" on the side of their house using the noxious mixture he was concocting back in the kitchen. Not only did it stink, it drew every fly in the Colony to their boat. Riley got all the way to the "THE" when his mother found him and promptly lit into him with her left pink house slipper. In flight, he dropped the bucket o' goo on the deck and her angry shrieks turned into wails as she quickly tried to hose the mess off into the fish ponds before more flies were attracted. Riley was made to clean the mess—he needed a salt-water hose and a heavy scrub brush before the greasy stink finally drifted away. Of course, he was fired.

Me? Well, I was stuck working the same hours. I wasn't ballsy enough to cheat my way out of the job, Dad woulda seen through my ruse almost immediately and he was famous for thinking of really diabolical revenge. It wasn't worth the trouble. The previous summer's pranks and mayhem faded into memory and I was back to the dull drudgery of another boring, lonely job.

The next two weeks settled into a sort of normalcy. Madison was learning the ropes and rapidly becoming my favorite line tender on Pen Patrol. We resumed our onshore sibling rivalry and pulled a few pranks on each other. We annoyed Dad, fought amongst ourselves for control of the single TV onboard (where I had enjoyed pretty much total control before) and I tried to pick up where me and Stacy left off. It was a quiet period and I was grateful for it. After the chaos of the last month I needed some kind of respite.

Dad was putting less hours in at the *Dixie* and we saw a lot more of him. The difficult part was that it made him more particular about house and fish-keeping. More often than not, he'd pull me aside for a fiercely-whispered conversation about how things were looking, all out of earshot of Madison because he would never lose his temper in front of her. I blew most of it off: I'm only one guy, come on home and do it yourself if you're so worried. Dad took Madison to the *Dixie* most nights when he had to work late … something he never did for me. On one level, I was mad but I had to remind myself that I had Dad to myself all last summer and it wasn't always fun.

There were a few other things that were happening at the same time. Steeplechase was in limbo this year. Pac Fish was looking for a way to close it down without losing all the money they brought in on the gambling. The Colony folk didn't want to lose what they made and so there was some negotiation going on. One night, Mongo, the guy from the Children of the Burning Man, visited me at the *Gun Range*. I pulled a late shift while Miguel attended a quinceañera over on the other side of the Colony. Mongo stumbled in, talking gibberish and mentioning between grunts that he was looking for Dad.

I tried to tell him that all he needed to do was go to the *Dixie* and ask for Rick but he must have been self-medicating or something. Mongo was talking a mile a minute and his eyes had a wild, violent look that creeped me out. Plus, he had a fishing knife tucked into his waistband. I stole a glance outside while he was rambling. Hopefully, Dad or Miguel would be coming by and see what was going on. All I saw was the Trash Man leaning against a railing, smoking a cigarette and staring at the paint. It was all too weird— Trash smoking outside and Mongo the Freak tripping inside. *Just another freak in the freak kingdom*, Dad would say.

Looking back on it now, I can see that there was some kind of tension. Maddy and I were cool but I think there was some kind of dramatic pause going on in the Colony. Dad was never around and Mongo pretended like the *Gun Range* freakout never happened. Trash Man was never far from sight—I would see him twice as often as Mongo and I knew there was something going on. Dad refused to tell me what it was.

So there you have it. We had drugs moving around the Colony, we had a sudden influx of people who were obviously illegal immigrants and meanwhile Pac Fish kept looking the other way. Something was very wrong on the Colony but nobody wanted to admit it. Things were getting out of whack and I guess everyone was waiting for an opportunity to restore some kind of balance. It was waiting for something. Yes, I can see that now.

Our current position is: 35° 8'52.84"N 120°47'6.98"W

Chapter Thirteen—The Meltdown

SO HERE'S WHERE everything goes crazy …

We had a fight on the first day that we heard the plague was loose. I had spent all night on the flying deck, shivering in my old sleeping bag, rather than down in the cabin with everyone else. Stacy and I were bored and we took a joyride on the *C Minor*. When Dad found out he almost threw me overboard. He yelled, I yelled and it ended with me stomping around on the flying deck before settling in for a long, cold night.

It was so cold that I was awake by 4:30. I was stiff and sore from sleeping on the plastic decking and I shivered in my sack thinking of all kinds of mean things to say to Dad when I saw him. I even took a leak off of the top deck into the water because I know it drives him nuts. The coffee was brewing around six … I could smell it. It made me want to go inside.

Dad had the coffee going and was working on some breakfast. Like I said, he's a cheap old man—he was making scrambled eggs out of that freeze-dried stuff they sell to backpackers. He said it was still good but I didn't believe him. It was well past the expiration date but Dad's adventurous like that. He mixed in some of the fresh salsa we had on board. It came from the stock of veggies he traded with Grandma Alice in exchange for some fish. The salsa was pretty good, actually but I wasn't in a mood to pay him any compliments.

He poured hot water into the pouch and let them cook. It starts out looking like corn flakes but eventually turns into something that looks like scrambled eggs with little bits of bacon mixed in. The trick is to pour out as much of the water as you can. It took about 10 minutes to put it all together and we didn't say a word to each other in all of that time.

I decided to risk it and try the eggs … we didn't have much else. The junk food was gone, the soda supply was low, and all we had was the diet stuff that Dad couldn't live without. A grocery run was almost two weeks away. I poured enough of the salsa on that I could barely taste them.

Madison was quiet as she entered the galley—she had disappeared into her room when Dad and I started yelling. She actually liked the eggs—don't ask me why. Dad gave me a triumphant look and started heating up more of those culture-grown sausage links for her to eat. People have started growing food like pork and beef, cell by cell, in factories. They've recently been approved for sale and you can't really tell the difference between them and regular meat. Even die-hard vegans are starting to eat them since they are definitely 'cruelty-free'.

I was happy that we had them but I knew he was doing it for Maddy. He would never have done that for me. Mad acted like she didn't even notice and disappeared into the salon to flip on a cartoon show.

I wanted to sleep for a while but knew better than to try and push it. I was still in my ratty t-shirt and gym shorts from last night and had to suit up for the pens. I took a cup of Dad's coffee with me and went outside to the docks. The *Horner C* isn't much for privacy after a fight and I wanted some distance between us.

I was sitting there in my wetsuit, drinking coffee and just enjoying the morning when Stacy walked up the dock. I was happy and a little surprised to see her: her dad wasn't happy about our joyride, either. It was still early … why wasn't she doing Pen Patrol? People are normally out doing their boat chores at this hour. I wouldn't expect to see her before noon.

"Did you guys hear on the news?" she asked as she approached.

"No—Madison and the cartoon brigade pretty much took care of that."

"They're saying that Los Angeles is under attack."

"What?" I asked skeptically. For a second, I was thinking that she was trying some weird joke on me. The look on her face told me that she wasn't. Dad was just over my shoulder, pretending to wash dishes while he glared suspiciously at us. I reached up and knocked on the window, startling him. "Turn on the TV."

I couldn't see him from where I was sitting but I knew he was trying to decide whether to be mad at me for making him jump like that. "What?" I heard him shout dimly through the window.

"Turn. On. The TV." I yelled again. "She says something's happening on the news." After a second, he lumbered off in the direction of the lounge. "That got rid of him," I said in what I hoped was a seductive voice. Stacy could be sexy hot when she wanted to … I was hoping that was the reason she came by.

"I'm serious, Jim," she said. "Something's really wrong." She started talking about the reports she caught before she went to bed—leaving her parents to watch the news like they usually did. Early in the morning, she woke up still hearing the sound of the video feed.

"It was weird … they never went to bed. Then I looked around and everything in the house was being packed up. I haven't seen the house like that since we moved in. We're supposed to go up north to Santa Barbara and help my aunt and grandma to evacuate. We're talking maybe 25 people on a 30-foot boat."

The fact that that many people were trying to get onto a boat that size and that her parents agreed without an argument scared me in a way I had never known before. Looking up at the window, I noticed that Dad hadn't returned to his dishes. "Hang on a sec," I said. I left Stacy outside and went inside.

Dad stood with his arms crossed and his feet wide to stay steady on the floor. The video feeds looked horrible—less dramatic than a movie but more terrible because it was real. Helicopter footage showed thousands of bodies in the streets, Wilshire Blvd looked like the pictures of Jonestown in 1979 that I read about in Wikipedia. Bodies were strewn everywhere—the chopper wouldn't get close for fear that the bug would spread. This kept us from seeing the horrible, close-up images of people dead from a weaponized flesh-eating virus.

"Dad," I said finally, after watching for a few minutes. "Dad!"

He looked up suddenly, I don't know if he knew I was standing next to him before then. "You think Mom is okay?"

He started to say something. "It's ... I don't know, son." He started to say more but then the colony loudspeakers chirped and they started announcing something. My stomach tightened—were the pirates coming back?

"Attention all colony members. Due to the emergency on the mainland, we are asking for all boat captains to meet at the Phoenix immediately for a response planning session."

Dad sighed and started pulling on his shoes. "Well, that's that. I gotta get over there."

"Yeah, but Dad—"

"I know, Jim—just slow down." He finished tying his shoes and stood up, thinking for a few seconds. "We're not going anywhere right now. I'll figure out what we're doing once I get back." He pulled on a hat and stepped out the door as another captain—the guy on the *AM Radio* jogged by to the shuttle boat ramp. He paused as Dad came out the door.

"You hear that?" he asked.

"Yeah, I'm on my way—they said it's a about the emergency on the mainland."

"I know," he said with a grin. "Which one?" He started walking quickly again, not bothering to explain himself. We stared after him for a minute.

"Dad—" I began but he shook his head.

"Don't ask, I don't know either," he replied. "See what you can find out." Dad started jogging toward the boat launch where a crowd was piling on. They motored off and left us—I watched them go and realized that Stacy was still standing there.

"Oh, dude ... I'm sorry," I said.

"It's okay," she offered. "Can I come in?"

"Yeah, sure," I said, opening the door. "He won't be back for hours."

She came into the lounge. "Hey, Madison."

Madison looked up from her place on the couch where she'd huddled with a blanket and her stuffed Tigger. "Hey."

"That guy on the *AM* said that there's more than one disaster," I said to Stacy.

"I know," she replied. "There's a bunch of things happening." She sat down and accessed the cable television menu we couldn't get on our boat because Dad refused to pay for it. The news channels came up and the carnage began to become very apparent to all of us. We stared in silence for half an hour—the bugs in LA and Baltimore. San Jose's downtown area had several fires that they were covering at a distance, afraid that a bug was spreading there, too.

My wetsuit started to get uncomfortable after all that time—dry suits bind at your shoulders; mine does, anyway. I went downstairs to my stateroom and almost had it all off when I realized that Stacy had followed me. She grinned at almost catching me with no clothes on—she knew that I never wore anything inside my suit.

"I just wanted to tell you, in case I didn't get a chance later ... it was fun." She stepped forward and kissed me on my cheek. Then, she put her arms around me and pulled me close. It was a kiss that I would spend many nights afterward reliving ... probably the sexiest moment of my life. Then, the roof caved in. "I gotta go," she said, turning to leave.

"No, wait!"

She was already upstairs and in the salon when I caught up to her. As Stacy turned around, I saw the tears going down her cheeks. "Sorry, Jim, I hate to tell you like this. My mom and dad are leaving today, after the meeting. I wasn't supposed to be gone this long but I had to tell you goodbye." She started crying hard and put her arms around me again. Sniffing, she kissed me again and again before tucking her head into my shoulder and giving me a whiff of her apple-scented conditioner. We held each other like that for a long time.

Stacy finally pulled away and gave Madison a hug. They had become pretty good friends in the month we were all together and Madison was crying, too. Finally, Stacy came back, put her arms around me and gave me the second best kiss I'd ever had in my life. Then, without another word, she was gone. She waved to Madison as she closed the door. I stood there, my wetsuit half-off with all of these feelings twisted up inside and no way to say any of them. Madison watched us in silence. Finally, she looked up at me, "I'm telling Dad!"

I looked over at her. "Really?" Madison wasn't usually one to narc on me.

She gave me that look that only a little sister can. "No. I'm sorry, too." For an eleven-year-old, Madison could be downright inscrutable sometimes.

Dad returned about an hour later, looking shaken. "Did you guys know that it's happening in other places, too?" he asked.

"We saw it," I said. "Stacy got us onto the cable nets." Mercifully, he said nothing about her being on board. Nodding, he went to the refrigerator and pulled out a beer. Sitting down, he started to tell us how the colony was organizing a boatlift evacuation for people on the mainland.

"No one thinks that it's 100% safe but they aren't giving us a choice. The President's declared martial law." So now, in addition to pirates, the Trash Man and whatever else is going on with Dad that he doesn't want to tell me, we have martial law, the mainland is in chaos and we're supposed to try to go to shore in this rickety tub. Can anyone else say 'between a rock and a hard place'?

"You've gotta be kidding," I said. "We can't make the mainland with our engines."

Dad sat there with his head down between his shoulders, staring at something no one else could see. It was one of those times where I could see what he must have been like in prison. He wasn't a large man but he had a certain strength that reminded me of a Rottweiler. For all his strength and ability to survive prison, this type of emergency was beyond him. I could see that he was scared, really scared, of something. Maybe he wasn't telling us everything.

"What is it?" I said finally.

He sighed. "The Coast Guard is ending their zone enforcement of the water south and west of us," he said. "They're moving in to assist with the emergency and have informed the colony that quote, 'it should not expect further assistance'." Madison looked confused but my heart sank.

I never got a straight answer out of Dad or Miguel about what Dad was involved with after that visit from the pirates before Madison arrived. Dad had called it 'harassment'. "The Coast Guard patrols these waters," he had promised. You could even see the cutters off in the distance every few days. "Anybody tries anything … the Coast Guard is right there."

At the time, it made us feel better. Now they were going away—there wasn't anything to stop these guys except Miguel and that big huge gun. Our world had suddenly become even more dangerous.

"So what does that mean?" I asked.

"It means," He said, "we're in trouble. Bad trouble. I give the pirates one or two days tops, and then they'll come for us." Silence ensued as my stomach turned to water. Dad had told us some hoodoo stories about the pirates, about them capturing small boats and what they did to the crews. I read something similar in an old paperback Dad had lying around … Clear and Present Something—I can't remember the title.

"Julian's got his gun," I said. "The sniper rifle?"

Dad nodded. "He's a good shot, too," Dad added. "The very last time pirates came around, he was up on top of the *Gun Range* and just let them come in. When they were in range, he fired one shot and punched a hole through the front of the boat. The bullet went through the entire boat and buried itself in the engine block; stopped the entire thing in one shot."

He sat back on the couch and pushed his fingers through his hair. "But he won't be here this time," Dad said. "He's going with us." There was silence in the room for a minute.

"This is going to sound dumb," he said. "But how good are you driving this thing?"

"Driving the boat?" I said. "I've never driven a boat."

"You've driven the *C Minor*."

"The *C Minor* is a wakeboarding boat, Dad," I said. "This …" I waved my hand at the air "is a ship."

Dad shrugged. "Just a question," he said. He sat up and stood, going to the refrigerator. I could hear the door open and the can snap. I squeezed my eyes shut in frustration—just like Dad to reach for the beer when we had a problem.

"Wait a minute," I said. Something was missing here. "Shouldn't you be driving the boat?"

"I can't," he said with a sigh.

"Why not?"

He was silent for about a minute, sipping at his beer and staring at the wall. It looked like he was trying to make his mind up about something.

"I'm in a bit of trouble," he said finally. "Your friend, the Trash Man, is an undercover DEA agent and he's trying to bust me."

"But why would …" I began before a sickening feeling crept over me. A very ugly piece of the puzzle just fell into place: this was why Dad was so successful. He was running drugs again. The room was silent while I tried to think of a way to ask the next question. "Mongo?"

He nodded slowly. "The groceries I've been running with Mongo … yeah." Children of the Burning Man and their grocery runs were how they were running drugs through the Colony. Whatever happened after that, I don't know. Maybe the Colony was just a conduit so the drugs could be shipped elsewhere or maybe that's what Mitch was selling. "If I make a move to leave, they'll be all over me and all over you."

"Who would, the cops or the pirates?"

He took a breath and let it out with a sigh. "Both of them," he said.

I made a little groaning sound in my throat and Madison looked at me weird. Dad was involved in the drug trade. He was also supposed to be running the *Dixie Star* and was probably funneling money to the wrong people doing that. On top of that, there were illegal immigrants running around. That meant he might have ties to the human trafficking and I'm sure the Trash Man would love to bust Dad for that even if he couldn't get him with the drugs. On top of all that, he had some low-rent pirates out of Baja looking for his nuts on a platter because he was probably trying to screw them as much as he was Pac Fish.

Madison and I were in a huge mess. My head ached when I even tried to think about it all at once. I'm turning 15 years old soon—are 15-year-olds supposed to be handling problems like this? Like I said, my head hurt when I tried to keep all the problems straight … don't even ask me about a solution.

"I don't know what we're going to do right now," Dad continued. "Might not even be an issue. Up there," he nodded toward the *Phoenix*, "they're still arguing it all over. I slipped out to get a jumpstart on getting the boat broken down." I couldn't believe he even said that … 'might not be a problem'. Dad was losing his grip and it pissed me off that he was doing all of this under our nose … doing it and inviting us out here to be a part of it all. Something snapped in me and I got very, very pissed off.

"So you already decided," I said flatly.

"No," he stared back at me, not liking the challenge.

"But you came back to start breaking down."

"That's what I told them, Jim," he said. "You seriously think I'm going to put you in harm's way?"

"You already have," I snapped. I didn't really want to and I hadn't planned on doing it but the oaf made me so angry that it kind of just slipped out. I shouted at Dad and I hit him closer to where it hurt than anything I might have done (or not done … I admit nothing) on the C Minor. But we crossed a line of some kind here and I didn't know what it might mean.

Madison jumped but I saw Dad just lock down like he was all of a sudden back in the joint. He tightened like he was going to either give or take a punch. His eyes tightened and his jaw clenched. I was terrified at the way I was speaking to him—this was nothing like the fight we had last night. Do you ever remember your first man-to-man argument with your father?

He stood up to his full height and went into his classic "I'm in charge" pose—hands on his hips and shoulders hunched like he was going to throw blows. "Don't you dare talk to me that way," he hissed thinly. "I may be a lot of things but I'm still your father."

It was a voice I'd never heard and it scared me a little … but not enough to back down. I roared back: "And you're the guy that has the DEA on one side and a bunch of drug pirates on the other. Everyone wants a piece of you!" Dad slapped me then.

In one smooth motion he stepped forward and gave me a big open-handed smack that knocked me to the floor. It happened so quickly that I was on the ground before I realized he'd hit me, but he wasn't done. Dad picked me up by the front of my shirt and slammed me back against the wall.

"Think you're so smart?" he shouted. "The stupid, drunk kid from rehab is going to tell *me* that I'm screwing up?" Madison was screaming with her hands over her ears. I could still talk and so I did.

"At least I didn't bring my kids into it! Screw you, old man!" His eyes widened with surprise. Oh, it was on now.

He slammed me into the wall. "So … smart! So … friggin' … smart!" He was punctuating his words by slamming me into the wall again and again and yet, he was watching his mouth in front of Madison. How ironic. In some back corner of my head, I was watching it all happen to me like it was a movie.

After a few more thumps, I could hear a crunching sound: he'd broken through the cheap paneling that hid one of our closets. He pulled me back toward him to see the damage and then pushed me away to where I slumped against the couch. Both of us were pinned to where we were by the sound of his voice.

He picked up the half-empty beer can and hurled through the window of the galley. The shattering glass made Madison start to cry and although I didn't want them to, some tears started rolling down my face as well. Dad's face was a mask of fury and something else … despair, maybe. His hands opened and closed and his entire body just vibrated with a dark energy.

After a few minutes, Dad went to the sink and leaned against the counter, staring at the floor and trying to compose himself. The cording in his arms stood out as he squeezed the cheap countertop with his hands like he was trying to lift it off the floor. Rhythmic squeezing—his muscles jumped with the effort.

I slowly became aware of his voice as he started talking about how much he hated himself, hated the colony … It sounded almost like crying, but no tears left his eyes.

"You know nothing about trying to keep it clean," he said, in a pause. "I tried to make everything work. Keep everyone happy. It never works." He looked at the two of us on his couch, like he had never seen us before. I guess that's how we looked too, starting back at him in fear. Who was this guy? Where was the nice guy? What had become of our Dad?

I guess everyone sees their parent lose it at some point. Some people wait longer than others but the effect, when it happens, is jarring. You get an idea that Dad or Mom are some type of rock-like characters who never snap regardless of how bad things get. Cold and remote, maybe, but imposing and strong nonetheless. But Dad snapped … all this stuff, everything that happened—Dad finally came apart and it wasn't pretty to watch.

He looked at us and he had the weirdest combination of anger and sadness I've ever seen on anyone. He didn't say anything, but he just kept staring at us and then back at the floor—his hands just kept working that part of the counter and I could hear the old particle-board that it was made out of creaking with the effort. Finally, he stood up from the countertop he'd been massaging. He left the ship by a side door and we didn't see him again for a couple of hours.

We had nothing else to do so we kept watching the cable feed from shore. The horror was non-stop and with every passing hour a new development would pop up. The attacks in LA were timed with some communique that claimed responsibility for dumping poison in the drinking water—using the water to put out the fire would expose people to poison-laced steam. Then there was something in Seattle—a dirty bomb or something. Then a plane crashed in Orlando and they said it was filled with Caesium-137. "What's 'Sezium'?" Madison asked.

"I have no idea," I replied. Why 137 and not 136? I should have paid more attention in chemistry. The bugs were scary and nobody really knew anything … the talking-heads just kind of gawped at each other after a while and I started ignoring them … trying to think and work things out as much as I could.

A tapping at the door got my attention and I looked up. Stacy was standing there, looking very upset with eyes red from crying. I opened the door and she almost fell into my arms (a nice diversion, even with all of this happening) saying "they can't leave—nobody is letting us leave!"

I got her a towel or something and she wiped her face, swearing endlessly about the idiots on the *Phoenix* who 'commandeered all boats for a rescue operation'. Her parents were on the *Phoenix* and all she could think of to do was pack her stuff and wait for them to put them off the boat. I noticed for the first time that her bags were on the front deck. This little stuffed bear that I won for her at the arcade on the *Phoenix* was sitting on top.

Her parents came for her and took her back to the *Seas of Cheese*—the 'rescue operation' was a rumor, they said, no one was taking the boat anywhere tonight. More news would come in the morning, Stacy's mom said, waving to us and cracking jokes—she said this would blow over in a day or so and I wanted to believe her more than anything. Even though she was smiling and laughing, I could see that the humor wasn't reaching her eyes. She looked very afraid and I think the fact that I could see that made me more frightened than ever.

They left soon enough and it was back to Madison and me … alone again. Madison came over to me and we huddled there next to the couch, just holding onto each other because there was nothing else to do.

Our current position is: 35°12'55.89"N 120°53'56.17"W

Chapter Fourteen—The Draft

THE SUN WAS getting toward the horizon again when we heard the PA system go off again. *"All boat captains report to the Phoenix for an update to the original emergency planning session. No exceptions—the meeting is in 7 minutes."* He repeated the announcement a couple of times and then clicked off. The snap of the switch echoed in the small speakers. I suddenly became irritated about them. The speakers were rigged haphazardly along the ring docks and you could barely hear what he was saying. Nobody cared about the Colony enough to get the place into shape. Even basic stuff like this was beyond them.

Madison and I huddled together under a blanket and watching the news. We hadn't seen Dad, I didn't know where he was or if he heard. My shoulder ached faintly from Dad's outburst, but it wasn't bad. I don't think it even bruised. The shock of it was worse.

Another hour went by, the pens were forgotten and we were eating from a half-stale bag of corn chips. Neither of us wanted to think about what Dad would do when he got back … if he got back. Finally, as the lights were winking on in other boats, we heard a familiar footstep approach the front door and he was inside the boat again. Wordlessly, he moved to the refrigerator. Another beer snapped open and he returned to the salon where he leaned against the stairway rail. It was a replay of an earlier conversation and both of us inched slowly away from him. Dad stared at the far wall for a long minute before speaking.

"It seems," he said, "that I've been drafted." We had stared at each other in silence for a few moments before he continued. "They're asking for anybody over 18 to go help the National Guard in Los Angeles with the evacuation. Actually, they want anyone over 15—I told them that you were 14 and that you needed to take care of your sister. No one asked for your birth certificate, so you're off the hook." He put the beer can down and pressed his hands to his eyes, hard, like he was getting a headache or something.

"But what about mom?" I asked. I wanted more than anything to get back onto shore.

"What about her?"

"Are we going to get her?"

"No. Right now it's chaos on the mainland, Jim. We'd just be in the way if we tried."

"So what are we going to *do?*" I was starting to get whiney. I hate that about myself.

Dad took a breath and tried not to explode. "I know. I'm getting to that. Someone needs to watch out for Madison." He was silent for a moment, thinking about something. Now that I think about it, I realize that he remembered a very unpleasant conversation. Something that must have taken place before he came to get us. "They told me I should leave her with the neighbors or on the *Phoenix* but screw that." He looked up at me from his seat. "I don't have a choice."

"What?"

"I need you to stay here on the *Horner* ... with Madison. It's probably the safest place in the world, right now. If it gets worse, you'll have to use the *Horner* to get her out of here and get to safety."

Dad had experienced quite a change of heart in the past few hours, I thought. *Didn't he put me through a wall on this boat a few hours ago,* I asked myself. What kind of crazy talk was this with his 'stay with Madison on the boat' crap? Again ... the right angles were coming too quick and too fast for me to keep up and so I said the most logical thing that came to my mind.

"Huh?"

"I need to trust you, Jim. You have to do this."

"What?" I asked, even though I knew what he was saying.

"You have to take care of Madison," Dad repeated. "You're probably going to have to sail this thing out of here."

"But ... me?"

"Yes."

You know how you imagine that moment when you stop being a boy and become a man? You keep imagining that it somehow happens like a show on the Disney channel—you have your dad clap you on your back and go, "Son ... today *you're a man!*" That's how I always pictured it, stupid as that might sound.

I imagined that reaching this stage in my life would have a little more pomp and circumstance, a little more drama to it. I start looking at my life like a big production number ... I wonder if everyone does that? Sadly, I wasn't going to get the big moment. Dimly, like I was watching myself on TV, I could see that this was the moment that I was always waiting for. It wasn't happening the way that I expected.

Dad turned and went to the counter underneath the stove. The stove didn't work ... we cooked off of the hotplate. He reached underneath and pulled out a flat metal box with *Sig Arms* stamped into the lid. It had been duct-taped to the underside of the stove back where you wouldn't find it right away. He opened it and pulled out a heavy automatic pistol. I was shocked to know that it was there. Dad had found a hiding place on the boat that I wouldn't have thought to check.

"You had a gun on this boat?" Madison was incensed. She picked up a lot of left-wing stuff from mom and hated guns on moral principle.

"Yep," Dad replied, not wanting to get into this discussion with my sister. "I'm leaving you the shotgun."

He went to his room and we heard a cabinet open a few seconds later. He returned to the salon with a scuffed-up shotgun. The nylon stock was nicked and faded gray with age. "That's a Remington Marine Magnum 870, Jim. It's loaded with double-aught buckshot and I've got some spare shells in the same place—you'll find it." He placed the shotgun across the bar underneath our flatpanel and then he stuffed the pistol into his waistband behind his back.

"Why don't you stick it in front?" I asked. That's what they always did in the movies and we never covered gun transport at the *Barco de Arma*.

"I'm not putting going to risk 'testicide'," he said. He stopped and looked up at me. "Please do not ask me to go into details." Dad returned to the galley and took a knee. He reached out to us, grabbed our hands and pulled us to him. "They aren't giving me much time, so listen close." He looked up into our eyes and I was struck with a wall of emotion. I guess this was what it might have been like if he was the normal kind of dad he was supposed to be. Even after all that had happened, it took this kind of emergency to bring it out of him.

"Wait 3 days for me," he said. "If you don't hear from me by then, leave a message for your mom." He went back to his room and pulled out a small backpack—he stuck in some food bars, water and a can of beer. Stuffing the items inside, he threw over his shoulder and continued the lecture.

"I have absolutely no idea what's about to happen," he said. He seemed like he wanted to say more but then he turned and started for the door. "They want us ready to launch in fifteen minutes." He gave Madison's neck a squeeze but skipped doing anything similar for me. "Don't let them take the boat—leave the colony if you have to. If you do leave, go north." He was about to leave but then backtracked to the bridge. He flipped open a cabinet underneath the throttle. Dad pulled out map after map before opening one and spreading it across the floor. It was a map of the coast from San Ysidro to Oregon.

"Here," he said, tapping a point on it. "We're here." His fingers moved up the chart. "If you head north, keep the land just in sight on your starboard side, you should be free and clear 'till you get up to Washington. Use the GPS and the compass; they'll keep you from drifting too far."

"Dad, wait …" I began. This was moving too quickly. Me? Boat? Take care? He was talking to the kid he just smashed into a wall, didn't he remember that? I was about to open my mouth to start screaming all of these things when he looked up at me.

There was so many things that we saw in each other's eyes at that moment. My dad probably wanted to apologize for what he'd done, how he brought us here and everything else after that, but he wasn't going to.

Dad was the kind of guy that would never apologize because it'd just open the door to all the other things in his life that he could never make up for. Leaving mom … leaving us. Failed jobs. Prison. The mistakes he made on the colony. The thousand and one things we had no idea about that took place when he wasn't in prison and wasn't making any attempt to be in our lives. You can fill up forty-plus years with a lot of regret. He knew he couldn't fix it and somehow he didn't want to acknowledge it … that would somehow cause the universe to cave in on him.

But the unstoppable force meets the immovable object. Were we supposed to chuck it all without talking about it? Does 'I'm your father' become the answer to every question? I haven't the slightest idea but the hole in the wall and my aching shoulder deserved something.

Someone should say something—maybe Dad could have at least said 'I didn't want this to happen.' I guess he had said that, but it felt more like he never wanted us around in the first place. You can't wrap a gold brick in a turd wrapping paper and expect everyone to want to clean it off. I wanted him to say he was sorry. I wanted him to apologize, just once, for all the messy stuff he put us through. What was the point? All of his plans, all of the scams and deals … they weren't saving us from this.

I wanted him to do something to make up for it. The sad part was that I knew that he never would. He'd never admit he was wrong and an apology from him was something I'd never get. Because I would never get it there was going to be a wedge between us for the rest of our lives.

We weren't going to solve any of this right now. Dad looked back to the map, clearing his throat. "The worst part is getting away," he said. "You can probably cut loose but they'll be expecting that. If there's a storm or something, that'll keep them indoors. It's your best option to get clear."

Madison and I were doing our best not to burst into tears. Mom in terrible danger, Dad off to who knows where. I wanted very much to be back home so that I could find my bed and go hide under it. I'm almost a man here and I want to go hide under the bed. I would never admit that to anyone else but that's exactly how I felt. Dad pulled us close and hugged us fiercely. Then, he let go.

"Take care of each other," he said. "I'll be back soon." With that, Dad was walking through the salon door and down to the dock, joining the other men walking in that direction. We got more of a goodbye from Stacy.

He waved once, then turned his back and walked toward the launches. We watched from the front porch door along with a lot of other people. The energy of all of these frightened people was so sharp that you could almost hear it buzzing like an old fluorescent light. Madison felt for me and I put my arm around her—right now, we needed to count on each other. As the launches left, people from the colony lined the docks to watch them go off. It's been happening in the same sick way since humankind began. The men go off to uncertain fortunes while the wives and children watch helplessly from behind. I can see that now … I just didn't know how it felt.

Madison began to cry as Dad disappeared from sight. The last I saw of him, he was walking stiffly toward the embarkation dock and then he was out of sight among dozens of other men. They all had the same walk almost as if they were all carrying a heavy load, and in a way, they were. It was the burden of the job that fell to them because they were here and because they were men. We were all safely left behind.

Tears began to roll down my cheeks, too—that whole end scene in *Empire Strikes Back* totally made sense to me at that moment. It's stupid how your mind works, sometimes.

The boats left harbor and disappeared into the horizon. Everyone was trying to find a way to get up onto the *Phoenix*, the *Dixie* or any other flying bridge to see our departing loved ones as long as possible. Madison and I climbed to the second deck of the *Horner*, looking for Dad. I looked for him but I didn't see him; the boats themselves looked like those troop carriers that have everyone all bunched up … you couldn't pick one person out if you tried. The sound of sobbing children and wives floated above everything else. I've never heard anything so depressing in my life.

Madison wouldn't stop crying and refused to let me get more than an arm's length away. I finally had to twist my shirt out of her fist just so I could use the bathroom.

Night fell cold and nasty that first night. We took all the blankets from the bed, twisted them up into a nest and slept in the lounge. The pilot for the gas went out sometime in the night and Dad never showed me how to relight it. It was dank and cold—the vague vibration of the motors keeping the colony in motion gave me some comfort but it did absolutely nothing to calm the raw pit in the middle of my stomach.

The next day, we made a half-hearted attempt at pen patrol. I swam the length of pens one and two but it became too exhausting to continue. I hauled myself out of the water repeatedly, gasping. Madison said nothing and helped me put my mask and hookah back on several times. After I caught my breath, I went back to it. I hated those fish and I hated pen patrol and I hated the colony but it was the only thing we could really do. Right then I felt like I had been cut loose from the planet to live out the rest of my life on a floating garbage dump. However alone or vulnerable I felt when I first arrived, it wasn't half of what I was feeling right now.

Stacy showed up around lunchtime. Her dad had left on the launch. Over cold sandwiches and warm soda, she told me that he didn't intend to stay with the organized group. She explained that if he could help, he would, but if it was obvious that he couldn't do anything then he would ditch the group and start finding his way north to Santa Barbara.

I listened to her story, thinking of my Dad. "If he leaves, will he take my Dad with him?" I asked.

"I don't know," Stacy said. "We didn't even talk about it." I thought my Dad a little bit more streetwise and smart than Stacy's dad. The problem was that, deep down, he was trying to be a decent guy. That might make him do something stupid to prove a point and that rarely worked out well for Dad. I was afraid he'd end up just another casualty of this holocaust in progress. Stacy left after turning on the sat-feed for us again and promising to come back later. She said her mom was really freaking out and needed to keep Stacy in sight at all times. Sure enough, as she left our boat to walk back to hers, we saw her mom standing with her arms crossed tight across her chest and pacing a tight little circle on the dock.

The news wasn't getting any better … we could see that. They weren't even trying to get live reports from the downtown area—the closest they would get were endless reports from high above the ground in choppers. Madison kept watching for any news about Mom, any news about people we knew or about our town. I tried to ignore it and get back to the business of the boat. It kept me calm to stay busy.

Pen Patrol took ten times as long as usual—I'm glad Dad wasn't here or he would be going insane with how long everything was taking me. *Not like any of it matters now*, I thought. I kept rerunning the argument we had before he left, thinking about how what I might have said different. It sounds weird but having arguments in my head with Dad was vaguely comforting. I thought that if I found the right way to say something that he might listen to me and agree with me once in a while.

I had just come inside from Pen Patrol to make myself some coffee when Madison came running down from the top deck.

"The Security guys are going door to door on every boat in the Colony," she said quickly.

I snuck a peek out of the side window to see guys in their official yellow windbreakers with SECURITY stenciled across their back. "That's never a good sign," I muttered. When was the last time we'd seen them around here ... Steeplechase? If you saw them, it only meant Pacific Fisheries business. But what did they want? It took me only seconds to figure it out. *They were checking for stragglers.* They might take me if they found out how old I was.

What should I do? Slip overboard and hide among the fish? This wouldn't be the only time they would check. I would be discovered eventually. But still ... I need to hide, right? I couldn't ignore that there was something very basic about *not wanting to be found.*

I grabbed Madison and slapped the OFF switch on the flatscreen. She screeched a protest but I clamped my hand firmly over her mouth and marched her to her room. I slammed the door and we huddled inside while I kept listening for the team to knock on the door. They had to be less than two or three boats away.

"What do we—" she asked and I shushed her violently. All of a sudden, we could hear the screams and the crying. The Security team was shoving an old Asian guy—an illegal probably—in the direction of the *Phoenix.* I'm pretty sure they weren't inviting him back to the ship for the hamburgers and crappy second-run movies.

It was terrifying. I peeked out of the small porthole in Madison's stateroom to see the team holding a group of women and kids back while they hustled off dad, uncle or grandpa. If a group of people couldn't stop them ... a pipsqueak like me didn't stand a chance.

While all of this was happening, a loud knock made us both jump. I told Madison, "Go answer it—don't tell them you're alone or they'll make you go up to the *Phoenix*. Tell them you're staying with Stacy and her mom." She nodded shakily and disappeared out to the salon to deliver the message. I slipped out of her room and went over to the Junk Room to find a place to hide.

The Junk Room was full of the stuff Dad inherited when he bought the boat from the old coot who lived there before. Old boat parts, books, and crap ... Dad had been trying to sell it or dump it ever since he moved in. The old parts and books had some value but at least half the room was pure trash. I found an open spot to lie in and pulled a heap of old moldy clothes down over myself. Big mistake.

This stuff was old in the last century, doused with either mothballs or old lady perfume and then left in wet cardboard boxes for a decade or two. It was making me gag and choke back some puke while I strained to listen to whatever was happening outside to Madison. I could hear Madison's muffled voice and one of the goons. I think his name was Ralph or something. Seconds turned into minutes and eventually I heard her slide the glass door shut. Was Ralph still here? Did he come inside for a peek around? I wanted desperately to look but I didn't dare ... I didn't have a chance to guess wrong.

All at once, I heard Madison's voice in the Junk Room with me. "Jim?" she called. I jumped out of my hiding place, making the clothes to kind of geyser up and freaking Madison out. I didn't want to scare her but the disgusting smell of putrid clothing was making me retch. I gagged and gasped for air for a few seconds before she could say anything.

"They were looking for you," she said when my stomach finally settled down.

"What?"

"Looking. For you."

"Looking for me? Why?" I asked.

She gave me a withering Little Sister look, the one that said: *you're the big brother, how can you be so stupid?* "I don't know but I'm sure you don't want to find out," was what she finally said.

"They got that old guy on the other boat," I said glumly, knowing full well what would have happened to me if Madison hadn't been up there to see them. Why were these guys looking for me? Dad told me that they would give me a pass! As per usual, Dad thought he had things covered but overlooked one or four major pieces. I was too scared to be angry, though. How were we going to get out of this?

We spent the rest of day watching the deck outside the *Horner.* I fixed up a nice little hidey-hole in the Junk Room and I hoped that it would be enough. Since I shut off the TV, we lost access to the satellite feed and Nancy would have to check in with the boats next door to see if they had heard anything.

We couldn't use the Internet because Pacific Fisheries was monitoring network traffic. Stacy was trying to watch all the major social networking sites at once for news and information. We couldn't post our contact information like they did—it was driving me nuts. I doubt Mom and Dad would even begin to know how to find us again, much less get in contact without getting us into more trouble. Trying to pay attention to site is exhausting, though. Everyone has their own version of the story and you have to go to two or three places to get a complete picture. After a while the data starts to blend together and nothing makes sense.

We fell asleep again in the lounge that night. This time I was exhausted but I couldn't stop thinking about everything that was happening. My mind kept grinding over and over different problems. Eventually I dozed off, only to wake myself up from a dream I was having. In it, Dad and I were arguing about him leaving us on the boat. We kept going back and forth on why we needed him here and why he needed to go ashore. Madison finally started screaming at me to shut up and the last part of my dream I was saying in a weird groggy voice, "Let me just make one last point ..."

I woke up on the floor of the lounge and Madison was awake, too. She was still on the couch but up on one arm looking at me. I took a moment while I sorted myself out of the dream—it was so real I wasn't sure exactly when I woke up.

"You were talking in your sleep," she said. "You said something about a final point."

I grunted wearily. "I'm sorry—I was arguing with Dad in my sleep."

I could see her grin in the darkness. "At least if you argue in your dreams you have a chance of winning," she said. I just smiled … we both were too tired to laugh, or even chuckle. Siblings can make the funniest jokes to each other. Somehow, they're never quite as funny if you repeat them to other people. "Did you win the argument?"

"No," I replied. "At best it was a draw … you were telling me to shut up."

"Wow," she said. "Realistic."

We went back to sleep again—I woke up several times but managed to go back to sleep again. When I woke the last time, the sky was that grey color that comes in the predawn. We alternated between watching the TV, trying to sleep more and scarfing down any junk food we could find.

Madison and I were both dreading the phone call we had to make— Dad had told us to try calling on the second day. How was I supposed to get over there without getting snatched up? I found ways to avoid doing it until the afternoon. It must have taken me an hour to make my up there, watching every direction at once for problems.

That turned out to be a waste of time … most the Security guys were gone. The ones that were left were guarding the ship and they ignored me. The *Phoenix* was a madhouse of activity: people were camped out on the deck of the ship or in the theatre where they were broadcasting news reports. The grocery store on the *Phoenix* was a complete shambles and some people were arguing violently over what was left. I had brought some money to snap up some chips or cookies but there was no hope of that. They were down to dented cans of olives by the time I arrived.

It took me a while to find the Colony Operations Office—I had never had a reason to visit before. It was a crummy room the size of a closet with stained blue carpet and ancient wood paneling. Inside, I found a very stressed-out lady screaming into the ship-to-shore radio phones. They were going back and forth about supplies and information. I guess the offices in Long Beach were being abandoned while the shore-based employees were being evacuated. What were we supposed to do? I hung around until a lull in the conversation appeared and then I waved to get her attention.

"Can I make a phone call?" I asked.

"Honey, *I* can't make a phone call," she replied. "Which boat are you with?"

"The *Horner C*," I said. "My dad—"

"I know, honey, I know," she said quickly, before I could cry or something. "The boat lift made it to shore and I'm sure your dad will be back with you before you know it."

"I just need to call my mom," I said. "My sister is worried—"

"All civilian traffic has been suspended," she cut me off again. "Don't you have a cell phone?"

"My dad did, but he left with it," I said. "He told us to see you."

"I don't know why he would have done that, we don't have public phone facilities."

"Well ... I guess he thought it was an emergency."

"He *left you* with no one to take care of you?" she said incredulously, like she suddenly realized that a fifteen-year-old kid was asking for his father and mother. I hated the adults who didn't keep up with what I was saying.

"They had a draft," I said.

"He should have gotten out of it," she said, "or gotten someone to watch you." That made me think: could Dad have stayed and took this as a chance to jump ship on us? That made sense, especially after our fight. I started feeling angry toward him again but I put it aside to see about the phone call.

No dice. She blew off my argument quickly and mechanically like she had practiced it. I'm sure she'd already had enough people in there for her to practice on. I'm sure she could patch a call through for us but she wasn't having it. Maybe I could try again later. I spent a few more minutes, arguing with her and hoping she wouldn't find a way to have me drafted. Then I left to go back to the *Horner*.

Our current position is: 35°20'10.25"N 120°53'31.64"W

Chapter Fifteen—The Phoenix Patrol

MIGUEL WAS GONE but somebody needed to run the *Gun Range*. This was the worst crisis any of us had ever experienced but people still wanted the *Gun Range* for the TV and cold beer. Priorities, I guess. I had just reached the *Horner* after my trip the *Phoenix* and here was some middle-aged white lady on our back deck waiting for me. She stood up from the chair she was sitting on and tossed me a ring of keys.

I caught them and looked at her. What was this about? "We need to open up," she said, turning to leave.

"What?" I asked. She turned and looked at me with withering contempt, like I was a bug or something.

"The *Barco de Arma* ... the *Gun Range*, you idiot," she snapped. "Get it open. We got customers."

Pause with me for a moment here: we had guys from Pac Fish occasionally sweeping the docks looking for people to draft. We had a national, maybe worldwide crisis that was *killing people* not 120 miles away. My Dad was gone, my mom and grandparents were dead ... maybe. Before he left, Dad was using me as his favorite verbal (and occasionally physical) punching bag. All that was going on, but now it didn't matter because this crazy lady showed up and I'm still an employee of the *Gun Range*.

It turns out that she was Miguel's wife. Where had she been all this time? She didn't think I was worth telling, apparently. Normally, I'd lose the keys and ignore her but Miguel was a friend and plus, he had Internet and a phone. Madison and I would start hanging out there and only going home to change clothes or sleep.

Even with the *Gun Range* being reopened, people were becoming increasingly ugly. Random guys would show up at the counter asking when the *Dixie Star* was going to be start again. I had to confess, I had no idea but nobody wanted to hear that. Pac Fish had used this emergency as an excuse to kill all access. Maybe they would have anyway ... the more conservative members of the colony were getting vocal about the *Dixie* being a 'den of vice'.

After my shift, I was puttering around the *Horner* and stretching out some hoses when the Bible Belt Lady appeared and had something she needed to speak with me about. I was surprised since we hadn't had anything to say since Dad introduced us on the first day of the summer. "She's from the buckle of the Bible Belt," Dad had explained. Her family arrived earlier this year and Dad had pointed out the Shakedown Boat with the crosses and vaguely Biblical phrases painted over the windows in white liquid shoe polish. After the introduction, Dad told me to avoid them unless I wanted a lecture. What did she want?

"It's about that den of vice your father is working in," she said, upset to the point of tears.

"Den of vice?" I asked. I wasn't trying to be smart ... what did that mean?

"That's right," my self-appointed conscience said. The charm of her Missour-ah accent was blunted by the trailer-trash lecture she was giving me. "That place is an abomination to our community and no self-respecting parent (she was looking right at me when she said it) would let their kids go work on there!"

"Well, good," I said. "The *Gun Range* sells beer but I don't drink it."

"I'm talking about the casino ... the *Dixie* Whatever!"

"Dad works on the *Dixie* but I don't," I replied. "He doesn't let me come aboard."

"Why couldn't ya'll have something like Branson?"

"Branson?"

"Branson, Missouri," she said. "They had all you wanted out of Las Vegas except for the gambling and the nekkid girls." I wasn't sure how to respond to that … I always want to crack up when someone says 'nekkid' instead of 'naked'.

I know she was probably trying to pressure me into convincing Dad to give up the casino when (or if) he returned but that wasn't going to happen. Dad would give me and Madison up before he gave up such a cherry gig. Who was she to suddenly start giving me all this advice, anyway? I was suddenly in charge of commentary on how Dad lived his life? Go take it up with him, not me! I was working myself into a towering rage of self-righteous hate at this crazy bag when someone joined the conversation.

"So in other words, they had everything you wanted out of Vegas except for everything you wanted out of Vegas," a voice said from over my right shoulder.

I saw the little wheels turning behind her eyes and she recoiled in outrage. I didn't even have to turn my head, I knew who it was. The *clink* of a Zippo and the smell of an unfiltered Camel simply confirmed it.

"I was talkin'—" she began.

"I know," Trash Man said in a soothing voice. "But right now, Jim and I need to talk about how we're going to keep vice and other bad stuff out of the Colony. There's a committee being formed, you know."

"A committee?"

"Oh, yeah," Trash said, pointing back toward the *Phoenix*. "Go on up to the main office and ask about it. They'd be glad to have you as a member." Her eyes lit up and she muttered a 'thanks'. Then, she started to quickly shuffle off as fast as her shower shoes would allow her on that wet dock. Trash tasted his smoke and squinted toward the horizon, watching her go. "That'll keep her busy," he said finally.

"Thanks," I said warily. I was happy to get away from that crazy broad but what did he want?

"It was nothing," he said. "This gives us a good chance to get acquainted. How's your Dad? I was sorry to see him go."

Trust the old fool to say something to get me upset. Of course we were freaked out since he left and every passing minute added to the tension. We were ending the third day after everyone left. No word from Dad, Mom, my grandparents or anyone and we were pulling our hair out. The news wasn't getting better as things really started to let go on the mainland. Madison and me … we wanted to be heading for shore even if we had to do it pulling the docks behind us. We wanted our Dad back, we *WANTED OUR DAD BACK*. I wanted to scream it in Trash Man's face. Why was that so hard to understand?

He was waiting for me to say something. When I let a few minutes go by, he goes: "So, nothing?"

"No," I said glumly.

"That's a shame … hope he's okay." He paused, just letting the smoke blow through the air at my face. "So, how much do you know?"

"Huh?"

"The drugs, kiddo," he said, finally confirming my suspicious about Dad and his sudden rise to wealth and prominence. "How much do you know?"

"Not much, I guess," I said bitterly. He nodded, taking his time and not rushing anything. He stood there like there he didn't have a care in the world.

"We've been watching your Dad for a while," he said. "He's got his thumbs in everybody's pie. Drugs, gambling … maybe even the illegals they got running through here. It's gonna make life difficult for everybody when he gets back here."

"What do you want?"

"A look around," he said. "You really don't know anything about the drugs? Does he keep any on board?"

"No … not that I know of."

"Can I look?" he said, moving to the *Horner*'s cabin door before I had a chance to say no. Was that how it was supposed to work? I started to protest but before I got a word out, he said over his shoulder: "Aren't you supposed to be up on the *Phoenix* or something? How come they didn't draft you?" My protests died after that. He had me and we both knew it.

He quietly stepped inside the *Horner* and his first obstacle was Madison bundled up in her nest of crappy blankets. She was staring daggers at him. "Hi, sweetheart," he said gently. "How are you doin'?"

"My Dad's not gonna like it when I tell him you were here," she said sharply.

"I know, baby," he said smoothly. "It'll just be our secret." He started rummaging through the entire boat, opening cabinets and poking under mattresses. I wanted to tell him to get out but what was I going do if he brought the Pac Fish people down on us?

"Jim," Madison said. "Stop him."

"I can't," I replied miserably. "He might get me drafted."

I followed him as he checked every drawer and potential hiding place on the boat. He finished with the upstairs and moved into the lower decks, starting with Dad's room and then moving into ours. He was efficient but it still took over an hour to toss the place. He looked everywhere on our boat for drugs, even my underwear drawer. This was so weird and creepy, what was I supposed to do?

I went back to the salon and sat on the couch with Madison. We couldn't stop him and I couldn't bear to watch him to it either. It felt like we were being violated. To cope, I held onto my knees and I just kinda … I don't know, *went* somewhere else. I pretended this wasn't really happening and we were watching it happen on a movie.

We heard a lot of drawers slamming open and closed, stuff getting overturned and something made of glass breaking in Dad's stateroom. God knows what he thought when he tried to look through the Junk Room. It felt like it had been going on forever when he appeared again in the lounge. He looked at us briefly and then let himself out without a word. We watched him walk away and then disappear around a boat … headed toward the *Phoenix*.

I spent the rest of that day on pins and needles waiting for the Security team to show up and cart me off. Every footfall on the docks outside, every voice I heard was the team preparing to raid us. I was planning to hide by jumping into the water and hiding. I even wore my wetsuit under my clothes and exhausted myself trying to watch out every window at once.

After an hour, Madison got tired of it. "If they were gonna do it," she snapped, "you'd be gone already." We both started arguing in heated whispers, me telling her to 'shut up' and her telling me 'stop it'. We started throwing little slaps and punches around and it was about to become a full-blown sibling brawl. Then a fist clanged against the back door … bringing our fight to a screeching halt. I leaped for the deck hatch that led to the front of the *Horner* and the water when a voice stopped me. It wasn't one of the Security guys.

Madison opened the door to one of the Gloucester West fisherman. I guess he was too old to go along with the boat lift. Maybe he was hiding like we were. "So where's ya dah?" he asked angrily.

"He's gone," I said, stating the obvious.

"You tell him I got a markah in that I want paid off or else." A 'markah'? What was that? And why was he threatening us? God, I swear this place is crazy!

I had reached my limit of crazy today. First the nutty religious broad, then Trash Man and now this. Outrage gave me some courage and so I decided to ask.

"Or else what?"

"Whattaya, gettin' cute with me?" he demanded. "All's I gotta do is walk over thea and this boat'll sink right out from undah ya. You along wit' it if yoah not careful." His East Coast accent was tough to follow when things were calm but nearly incomprehensible to me now, angry as he was. He pointed a talon-like finger at my chest and poked it for emphasis. "You tell him 'Eddie says we're squaah' or I blow the lid right off and I don't caah who goes down wit'im." He reached out and gave me a slap across my face. I jumped back, startled and rubbing the spot … it hurt but the suddenness of it was what shocked me. "Get smaht with me again, I'll slice yah balls off."

He disappeared and I felt myself beginning to cry as I watched him leave. Who were these freaks? The neighbor culture that I'd grown so comfortable with here was suddenly gone. All that was left was a bunch of sewer rats … a bunch of sharks circling and moving in for the kill now that we were alone. The tears were standing in my eyes but I couldn't let it show.

"Stop it," I told myself … trying not to break down and cry. When the tears did not go away, I tried slapping myself. "Stop it!" The first one didn't hurt that much so I did again, harder. Then I did it again and then again and again and again. I was slapping and pounding on my forehead until the tears were gone … it took a while. When I was calm again, I went back inside to find Madison drawn up and looking at me in fear from the couch.

"I'm okay, Madison," I said. "I … I just can't cry right now." I left to my room and start looking around for Dad's shotgun. I found it and loaded it—my time on the *Gun Range* had taught me that much—and then I set it by the salon door.

"Don't touch that thing … don't even look at it," I ordered Madison sternly. She stuck her tongue out at me but she didn't argue. We didn't talk after that for the rest of the day. People continued coming to the door to ask about Dad, the *Dixie*, the *Gun Range* or whatever. The really freaky ones were the sketchy-looking fools, nobody wanted to ask about drugs but it was obvious what they were after.

Meanwhile, Security teams were rumored to be still looking for people to round up. You'd hear the kids of the Colony singing "Phoenix Patrol!" and then suddenly the docks and upper decks would empty of people. It would have been funny to watch if the situation wasn't so serious. You'd hear the cry from far away and any kid under 10 would take up the sing-song. You'd suddenly hear "Phoenix Patrol, Phoenix Patrol!" and then less than 30 seconds later there'd be nobody anywhere on the rings. Better than a fire drill … it was like yelling "Five-Oh!" on the block in LA.

We steered clear of the *Phoenix* but I still had the same problem: I had to call Mom. I went back to the *Gun Range* for another shift, thinking that I would try to make a call from there. Miguel's wife was parked on the lounge sofa with a Long Island Iced Tea in a plastic stadium cup in one hand and an automatic rifle across her lap.

She helped herself to something in the hidden gun rack one afternoon and it never left her side after that. She called it something … S4, M4, A4 … I forget which. Nasty looking thing, that's all I knew. She nursed that drink all day and refilled it whenever it got shallow. I manned the counter but nobody came by. I spent my time surfing the Internet on their slow satellite connection—it was awful. No info on Mom or Dad but the situation on Shore was still getting worse. The sun was dipping low on the horizon when I finally screwed up enough courage to ask her to borrow the phone.

"Wha?" she said, slurring a bit.

"The phone, ma'am," I said, going for the respectful-kid thing. "I need to call my Dad."

She looked a little bleary and confused but finally said, "Oh yeah, here." Reaching into the pockets of her stained white tennis shorts she tossed me her phone which landed about halfway between us.

"You're not bad looking," she said quietly when I bent to pick it up. "You ever think about me?"

I was stressing about my Dad and missed what she was talking about. "Huh?"

"You're kinda hot," she ventured. "Ever get lonely?"

My jaw pulled back into my throat when I realized what she was saying. Ugh. I mean, *UGH* … I gotta deal with a drunk broad trying to put the moves on me on top of everything else? I don't even know her name and she's coming onto me! Miguel's wife was a white chick, maybe this side of hot trailer trash with the blowsy blonde hair and a rack that might have been interesting if it wasn't sagging for the floor. Her butt was fat, not badonkadonk fat, just *fat*. Gross, if you will. Anyway, I just played it off and ignored her but managed to put the call through finally.

I let the phone rang to voicemail three times before I finally left a message. "Mom, it's us. We're here and Dad's gone to shore on some boat lift. We need you to come get us. Call me …" and suddenly I realized I had no idea how she might get ahold of us. "Just call Pacific Fisheries and put a message through. Hope you get this … bye, Mom."

I left a message and moved on, calling Mom at the house, on her cell, then Marty's cell, then her work number and then Marty's. Nobody picked up and it was just kinda mechanical—I'm glad I had all those numbers memorized. Miguel's wife watched me in silence, cradling the wicked-looking rifle in her lap and sipping daintily from the stadium cup full of hooch. For the next 20 minutes, I sat there waiting for the phone to ring, but nothing happened. No pickups, no nothing, no call backs.

We both continue watching the news in silence. She finally fell asleep on the couch with the rifle in her lap after an hour of no customers. I slipped out to go back to the *Horner*. I was half-hoping that Mom had gotten our message and that a Security team would be loading us up to leave. Half-hoping? Nah, I was praying for it. I really wanted to be out of here … if it wasn't for Madison, I would jump in the water and start paddling right now. We ate another dinner of cold canned spaghetti and then I had Maddy sleep next to me in my stateroom. My back was starting to hurt from sleeping on the floor in the living room and I wanted to keep an eye on her.

I fell asleep at some point because the next thing I knew it was one in the morning and the general alarm was *a-HOO-Gah*-ing out into the foggy air. "What the—" I started to say and then I jumped when realized what was going on. Terror pushed up through my nose and I vaulted out of bed, not even touching the ground between my bed and the stateroom door.

"*Colony Patrol—man your stations. This is not a drill, repeat, not a drill. Bogies approaching.*" The voice droned again, a scary repeat of that other time a month ago. "*All individuals in the dock area, stay in your boats and lock your doors. Do not attempt to go outside for any reason. CIWS systems are armed and preparing to fire.*" The echo rolled out into the distance while I grabbed Madison and we made for the hiding place I made in the Junk Room a few days ago. I pushed old cartons of records aside and shoved Madison into the space.

"What're you doing?" she whined. "This stuff smells gross!"

"Shut up," I whispered fiercely. Pulling the boxes into place behind us I threw an arm over Madison and pulled her close. It was a tight squeeze. We would have had more space if we were sharing a sleeping bag. I could hear the buzz of small boat engines approaching us and in the darkness it was ... terrifying. The boats were on us and then we could hear the feet. Male feet, some bare and some wearing heavy clod-hopper boots, slapping and clunking around the docks and boat decks. They had slipped in between two boats maybe three or four spaces away before we even knew they were there.

Before this year, I thought it was hilarious, the idea of pirates out here. Pirates were guys who stole software or took over cargo ships in Africa. Who ever heard of pirates off the coast of LA? All of Dad's talk about 'colony folks being good at taking care of themselves' echoed in my head but none of it mattered now. Now he was gone along with half of the Colony and we were laying here in the dark like two scared puppies.

I heard the staccato rip of gunfire—a machine gun and then the louder crack of something else ... Maybe a shotgun. "Is that Dad? Is that Dad?" Madison wanted to know. It might have sounded like a dumb question but she had a point, kind of. Who doesn't want their dad to be nearby when there are scary things around?

We could hear another motor launch near the back deck. Several voices were shouting in Spanish and I could hear the boat scrape the sides of the *Horner* as they squeezed in between us and the next ship. The pirates grabbed handholds and pulled themselves over the railing—glass was breaking and sudden shouts as they entered the boat next door.

Terror ... abject fear. I thought I knew what it was to be scared, but I didn't have a clue. Madison and me huddled tightly together and listened. I could hear them crashing around kicking in doors and breaking glass. No screams from the residents. They must have been there to smash and grab, not hurt anyone. I started to breathe a sigh of relief ... *maybe it wouldn't be that bad.* But then there was another sound.

My heart kicked up another hundred beats when I heard a soft footstep on the back deck of the *Horner.* No way was it Dad or Riley ... I knew what their footsteps sounded like. The back door quietly clicked open—it was rarely locked—and then he was inside.

The footsteps were evil—soft and light—someone didn't want to be heard even as his amigos were busting things up next door. I heard the hissing sound of someone lightly dragging their fingertip along the bulkhead. We both started breathing shallowly as the step stopped at the door of the Junk Room. The creaking doorknob turned slowly and the door opened.

"I know you are here, little ones," a Spanish-accented voice said lightly. "I ca' smell joo." He spoke into the silence of the room and his feet weren't eighteen inches from my head. I closed my eyes—if we made a sound, any sound, the game was up.

I don't know why I knew this guy was bad news. I just knew it, right? Like when you're watching a horror movie and there's that innocent-looking white guy. You *just know* he will be hacking people up later. I had no idea who this dude was but if he found us ... there was no telling what he would do.

Wait a minute ... this was so weird. How did we know this guy was bad news, worse than the pirates outside? Maybe it was Riley pulling a prank—ready to pull the box back and film our reaction with his camera phone. He was clearly not above it. I really wanted this to be one of his pranks but I knew in my heart that it just wasn't. This was bad, the real deal … trouble with a capital T. I would never question that instinct again.

The three of us were like that in the junk room for what seemed like an eternity. Madison's breathing was sharp but mercifully silent. I held my hand clamped down brutally over her mouth, to keep her from making a sound. Afterward, neither of us could say how long we lay there like that. It was only a matter of time until we made a noise and then this scumbag would be on us. I prayed … Dear God I prayed like I never had in my life before. I didn't pray for my Dad to come home or my Mom to be okay—I just prayed for this guy to leave.

I don't think God uses an M4 carbine, though. Fortunately, Miguel's wife does. Apparently, she had woken from her buzz to hear the sirens and, taking up her little piece o' nasty, started looking for someone to shoot.

The burst of machine gun fire made us jump. Loud, almost like it was inside the *Horner*. I heard a burst of lurid swearing in Spanish and the guy's footfalls as he made for the back porch. "I got you, wetback!" she screamed through the cheap paneling. The guy was screaming as he dove for the boat and I heard her run through the boat toward the back deck. More shots as the boat grumbled away staying close to the other boats for cover.

The whole thing happened so quickly that I didn't know what was going on until she was saying "Jim? Jim!" in the darkness. In hindsight it made perfect sense: she was protecting us. At the same time, like everyone else in the Colony, she was looking for someone to take her fear and anger out on. "Well, thank God she's on our side," I heard one of the Security guys say later.

Speaking of which, the Security team finally started doing their job instead of harassing us. I could hear them as they shouted threats in Spanish and tried to run the pirates off. Later on, I would hear that they fired into the air to make noise, not wanting to shoot into a boat and risk hitting a civilian. Someone onboard the *Phoenix* decided to give them a display of firepower and we heard that CIWS gun go off. The sound was between a fog horn and a massive fan … the heavy, groaning sound of the space invaders when they arrive to destroy the humans … zzzzzhhhhBbrrrraaaaAAAPP!

Well, that did it … they didn't wait to hear anything else. The pirates broke and made for their boats. In seconds I heard the various groans and buzzes from broken-down outboard motors. They were out of earshot in a minute or less. I'm surprised that the *Phoenix* didn't wait until they were away from the rings and then turn them to chum but I guess they didn't want to worry about reprisals. The Colony Patrol, such as it was, had some fun taking pot shots at the retreating boats and I found myself hoping at least some of those shots landed.

I've never been in the position of deliberately wanting to see someone die. I guess the terror I felt from a few minutes before made it inevitable. I didn't want to think about what might have happened if Miguel's wife hadn't shown up when she did. I had nightmares of her going the other way and this guy grinning as he slapped the boxes away from our hiding place to find us.

We stayed in that little hiding place for another hour after the sirens stopped. Miguel's wife came stumbling through there again, calling for me. Still drunk, she was bouncing off of the walls like she was avoiding incoming artillery and while holding onto that gun. I could hear the metal clank against the walls, door knobs and anything else in her way.

"Jim! Jiiiim!" No way was I coming out, now. If I popped my head up she might blow a hole in it thinking I was a Mexican pirate. Laying there, I thought about how this place has taught me to always assume the worst case or the weirdest-case scenario. 'Crazy begets crazy,' is a saying among the Colony folks. I smiled slightly … it was something I was going to have to explain to Madison in the morning.

We lay there for so long that Madison's breathing became deep and regular—she fell asleep among the moldy boxes and mildewed trash, the poor kid. She was sleepy and a bit grouchy when I got her out of there and I think she was sleep-walking when I led her way back to the stateroom. It took a long time for me to fall asleep.

Our current position is: 35°25'48.39"N 120°57'0.54"W

Chapter Sixteen—"We Gotta Go"

DAWN BROKE GRAY on a heaving sea. It was quiet after the attack and still we were still asleep at 10 in the morning. A knock on the back door woke me up. Not an old crazy coot who was looking for the *Dixie Star* or a sketch-head looking for Dad. Instead, I saw Ralph, the security goon, staring in at me through the door. Not much of an improvement. Last time we saw him; he was snooping around and looking for people to draft. Why was he here now?

Ralph carried an old M-16 slung over his shoulder. After last night, everyone was in an 'enhanced security posture.' Well, good for them, I guess. "What's up," I asked.

"We need you to come up to the *Phoenix*," he said. "We need to talk about last night."

I was suspicious. "And then what?"

"We'll see," he said. "Don't worry—nobody's drafting you." He waited while I got cleaned up and dressed. Madison insisted on going even though I wanted her to stay with Stacy.

"Don't worry, they're up on the boat with us now," Ralph said.

So that's where they ended up. We were silent on our journey to the ship, passing boats with kicked-in windows and trash all over the place. I saw clothes and paper floating in the water inside a pen and it made me sad about our own fish. Nobody had been taking care of them and I was starting to see a few Tilapias floating to the top. Would we ever get back to them?

Onboard the *Phoenix*, Ralph steered us toward the administration offices. We passed groups of families huddled together in random places on the deck. Riley was morosely working the counter of the Grill, turning out sandwiches and hamburgers and apparently not taking a dime for any of them. If Jeb saw this, he'd hit the roof ... if he was still alive to care, that is.

As we passed the families, we saw people stopping whatever it was they were doing to look at us. I thought they were staring because they were concerned, but there was more to it. The one crazy lady slobbering about Branson I met yesterday, she was glaring at me with eyes like needles. I kept hearing people mutter "Rick's kids" as we passed. Nobody planned it ... they just kept saying it.

Yeah, we were 'Rick's kids.' So what? Did that matter, all of a sudden? Aren't we survivors like everyone else? Trash Man's visit yesterday confirmed that Dad was into some bad stuff. How was that our fault?

I didn't like that Dad was involved but seriously ... drugs were *everywhere* in the Colony. The kids of Burning Man started tweaking at earlier and earlier ages. You'd see the men of different boats smoking pot on their back decks—it was the worst-kept secret here. Random kids getting high and too many infirmary visits listed as 'allergic reactions to cold medication.' None of this was a surprise ... drugs were just part of the life here.

There was no better anti-drug commercial than seeing people slowly turning into human garbage. You could watch it happening to them from one summer to the next. The light in their eyes died. Everything about them seemed to fall apart. I'm not trying to sound like a DARE program or something ... they became a mess. I knew that I didn't want to go down that road. But why would Dad?

See ... this is why we need to talk! I mentally screamed in his general direction. After all of his lectures about booze and drugs—Dad was part of a drug ring right here on the Colony. Everything he said to me was so much crap. I just ... I don't even know what to say.

Everything about Dad was a waste. He couldn't be content to just build his catch and make it work. He had to scam somebody ... He was always trying to cut corners. He had more energy to make excuses than to just do the job right. Did he understand what it was like to want to look up to someone and realize you couldn't? What are you supposed to do with that?

I guess I wasn't the only person who was disappointed in Rick Westfield. Ralph steered us around makeshift areas of people living on blankets and ratty-looking lawn chairs. People continued to look up as we passed. The whisper grew in volume and bitterness as we drew closer to the ship's office. *Rick's kids … those are the ones … right there.*

We were almost there when a raucous shout came from behind us. An old Chinese lady was standing in the aisles of families and pointing us accusingly. "You no good! You Daddy bad man!" she shrieked. "Go 'way … you no stay here!" We were stunned by her outburst but what followed was worse. An old lady was standing there, still pointing when the people on both sides of the aisles came to their feet cheering. They were leaning against bulkheads or lying on the deck, but they all got up together to give her an old-fashioned standing ovation … it was quite impressive.

Madison was not impressed. In fact, she burst into tears. It was too loud for me to hear it but I could still feel her shaking with sobs next to me. Ralph tightened his grip on our shoulders and used his big, fat body as kind of a shield to get us away from there and out of sight. He sat us down in at a desk in the Admin Center and then disappeared.

The Admin Center was next door to the Colony Operations office I was trying to make a phone call from. It had the same old blue carpet, smelled of burnt coffee and the décor was straight out of Old Gross Office Monthly. No one went to any trouble to make it look nice, just more cheap wood paneling. Where was everybody? Normally this place was jammed with office people but for right now it was deserted. The door opened and Trash Man walked in.

I didn't recognize him at first without that nasty coat he always wore. His beard was trimmed back and it was the first time I'd seen him with combed hair. His usual fuzzy and bloodshot eyes were sharp and pointed. He was wearing blue jeans, a polo shirt and a waistband holster in he carried a chunky-looking pistol. He dropped a thick manila folder full of all kinds of paper and then sat at the desk in front of us.

"You're in a lot of trouble here, Jim," he said. "You could help your sister here and tell us where your Dad's been hiding his stashes."

"I don't know …" I began but Trash cut me short.

"Spare me," he said bluntly. "Spare me, okay?" You could see that he was trying hard to hold his temper, but why was he so mad at me? "I've been up all night and I'm a little tired. Maybe you're telling the truth and maybe you aren't. Your Dad is involved in some seriously illegal activity." He paused, like he expected me to fall off my chair or something. If he was, he was going to wait a long time. I knew Dad was scamming like everyone else and that it probably constituted illegal behavior to someone. But he always stayed on the right side of wrong ... so far as I knew.

When the Trash Man saw I wasn't going to respond, he continued. "Now he's on shore and I'm having a hard time holding these people back. Maybe you saw what's waiting for you out there?" He paused while I tried to make sense of all of this.

What was Dad really into? Did he leave us to fend for ourselves knowing these freaks were going to come after us? What kind of parent would do that? Trash wasn't going to let me take much time to think ... he already had it all figured out.

"Your only chance at this point," Trash continued, "is to give it up and let us take you into 'protective custody'. That way, they'll see what we have you and that we have the drugs. After that ... you'll probably just end up losing the *Horner*."

"Lose the *Horner*?"

"Yeah, Jim," he explained wearily. "These people gotta take their rage out somewhere ... I'd much rather it be on some crummy boat than on you and your sister."

"But ... wha ...?"

"Jim!" he slapped the table and thundered at me. "Wake up! Those animals are getting ready to rip you apart. Now where are they?"

"I don't know!" I said, feeling myself start to cry. Dad really had abandoned us, hadn't he? He left us to this and never even bothered to warn me. I didn't know what I was going to do at this point. I guess I still love him but at that point I wasn't worried if I ever saw him again.

"Think, kid," Trash said. "Think hard. Did you ever see him with bags or boxes?"

"Of course ... he always has something. He's scamming with different people all the time."

"Who?"

"Everyone," I answered. "He's always trying to do something with somebody." I wasn't lying: that was the truth. Dad's 'pickle test' philosophy means that he is constantly throwing pickles at the wall and looking for one of them to stick.

"Anyone in particular?"

"Miguel," I said, feeling like the world's worst traitor. I knew that giving Trash Man the names of anyone on the Colony meant they would become targets. I hated myself for doing it but I didn't know what other choice I had.

Trash surprised me. "Nope ... Miguel's not involved," he replied. "Who else?"

"I dunno ... The Burning Man people?"

"Big guy named Mongo?" he asked in reply.

"Yeah. Dad and Mongo are tight." Trash grunted thoughtfully and it made me think I'd just confirmed something he already knew.

He kept at us for another hour or so until he was convinced we had told him everything we knew. Meanwhile, Trash Man told us how he had been working as an undercover DEA agent on the Colony to put a stop to the drugs and his real name was also Rick. I had to tell him the same story, over and over again. He'd ask the same questions in different ways to see what I would do. It was exhausting.

After he was done, Trash Man assigned a Security detail to walk us back to the *Horner* and keep an eye on us. "For our safety," he said. I think it was more like they wanted to use us as bait. Madison was still crying. She had heard everything we said and it was way too much for her to absorb. After we went inside and the security goon was gone, I grabbed her and pulled her close.

She cried for a few more minutes, sobbing into my shoulder but stopped when I said, "Maddy. Mad, listen to me!" She choked back a sob and started breathing heavily. "Listen to me," I said again, grabbing her by the shoulders and looking right into her eyes. "We gotta go."

"What?"

"We have to leave here."

"On the boat?"

"Yes. I have to take the boat and you and get us out of here."

"But why can't we stay here?"

"You heard 'em from before?" She nodded. "They're talking about letting people take this boat and it's all we have right now. Do you want people to sink our boat?" She shook her head vigorously. "Well if we stay here, they will. That's why we gotta go."

"But can you drive this thing?" she asked. Dang ... Why are little sisters so good at that? That was the question I was hoping she'd overlook. I wanted to say something like "I don't know but I'll try" but it sounded so phony. When I looked into her eyes I saw something like hope and trust. There was no way I was giving that up.

"Yes," I lied. "Yes, I can. It's easy. I'll even show you how." *Good answer*, I told myself when I saw her shaky smile. We quickly hashed out a plan for escape.

"We need food and we need fuel," I said. "You're in charge of getting the food together. Find out what we have and then check the boats next door for whatever is left." She nodded and went to the kitchen to get started. I would work on getting the fuel and this was going to be a lot more difficult.

The *Horner* did have some fuel but I had no idea how much. Assuming that Dad never took it anywhere, I thought the tanks might be empty. The fuel gauge showed that we were about half-full ... how much was that? I knew that the boat ran on diesel and that the engines should run okay. Ever since I got here, Dad had me start the engines every week and run them for 10 minutes to keep the batteries charged. It was a boring chore but now it might be the thing that saves our lives.

I found a binder under the console on the bridge that gave me some basic numbers about the *Horner*. Forty-six-foot pilothouse, built in the nineties ... blah, blah, blah. Fuel capacity ... it was a thousand-gallon tank. Half-full meant five hundred gallons of fuel. How far would that take us?

I checked that map again—from here to Puget Sound was over 1200 miles. Cruising range of the boat is 2000 miles. That's how far it can travel, right? I was going to need some more diesel. So where was I going to get fuel? And how would I do it with the Security goons breathing down our necks?

Pacific Fisheries made a tidy profit hauling diesel out from Los Angeles in rusty green Castrol drums. Then they bring the drums out to your boat on a dolly to be siphoned into your gas tanks. Getting gas for the boat is miserable work and you wouldn't believe what they charge for it. One of the good things was that Dad had an electric pump system that allowed him to run a hose out to the dock and pump the gas directly into the tank. It used to be somebody's bilge pump but he figured out a way to re-purpose it for fuel. It wasn't a bad system and it saved hours of back-breaking labor when you were miles from the nearest gas station.

The security detail, whoever they were, weren't close enough to see me slip out the door to the bow, over the rail and onto the fishing porch. Madison ran the hose over to me and I was able to stretch it over as far as the gas tank on the ship next door to us. I gave her a little wave and she hit the switch to start the pump. Gas was sucked up through the hose—it was old surgical tubing, I think—and into our fuel tank.

From the bow, I noticed that we were totally exposed if someone wanted to swim around and get to us that way. The goon squad wasn't watching the back side of the Colony. They certainly missed the one pirate who almost found us. I shivered just thinking about it. The guy next door didn't have much and he ran dry in only a few minutes. Madison heard the air bubbling into the tank, hit the OFF switch and then we went through the process again of moving the hose to another nearby boat and emptying their tank.

I felt rotten to be stealing from our neighbors and it was a hard job, too. I found extra hose and connectors in the Junk Room buried under a box of old software CDs. I figured out how to connect the hoses but we had to be careful to keep it out of the water and keep salt water out of the gas tank.

Each boat was a nightmare. There would be a few tense minutes while I scoped it out and then climbed aboard. Each time, I was risking a serious beating or worse for being a looter. I ended up checking four or five boats near us and they each had less fuel than Dad did. It was still something and we were able to empty their tanks with the help of Dad's little home-improvement project.

It took hours to find hose, move to different boats and avoid anyone who might see us. We were completely exhausted and terrified at the same time. All we got for our trouble was a hundred gallons of fuel. Not enough, but we were out of options.

I made the decision to let the fish go while Madison was out checking other boats for food. She called it 'grocery shopping'. I took a pair of heavy shears and started cutting the nets open from their plastic housings. Part of me was sad to see them leave after working so hard to take care of them but at the same time, it was great to see them go free. I had to remind myself that they knew how to take care of themselves. They didn't really need us as much as we needed them. I didn't finish the cuts ... I just went about halfway and let them figure the rest out. Then I cut loose the rig of plastic pipes that held the nets together and let them drift away.

Since the decking was hooked to us and to the E-Ring docks, it wasn't going to give us away if I unhooked them. They weren't going to float away or anything. It felt historic and sad to unhook the big rubber-coated chains that held the decking to our ship and let them fall into the water. They were free and now ... so were we. There was nothing between us and the horizon but water. The only thing holding us onto the Colony was a few feet of rope.

We completed our preparations about six that evening. Maddy had raided a number of abandoned boats for food and whatever else she thought was worth taking. She did okay but we ended up with a lot more junk food than real food. While she put the food away, I slipped over to the *Barco de Arma* one last time.

"Hello?" I called. The place was tore up ... someone else had gotten to the *Gun Range* before I did. Miguel's wife was gone and so were all of the rental guns we rented to customers. The empty green velvet racks looked sad and pathetic without any hardware sitting in them. I remembered long days, checking them out and back in again maybe an hour later and endless afternoons with rods, patches and a bottle of Hoppe's No. 9. The silence of the room was so heavy that I had to spend a few minutes to get it together. I remembered a line from a book that said 'the time for grieving would come later.' Right now, I had a job to do.

Whoever raided the gun cabinet may have missed the hidden stuff. The small lock that kept the back cabinet closed was still locked and that gave me hope. I spent a few minutes looking for a something to use as a lock pick. Have you ever tried to pick a lock with absolutely no training or experience? I jammed pieces of wire and straightened paper clips into the keyhole like I'd seen guys on TV or movies do it. After a few minutes I gave up … I didn't know what I was doing. I went back to the *Horner,* rummaged around the Junk Room and returned with a rusty crowbar. That was much more effective.

"Miguel's gonna kill me," I muttered and rammed the point of the crowbar into the space between the two doors to wedge it all open. When that didn't work I started on the hinges and eventually, the door popped loose and one of the large shelf pieces crashed to the deck. I had no time to lose … if anyone heard me they would be here in seconds. I heaved the shelf out of the way for a peek inside.

It turns out that there was nothing to take. The interior shelf unit that nobody was supposed to know about was just as bare as the one outside. That big machine gun was gone and so was everything else.

He told me later on, after the pirate run, that the gun was a 'PKM' … whatever that is. He also had an automatic shotgun, some nickel-plated handguns and a Mac-10 with a fat suppressor screwed onto it. That thing really would have done some damage against the pirates. I guess it will still do some damage when it gets used wherever Miguel ended up at. I wondered if he was still alive.

I looked at the mess of torn green velvet and splintered wood, smelling gun oil and wondering what I was supposed to do now. Dad had left us the shotgun. What good was that when I might be dealing with 50 bad guys from Mexico looking for money or drugs that I didn't have? Maybe I could use it to shoot myself.

I stole around the Colony a few more times, looking around for anything else that might be useful on our trip. A few boats were still inhabited and the ones that weren't were looted and wrecked. In fact, one of the shake-down shacks was swamped and starting to sink. These boats were the homes of our friends and family … what was I doing? I stopped looking for things to take and started making my way back to the *Horner.*

On the way, I kept looking at things, looking again and then looking a third time. I wanted to remember everything. If I had the camera, I might have taken some pictures but even then, the flash might have attracted unwanted attention.

As I turned back down the ramp to the E-Ring, I saw one of the 'Monopoly' street signs that I'd admired last year when someone hung them up for the first time. It was hanging lopsided, by a single wood screw, and just looking at it made me sad. I used the crowbar to pull the screw out. I really should have used a screwdriver but something male inside me said "Hey, I'm a guy …" and got to it.

I enjoyed rolling the phrase around my mouth a few times between grunts of effort. Yes … I'm a guy. I am a man. It was a thought that I would use to comfort myself in the nightmare that would follow.

With the 'Monopoly' sign in my back pocket and the crowbar in my hand, I returned to the *Horner*. On the horizon I could see a dark smudge and the wind was blowing it toward us. A storm was coming … *that might be our way out*. Just need to hold it together for a few more hours. The sun painted the Colony with shades of pink and purple and it reminded me of happier days. I sat on the floor of the salon with Dad's shotgun across my lap and ate a dinner of canned beef stew that Madison warmed up on the hot plate. After she cooked dinner, Madison sat in the pilot's chair bundled up in a fleece comforter with a death grip on George, her stuffed rabbit.

"I can't believe you brought that thing here," I commented. George had been through a lot with Madison. From age three onward, she faced all her doctor visits, scary dreams and other childhood trauma with George under her arm. I thought she'd keep him in a safe place back on shore rather than risk losing him to the ocean but here he was again with Madison, staring out of his one shiny button eye. George was a survivor. I just hoped we were, too.

"George will bring Mom back," Madison said simply.

"Really? How's he gonna do that?"

I shouldn't have said it but I guess I was feeling a little snotty, being in charge and all. She gave me an annoyed look and resumed her gaze at the horizon while listening to the TV for news. I finished eating and kept an eye on the deck outside, the TV and whatever part of the sky I could see outside our windows. The Colony was still rotating, just like it always did. Someone on the *Phoenix* was still making that happen. I hadn't seen anyone walk past our door on the deck outside in hours … it felt like we were last persons here.

Night fell very quickly. The sun disappeared behind some approaching clouds and slipped us into a dirty, smudgy twilight. Outside, on the docks, the automatic outdoor lights snapped to life. Everything looked pretty normal, if you didn't know what was happening. The wind picked up and the Colony started to roll and pitch. Madison was starting to get scared and I spent a lot of time reassuring her that the storms were normal and that the *Horner* could ride it out just fine. I wasn't so confident myself but I didn't want to tell her that.

I took a quick look around on deck just before the rain started. The docks were all shipped and everything looked like it was in order. Just a few more minutes and I'd try the engines again. I've only started the engines … I've never piloted this thing. I tested them again today but I would have liked to take the *Horner* just to get used to it. That wasn't going to happen. I was starting to get freaked out by all of this. I was taking charge of the boat—Dad's boat! I had no sailing experience and I have to sail through a storm on my first try.

Hopefully this helps you understand how desperate the situation was for us. I was pretty sure that I would get us killed, taking off like this. We just didn't have a choice.

I guess it made me mad to contemplate just how difficult the task was but being angry was better than being scared. *I'll do it*, I told myself. I'll bring this tubby old scow up to Washington, park her on a sandbar where Dad'll be standing there. His arms will be crossed and he'll have a proud grin. I'll grin back and then put the nylon stock of this shotgun across his eyebrows. *Half for putting me through the wall and half for putting me through this, Dad, I'll say. He'll take it because he knows he did me wrong.* I spent quite a bit of time mentally rehearsing a cool monologue that I'll deliver when we're on dry ground and out of the danger zone. That's right … Dad and I will finally have that man-to-man talk.

I felt the drops of rain and heard them begin to patter against the windows of the ship and decks outside. The rain hit fast and in seconds I was soaked. I held onto the lifeline and started back for the bridge. Time to go. On my way back, the siren on the *Phoenix* started again. I groaned. "Not now!"

"*Pirates! Pirates closing fast!*" I could hear the panic in their voice through the scratchy sound of the speakers. "*E and D-rings are within the fire zone. Repeat: E-Ring and D-Ring are in the fire zone! Anyone out there needs to get onto the Phoenix now! This is the last warning—we are expecting hostile pirates in ten minutes.*"

I was stunned ... E and D-ring was in the fire zone. The *Phoenix* could use those CIWS guns to take any bad guy apart that didn't wasn't packing anti-ship missiles. We had heard them firing during the last visit from the pirates a few days ago. The guns were huge, barrel shaped things roped off on the *Phoenix*. We were never allowed anywhere near them. They were only useful to a point, Dad had told me. He went into this whole explanation and used phrases like 'defilate' and 'dead space'. He explained it three times but I'm still not entirely clear on all of it.

The CIWS guns could draw a continuous line of fire in a complete circle around the *Phoenix*, but that circle was 200 yards wide. I knew that they would cheerfully sink every boat in that circle than let the pirates get close and that they didn't know we were here. The spent Uranium projectiles would turn any boat, dock or person into shredded rags and we were right in its path.

It just keeps getting better and better, doesn't it?

"What am I supposed to do?" I suddenly screamed. Standing outside in the rain, I was looking toward the lights of the *Phoenix* and imagining the guns tearing us to pieces. I guess it was building inside, the frustration and fear. The question had been hiding at the back of my teeth ever since Dad left and now I picked a perfect time to vent, screaming into the storm.

I started screaming "What am I supposed to do?" I was losing it more and more each time. I started screaming and cussing and swearing, just like I did on that cold day at Mugu Rock. I started wailing and crying like the lost kid I was.

One time when I was 4, I got lost in the sporting goods section at the Wal-Mart in Torrence. They almost called a "Code Adam" over it but Mom showed up as soon as they paged her. I can still remember it—Lost boy wearing brown shorts and white t-shirt. I was crying that day because I lost my Mom and she wasn't where I thought she was and I was out of ideas on how to find her. I cried in the rain while standing on the deck on the *Horner* because I was lost again and I had absolutely no idea what I was supposed to do.

Over the sound of my voice and the storm, I could hear engines. *Time to get out of here, buddy.*

I stormed through the cabin quickly, soaking wet and crying. Madison must have thought I looked like a crazy person but I didn't bother explaining. I tore out the back door to grab Dad's 'Emergency Axe' and cut us loose from the ropes that still held us to the dock. At the center of the Colony, the *Phoenix* kept its engines running to maintain a slow, clockwise motion and keep our fish moving through fresh water. It moved the docks and all of the ships along with it. If the *Phoenix* sank, it could take the docks and every boat attached to them, down with her. If you needed to cut your boat loose in a hurry, the theory was, you had an axe to do it. Every boat was supposed to keep an 'Emergency Axe' on hand. Nobody had stolen ours, thankfully, and I yanked it loose to start cutting.

Have you ever tried to cut a taut rope? It isn't easy ... much less one that was moving and wet and holding a large boat in place. I took a big swing, missed the rope entirely and fell to the deck in a large puddle. I got up and tried it again, slower this time, but the rope simply bounced the axe head back the way that it had come.

We're getting nowhere fast. I tried it again, this time aiming for the rope near the cleat on the dock. My first swing cut the rope, shredding half of it and my second swing cut it entirely. Whooping like an Indian on a war party, I made for the other three lines. As I cut the second, the normally stable ship, cozy inside her taut lines, started to bounce and drag against the dock. I couldn't hit the ropes any more, they were moving too much. I settled for chopping the cleat out of the dock on the last two lines and then we were ready to go.

The *Horner* was loose of the Colony. She groaned and slammed against the docks. There were never any fenders out ... Dad didn't see the point with the lines in place. She scraped and thumped, taking all kinds of paint off of the hull in the process. I could hear Madison screaming inside and I realized that she thought I might have been hurt or killed. With a flash of shame, I realized I should have been working to keep her calm instead of going to pieces.

"*Stop it you big baby!*" I yelled at myself. "*You have a sister to take care of ... nut up and get to it!*"

The *Horner* was careening in the storm, first slamming into the docks and then away from them. I realized in horror that she was loose and I was still on the dock. The gap of water between us was getting bigger. I threw the axe aside and leaped for the after deck ... not quite making it. I caught the metal rails in my hands but my sneakers slipped right off the decking. My feet dropped into the water and my face slammed into the metal. The pain was so bad I actually saw stars, but by some miracle my hands stayed locked to the handrails. I was groaning and trying to pull myself up out of the water when the *Horner* lunged for the dock again.

I still don't know how I managed it, I could barely see. The pain, the fear and the cold ... all of that stuff suddenly disappeared. I yanked myself out of the water like a gymnast and away from the deck as the boat impacted. Man, that was close! That would have cut me right in half. The dock was splintering under the repeated crunches. No telling what this was doing to the *Horner* but I didn't want to hang around to check.

I got up from the deck and slammed through the back door into the salon. Madison screamed "Jim" as I entered the salon and then screamed again. I looked down at my t-shirt and saw the reason why: I was covered with blood. That little face plant popped my nose loose and now it was bleeding like a waterfall. That's the first time in my life it's taken so long to realize I had been hurt. My front teeth felt a little loose too, but there wasn't anything that I could do about it.

I got into the Captain's chair and prayed that the engines would fire when I started them. I turned the key and pressed the starter. We could hear the engine cranking over the storm, the sound of boat engines and the alarm. Would they start? A few agonizing seconds went by.

"Why aren't they starting?" Madison asked, beginning to panic.

"I don't know ... they're gonna start, though. Just a few more seconds," I replied. Normally, I would tell her to just shut up or something. I realized with a sudden wave of sadness that if things didn't start going our way this might actually be the last time we would see each other. I wanted

Madison to know that I loved her. Even if all we had left were a few minutes.

At a moment like this, I found out that your mind slows down and everything breaks into little pieces that you can look at. Dad, Stacy, Miguel, Mom and my grandparents—they were all important people in my life. I might never know what happened to any of them ... they may never find out what happened to us. Madison must have been feeling the same way because she grabbed my hand from the wheel and squeezed it.

I squeezed back and then suddenly we were hugging like crazy, both of us crying. All the silly stuff we used to do, used to put each other through ... it was running through my head on fast-forward. I didn't realize how much it all meant to me before. It has never been clearer to me that what I'd been doing with my life, the drugs and the drinking ... what a waste it all was. I had been able to pull things together out here but before now, I'd killed a lot of happy moments because I wanted to be drunk or partying.

So, look, this isn't a 'moral of the story' moment, okay? I don't know ... I can't tell you why I was such a screw-up and why getting high still looks good after what I've put myself through. I couldn't tell you what made me want to be a hero for my sister right at this moment, either. I just knew that I really, really, *really* didn't want us to die right now. I said the silent prayer of a person who just needs it to go right this time—not even sure what all needs to be done, but please make it work. *Please*, I kept thinking ... *please*.

All of a sudden, with a grumbling roar, those engines came to life.

We cheered when we first heard that coughing growl. "Go, Jimmy! Go!" Madison screamed.

She grabbed the back of the Captain's chair and I gunned the motors to warm them up. Those twin diesels had a lot of power and I was saying silent thanks that we were able to find as much gas as we did. I threw the *Horner* forward by shoving the throttle balls out and up as much as I dared.

The *Horner* seemed to jump a bit as she pulled away from the docks and the Colony for the first time in years. It occurred to me: *maybe she was happy to finally get out of the house.* The full power of the ocean had us ... it felt like the trip out on Ignacio's little pilothouse. With the *Horner* yawing and pitching, I honestly saw her as a boat for the first time instead of a dirty bunkhouse.

The E-ring decks were about fifty yards away from us when I spun the wheel hard to the right and eased the throttle up. Madison and I both cheered again as we surged forward … we were on our way. Obviously, we had no idea what was about to happen.

Our current position is: 35°31'6.91"N 121° 5'14.02"W

Chapter Seventeen—Into the Storm

WE WERE A few minutes into our trip and the lights of the Colony were still pretty close. I had a few minutes to think about what just happened. I looked at the compass—we were facing east when we left so all I had to do was turn the rudder until the compass was pointing north and then keep it there.

Rain was pounding against the windshield and the sound of the water ticking against the glass was all I could hear ... then I heard the CIWS guns go off. The initial joy of surviving everything that had just happened was making me smile like crazy while trying to hold the wheel steady. When I heard the guns, I recognized them immediately ... there's no other sound like that. The smile dropped off of my face.

The sound of the rain against the glass returned and then I heard it again. *ZhhhbbBRaap!* With the sounds of our engines to drown it out, I had no idea where the pirates were. I didn't know if they were on the far side of the colony or if they were right next to us getting ready to board. They could be twenty feet away pointing a gun at my face and I wouldn't be able to see it in this weather. In the excitement I totally forgot about them but now I was terrified. We'd left the safety of the Colony, such as it was, and now we were just one big bright cork floating in the ocean. Would they come after us?

We were moving north and the Colony lights were barely visible through our right windows. Not much was showing through the darkness and rain but a burst of fire caught my attention. I watched the line of tracers again disappear far out into the water. I guess you could tell that they were pointing away from you because you could see a line of them. I wouldn't want to know what they look like when they come straight at you.

"How do they know where to shoot?" Madison asked.

"They must have night vision," I said. The difficulty of steering the boat kept me distracted and I ended up ignoring the next few bursts. "Wish I knew what was going on."

"Don't you have the radio that talks to the *Phoenix*?" she asked. Oh yeah, the ship-to-ship intercom ... I forgot about that. They issued a bunch of walkie-talkie and console sets to people a while back and Dad made us learn how to use them. If you had to talk with Pac Fish, using the radios was a lot better and faster than tramping around the docks to deliver a message. I had her look for it while I kept my eyes on the darkness outside. It's a big ocean but who knows what was out there in all this? We had a GPS unit mounted to the console—I farted around with that for a few minutes to figure out how it worked. After a few minutes I had the display working correctly. We were east of San Nicolas Island and south of the Channel Islands. We wouldn't have to worry about rocks or anything for a while.

I heard a lot of noise behind me. Now that the *Horner* was moving, we had a new problem I hadn't thought much about. Since she was, as I mentioned, a big, dirty bunkhouse ... we didn't have a lot of secured storage. All the dishes piled in the sink had slid out to explode onto the floor of the galley. In the salon, all kinds of clothes and junk were swimming back and forth on the deck. I could hear the contents of the Junk Room crashing around below. Since I was in the Captain's chair, the motion of the ship didn't really bother me. Once you left that chair, though, you were subject to all kinds of things to stub a toe or bang a shin on. The galley cabinets popped open and merrily dumped cans of food all over the place. No time to worry about it now.

Madison had to use her hands to steady herself while she looked for the radio. Two geological ages later she returned holding the little console radio as her prize. "Not sure how well it'll work," I said. "Supposed to be good for two miles and I know we haven't gone that far." The batteries were still good and it as soon as it crackled to life we found out how things were going back home ... back on the Colony.

"*Pirates bearing Red 45 ... forward gun, do you see it? About 1500 yards?*"

"*I see it, stand by ...*" I turned to look at the sudden shaft of pink light that appeared through the rain.

"*There's another*"—we heard them say—"*closer to us at 180.*" Another line, this time from the other side of the ship, appeared and then sank out of sight. So far, the pirates were attacking from the north and south ends of the Colony. I was silently applauding whoever decided to attack from where we weren't. I turned the boat to face farther east and get us away from the action. The calls of 'pirates sighted' and responding bursts were coming faster now and we continued listening to the radio as it all happened.

"*Gotta keep these bursts short ... only call out the ones we can hit.*"

"*They're getting closer to E-ring now, is it time to sink the ships?*"

"*Give it a few more minutes ... did I see a ship leave?*"

"*Yeah ... I saw one. Idiots were out there on the E-ring ... they must have been there the entire time.*"

"*Which boat was it—new contact on zero-niner-five!*" An answering 'got it' and burst from the CIWS followed this announcement. I realized that they had seen us and if they were going to sink the E-Ring, we got out of there just in time ... maybe with only minutes to spare. So far—contact was north and south and I knew that wouldn't last. I eased the throttles up to move faster but even then, I knew we wouldn't be out of the danger zone before morning. No sleepy-time for Jim-Jim tonight. The radio crackled again.

"*Was that Rick's boat? The Horner?*" My heart leaped into my throat when I heard the question.

"*Yeah ... think so. His kids are on board the Phoenix, right?*"

"*We're checking ...*" A few minutes from now—they would realize we that we were not aboard the *Phoenix*. What would we do then? The grumbling of the engines was becoming hypnotic and I noticed Madison's eyes beginning to droop. The full scope of everything that had happened hit me like a wave ... all I wanted to do was lay down and sleep.

In between the contact reports, I could hear that they were still looking for us. "*The Horner C crew isn't in the mall with the rest of the civilians.*"

"*Roger that—coordinate with Rick and do a sweep of the entire ship.*"

Rick ... they must be referring to the Trash Man. The Security team would eventually figure out that we were the people they saw leaving on the

Horner. They wouldn't be able to do anything about it but other people could. Pacific Fisheries had several colonies along the coast north of here. We were not out of the woods yet.

I pushed it out of my mind and continued piloting the boat in the storm. The rain lashed against the windscreen and I could hear the rough water slapping into the hull. Late at night on a dark sea with no one to talk to is the perfect time to imagine every worse-case scenario you can think of. I kept thinking of the fiberglass hull parting under the heavy seas and leaving us with half of a life-jacket to cling to.

Madison brought me a raggedy old t-shirt and held the wheel while I mopped the drying blood off of my face. I spat dried blood out ... My mouth tasted like I had been sucking on rusty metal. I checked my loose teeth again and was grateful to find that none of them felt loose after all. I had simply imagined it.

For the next hour the boat pushed north on the same course as that run to Mugu Rock last year with Mitch. The radio had better range than advertised ... we were able to continue listening to the Battle of the *Phoenix*. Every time we heard the "contact!" and "got it" calls ... someone was dying. Even if he was a pirate—he was still a person. How are you supposed to feel about that? The sound of the CIWS guns faded out after a while and that was fine with me. I never wanted to hear that sound again as long as I lived.

"We're losing the battle, chief."

"I know it—set condition Delta."

"Condition Delta, sir?"

"Yes ... remove D-ring."

I started to cry when I heard that. They were going to shred every boat that was still moored on D-ring and E-Ring to create a buffer between themselves and the boarding pirates. They may not have guns as powerful as the ones mounted on the *Phoenix* but they were a hundred times more mobile. That old tub was powerful but it couldn't corner like an old Sea-Doo. It was just a matter of time before someone slipped in with explosives or took aim with a surplus bazooka round.

But still ... they were going to do this? They were going to destroy people's homes? This is where our friends lived. I know some of them are weirdos but most of them were good people who didn't deserve this. Everything I knew about the Colony, even what I hoped would remain after the Meltdown, was gone forever.

I know the Colony wasn't much to begin with. My initial impression of the place was to call it 'the garbage on top of the water.' That's how everyone describes it when they first arrive. You have to look for a while to see how people relied on each other and to see the community. Ethan, Stacy's Dad, was the one who got started talking about how the Colony was a boom town 'from a social standpoint.'

"A what?" I had asked.

"A boom town. Like in the Gold Rush Days," he replied. Back then, he had explained, towns could grow overnight when they discovered gold and disappear just as quickly. It takes a certain type of personality mixed with drive and weirdness to carve out a living in a place like this. People have to be willing to live and operate in a way they had never known before. "It's always a surprise to me," Ethan had said, "that people could abandon something they had worked so hard to create."

"But they do," I said. He nodded and took a sip of the beer he was holding.

We were sitting in wheelhouse of a boat that was part of a failed social experiment. We were leaving it and our friends behind to face an uncertain future. On top of that, our neighbors were in danger because of things that my father had done. The sum total of the loss and the shame of how things were ending brought the tears to my eyes. I couldn't help feeling very glad that we were away from the immediate danger. I couldn't help feeling very guilty, too.

I looked to my left and saw that Madison's eyes were drooping. Knowing how tired I was, I was afraid that if she dropped off I would fall asleep as well. Stopping for the night was out of the question. That might give the pirates all the time they needed to catch up to us. "Talk to me, Mad," I said sharply as she was about to doze off. She jumped and sat up, rubbing her eyes really hard.

"I'm tired," she complained.

"Me, too. We can't go to sleep yet … I need you to talk to me."

"About what?"

"Anything—just pick a topic. I need you to talk to me so I can stay awake and we can get away."

"Can't I get 20 minutes?" she whined.

"If I go to sleep, we sink or we get boarded by pirates," I replied. Madison's eyes widened in fear. "Talk to me ... about anything." She let a few moments go by in silence and I looked toward her in frustration. "Well?"

"Why do you have to get drunk all the time?" she asked. Ouch.

Trust your sister to find the *one thing* you don't want to talk about right after you get through telling her that she has to talk to you about anything. Classic. I put my head down on the cool aluminum of the helm and groaned. Is this what they mean by 'be careful what you wish for?' She wouldn't accept a groan for an answer.

"Well?" she mimicked me. Very annoying.

"I don't know." I kept my eyes on the windshield so I wouldn't have to see her staring holes through me.

"Where are we?" she asked.

I looked at the GPS. "About ten miles north of the colony."

"Are there any islands out here?"

"I don't think so."

"Why do you do it, then?"

"Do what?"

"Drink." I grumbled again and asked her to find me a Coke or something. She dropped away wordlessly and disappeared. I wish Madison hadn't brought it up. The drinking was something that I did and then didn't do and after it happened it was like I had been watching someone else. Getting drunk or high was like taking a vacation from me. It felt so out of character to me that it was like I was watching it happen to someone else.

But what did all that mean? I'd get hammered and then I didn't want to drink ever again ... until the next time. What was wrong with me? I got depressed thinking about all the mistakes that my Dad had made. What would keep me from following in the same loser path that he was on? Dad's little scams had graduated from painfully embarrassing to irresponsible and dangerous. He clearly hadn't been thinking about us when he did it. Dad was doing what he did best: thinking about himself. Madison reappeared with an open can of Coke that we could share. I reached for it and she pulled it back, taking a sip first. Then she held it out of my reach … I knew what was coming.

"So?" She wasn't about to give this up.

"I don't know why I drink," I said, half in frustration and half in surrender. I admitted to my little sister the thing I wasn't able to say to myself or anyone else before: I had no idea why I drank. "I don't know why I do it and I'm sorry every time." I looked at her and then added, "You should know that I love you more than I like to drink but sometimes it ain't enough."

"Why not?"

"I don't know. The older I get the harder it becomes," I said. "The older you get the more you see that everyone else makes excuses. Excuses for not trying hard enough … excuses for giving up when you know you can keep going. Everyone does it … even Mom." Madison was aghast.

"No she doesn't!"

"Sure she does."

"She does not."

"Does, too."

"Whatever …" She gave me a dirty look and we continued on in silence. This was frustrating because I was fighting fatigue and I knew she was, too. In the back of my head were all the problems that could still be waiting for us. We were definitely out here with no protection and no help. It's terrifying at any age but I was 15. I was *a kid*. What made me think I could do this?

It's times like this that I usually get dark and depressed about everything. Anyone would have trouble surviving the last few hours like we did. Would they also have the crushing weight of their own problems making them feel like this was going to be yet another item in a long list of failures? All of this negative junk was making me upset and Madison could see it in my face. Falling apart was definitely not an option right now.

Stop it, I told myself sternly. *Whatever else happens, you still managed to get away. You and your sister are still alive because of that.* Dad would often say that 'hindsight is 20/20.' I guess I'll know better for the next time me and

Madison have to bust out of a fishing colony ahead of a bunch of Mexican pirates. In case you're wondering: yes, I am being sarcastic.

I had to knock off this constant stewing in my own juices and *just try to do the right thing now*. That was the only way we were going to get through all of this. I pushed all of the mental debate out of my mind and checked our heading, the GPS and the depth finder. I wanted to know if we were about to run this old tub up on the rocks.

As time passed, I felt calmer. I was piloting the boat, I could see my compass and my GPS ... we were doing okay. I had done well so far and I would probably be able to handle whatever came after this. What would getting upset accomplish, anyway? I was a teenager steering a boat for the first time, a beat-up yacht, in a horrible storm. Of course I was having a hard time ... this is a hard problem. All of the negative stuff in my head gradually dropped off. It didn't matter whether I sucked or not—I had to do this because no one else could. *Our lives were in my hands*. The thought got me out of my slacker funk and focused on the problem of saving our necks.

On the radio, the Colony was dying. They turned our friend's boats into confetti but the pirates kept coming. When I had a second, I leaned my head as far as I could out to the starboard to see if I could see anything. There was an orange glow on the horizon. That had to be the E and D-Rings sinking into the ocean.

We listened to the fight as long as we were in range of the radio. The pirates boarded and among other things, they were looking for Dad. When they couldn't find him or the *Horner*, they started trying to fight their way aboard the *Phoenix*. Security tried to hold them off but the pirates weren't leaving this time. I guess there was some vicious fighting at the A-Ring gangway. The *Dixie Star* was somehow damaged or sunk in the process. I couldn't make much sense of it from what they were screaming to each other. Finally, someone on board the *Phoenix* decided that enough was enough.

They cut loose their moorings ... the big crossbars that attached the *Phoenix* to the rest of the Colony and then, they gunned the engines. It must have been quite a sight to see: that big old iron hulk smashing through docks and boats. The *Phoenix* was a military ship—a destroyer—and it was designed to take a beating. I didn't have to be there to imagine the shriek of metal on metal as it cut through the docks.

Maybe they hit some pirates making their blind charge ... they might have hit some Colony folks, too. I don't really know. The 'civilians' ... our friends on the Colony ... they had to hold on for dear life while their homes were shredded underneath them. We heard also that the Navy was coming in to 'secure the area' long after it was too late. The Navy was unable to reclaim the Colony and, since they didn't want the pirates using it for a base of operations, they cut loose some artillery and destroyed it.

I'm glad I wasn't there to see it. Our little Colony was a tiny corner of the world and holding onto life as best as it could. It wouldn't have stood a chance under some serious ordinance. I shiver now when I think about what a tremendous loss it all was. A boom town that grew to be a fledgling community and then gone again in less than a few minutes of sustained fire.

Ethan was right. The Colony was a boom town and a community like that couldn't last. It makes me wonder if Dad knew that and deliberately involved himself in what would lead to its downfall. I wonder if he felt responsible for helping to kill the neighborly spirit that brought us here in the first place. To believe we could or should help rebuild the fish population. To believe we could all get along together just by believing in a common purpose. To believe that a common purpose was all we needed in a place like this. I wonder ... I doubt if he thought about it all that much.

The radio eventually faded and all that was left was us, the rain and the steady grumbling of the engines. We were still heading north and already we were fifty miles away from the remains of the Colony. I could see that the idea of us getting up to Puget Sound was crazy. It's over a thousand miles away ... I just didn't know what else we should do. I was beyond tired and into that weird, euphoric state where you're running on adrenaline.

The storm passed and the sun came out around eight the next morning. I needed to rest and I couldn't leave Madison to drive the boat alone. As a matter of fact, I couldn't ask Madison to do anything ... she fell asleep about seven and there was no waking her. What were we supposed to do? I was watching the GPS for a boat dock or a beach we could pull up next to. The coast north of the LA basin is rocky and dangerous. There are big tall cliffs, rocks and then water. We just kept going and going.

About four the next day, I saw something on the horizon that might work. We had skirted Vandenberg Air Force Base and other places during the day ... now we were almost 200 miles from the Colony. The sun was setting when we pulled in and I tied off the boat on some pilings that were too tall for a boat dock.

The beach looked soft enough but I didn't want to try beaching the *Horner.* I doubt I could get it off of the sand again. It took everything I had to pull up, put the fenders over and then tie her off. Stupid things that Dad had taught me, like knot-tying and basic boat handling, were saving us right now. It made it difficult to hate him. I had just finished cleating the last line down when I saw an old man in a rain slicker peering down at us curiously. He was wearing a green rain slicker with brown docksiders and carrying a fishing pole. We were tied up at somebody's fishing dock.

"You guys alright?" he asked, pitching his voice over the noise of the surf. "Not the best place to stay."

"I need to stop," I called back. "I've been up for two days."

"For *two days?*" he called back. He sounded impressed. "Where were you?"

"Down in the Colony," I called back. "Off of the Channel Islands?" He nodded, understanding. "It's gone now."

"Gone?"

"Yeah ... they killed it." My voice was catching suddenly. "They killed the Colony and my friends and now I can't find my Dad." Tears were running down my cheeks before I could stop them.

Without a word, the old man his way over the chest-high rail and then worked his way to us to drop down on the forward deck. With practiced ease, he added expertly tied a few more lines to hold us even more tightly to the dock. "That'll hold you for a while," he announced. "You need to rest up a bit." He noticed Madison and pulled out a phone to dial a number. Whoever answered his call was told to make arrangements for us to stay somewhere and get a hot meal. "Where were you going?"

"My Dad said to get to Puget Sound and he'd find us there."

"Puget Sound?" he asked. "All the way up to Canada?" I nodded. "Wow ..." he said, thinking hard. "Well, you guys won't make it tonight, that's for sure. You were supposed to get all the way up there on your own?"

"I guess so," I said.

He shook his head, thoughtfully. "It's dangerous, kid. That's a tough job for grown men with years of experience. You won't make it on your own." He looked at me. "I guess you guys have had it pretty rough if that's what he told you to do." I nodded and wiped a few tears back … it was a relief to finally find someone who understood. "Com'on," he said kindly. "Let us help you figure this out."

We left the *Horner* tied up at the dock and piled into his old green pickup. After everything that happened I wasn't ready to completely trust him, though. I didn't bring the shotgun with me but I did slip a nasty-looking pocketknife into my jacket. It was one of my souvenirs from sorting through all of that junk with Mitch Cutter.

It was a dirty evening, foggy and cold. Eventually, it started raining again. The old guy was retired and lived with his wife in a home nearby. He had come to the docks to fish and distract himself from worrying about their family that they couldn't get in touch with. That sounded familiar. "Then I found you," he said.

We exited the parking lot of the beach and turned onto the highway. "Where is this place?" I asked.

"San Simeon State Beach," he explained. Pointing off that way, he said "up there is Hearst Castle. Not a bad place to leave your boat … One of the richest men in the world has done the exact same thing." Beyond exhaustion, I managed to stay awake long enough to arrive at his home and eat the bowl of soup his wife placed in front of me. Then we sank into beds in their guest bedroom … just two more dirty, scared and tired children. Before I fell asleep, I wondered idly how we were going to get to Puget Sound and *how* we would find Dad. Our troubles weren't over yet.

These problems were so large that I wasn't even sure if there was a solution. Finally, bone-tired and burned out, I came up with an answer that would have to do …

I'll figure it out in the morning.

Our current position is:
Docked @ 35°38'27.17"N 121°11'16.32"W

Jim and Madison continue their adventure in

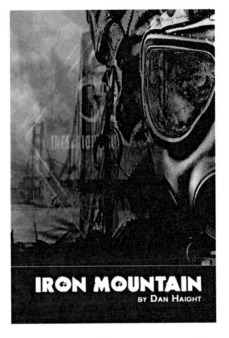

Iron Mountain

Now available at www.flotillaonline.com!

About the Author

Daniel Haight is an emerging writer whose credits include the Flotilla series and many published short stories. As a native of the San Francisco Bay Area, he's a 'blue collar geek' with a passion for writing, working with his hands and being a dad. A former disk jockey, Dan is talking about the Flotilla series on radio and podcast shows all over the world. He works as a 'computer guy' during the day and writes in his off-hours, releasing new titles several times throughout the year.

Learn More: www.flotillaonline.com
Contact him through Twitter: @Flotillaonline

CPSIA information can be obtained
at www.ICGtesting.com
Printed in the USA
FSOW01n1110170914
3126FS